SONG
OF THE
ABYSS

SONG
OF THE
ABYSS

MAKIIA LUCIER

HOUGHTON MIFFLIN HARCOURT
Boston   New York

Copyright © 2019 by Makiia Lucier

Map illustrations copyright © 2019 by Leo Hartas

hmhbooks.com

The text was set in Adobe Jenson Pro.

Library of Congress Cataloging-in-Publication Data

Names: Lucier, Makiia, author.

Title: Song of the abyss / Makiia Lucier.

Description: Boston ; New York : b Houghton Mifflin Harcourt, [2019]

Series: Tower of winds | Companion to: Isle of blood and stone.

Summary: When men start vanishing at sea without a trace, seventeen-year-old Reyna, a Master Explorer, must travel to a country shrouded in secrets to solve the mystery before it is too late.

Identifiers: LCCN 2018052136 | ISBN 9780544968585 (hardback) ISBN 9780544968615 (e-book)

Subjects: | CYAC: Explorers — Fiction. | Adventure and adventurers — Fiction. | Kings, queens, rulers, etc. — Fiction. Missing persons — Fiction. | Fantasy.

Classification: LCC PZ7.L9715 Son 2019 | DDC [Fic] — dc23

LC record available at https://lccn.loc.gov/2018052136

Printed in the United States of America

DOC 10 9 8 7 6 5 4 3 2 1

4500766629

For Reyna

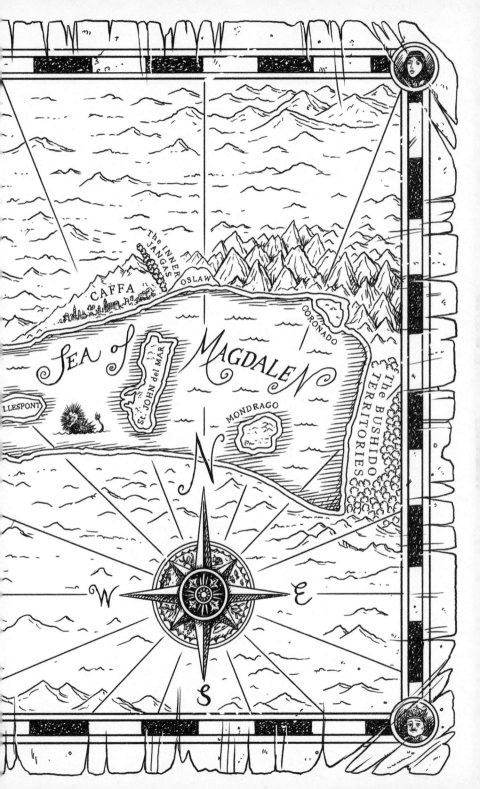

ONE

THEY CAME IN THE NIGHT as she dreamt, in her berth, on a ship sailing home to del Mar.

After, they would be all Reyna thought about: two carracks painted scorpion black. No emblem on either forecastle, no pennant flying above the mainmast to hint at a kingdom of origin.

Never a good sign.

She had not meant to fall asleep. Her cabin was the size of a leading stone, her berth within the only comfortable spot. She had taken a chart to study there and had dozed by the light of a candle. A rough shaking woke her. In that dazed state between sleep and wakefulness loomed a face, inches from her own.

"*Quiet*," Gunnel ordered before Reyna could scream. The gruffness of her voice suggested she too had just woken. But Gunnel wore her sword on her back and two daggers in her belt, something she hadn't done since they had boarded this ship seven days ago. "Good, you're dressed. Up, up. Quickly, Reyna!"

Reyna rolled from her berth and dropped lightly onto bare feet. From overhead, so peculiar she thought she must still be dreaming, came the sound of a man singing. A gentle, soothing tune, soft as a child's lullaby. "What is that?" she said.

"Sea raiders."

Reyna's grogginess vanished, replaced by a deep, thrumming fear. "Where is the captain?"

"Captured." Gunnel pointed directly upward. "With the others."

Reyna crossed the cabin in two steps and threw open her sea chest. There were rules that must be followed, for an occasion such as this. The top half of the trunk was filled with maps and portolans, each rolled and secured with twine. She crushed an armful to her chest and spun around. Gunnel, a sea captain's daughter long before she'd become Reyna's guard, had anticipated her next move. The older woman shoved open the window so that the maps could be flung into the darkness and open sea.

It's fine, Reyna told herself. *Fine*. Those had been copies of copies, the originals safe on del Mar. Better she lose them than let their trade routes be known to the enemy. Whoever the enemy was. As they emptied the chest, the light from the candle cast shadows onto the walls. Gunnel explained what she knew; it turned out to be very little.

"There are two ships to our west. Both much larger than ours."

"We had no warning?" There were lookouts aboard the *Simona*. How had anyone managed to come so close without setting off the alarms?

"None."

Reyna's map carrier lay on the table, a leather tube three feet in length. She uncapped it, glanced inside, and felt her heart spasm in protest. These maps were not copies, but the result of twelve months of labor. A year of her life. And she was expected to destroy them. What would Uncle Ginés do? Or Lord Elias? She knew the answer, which only made her decision more agonizing. Above, the strange humming continued. An eternity passed before she replaced the cap and slung the strap over her head. The carrier lay against her back.

Gunnel looked down at her with a disapproving expression. Quite a ways down, for she stood a good three inches above six feet, unnaturally tall even among her people. She indicated Reyna's carrier. "It's a bad idea," she said.

"Yes. I realize."

If Lord Braga learned she had kept these maps, and they were stolen as a result, he would suffer a seizure. He would banish her from the Tower of Winds. He would string her up by her feet and toss her over the cliffs at Alfonse to die slowly, her eyeballs pecked away by the gulls. And she would deserve it all. There were rules that must be followed, for an occasion such as this.

She left the carrier where it was.

Gunnel shrugged as if to say, *It's your bed*, before pitching the last of the charts out the window. "Listen to me," she said. "There's something wrong with the men."

Reyna shoved her father's dagger in her belt. "They're injured?"

"No, something is wrong *here*." Gunnel tapped the side of her head impatiently. "I heard footsteps outside my cabin, and when I opened the door, they were shuffling past. Like cattle. And their faces . . ." Her brows, unkempt, sprouting everywhere, drew together. "There was nothing there."

Gunnel was not making sense. "They had no faces?" Reyna asked.

"Of course they had faces!" Gunnel hissed. "Don't be an idiot. They looked like . . . like your parchment before you begin painting."

Blank, Reyna realized. That was what Gunnel meant. "But how? And why were we missed? And who is that man singing?"

"I don't know, and I don't care to find out. Not a sound from you." Gunnel reached for the door just as Reyna snuffed the candle with pinched fingertips, plunging them into darkness.

Luck was on their side. The door hinges, well oiled and silent, did not give them away. Reyna followed Gunnel down the narrow, stifling passageway. They crept along the edges like mice. Ahead, torchlight trickled in through the open hatchway. The humming had stopped. A man spoke in a language she thought was Coronad at first, until she realized she could only make out a smattering of words: *Yes. Lame. No.* The inflection was guttural, like Coronad, but not. A dialect? From her ship-mates she heard nothing. No begging or threats. Not a word of protest. Were they dead already? Killed while she slept in her berth? As they tiptoed beneath the hatchway, a man stepped into view on the deck. Reyna and Gunnel moved as one, flattening their backs against the wall.

Don't look down. Please do not see us. Sweat trickled between Reyna's shoulder blades. After a minute, she chanced a glance upward, long enough for her to see a man caught half in shadow, half in light. Younger than she'd expected, bigger than she wished. His face, wide, with sharp cheekbones, bore the toughness of a Coronad and was heavily pocked. A knot of hair, perfectly rounded, perched atop his head, a feminine style that contrasted sharply with the assortment of weapons hanging from his vest and belt. Axe, whip, daggers for every occasion. Perhaps strangest of all were the ear covers draped around his neck. The night was warm and pleasant. Why would anyone need to keep their ears covered in such temperatures? He exchanged words with someone out of sight, then reached up and sliced a finger across his throat, an ominous gesture that needed no interpretation. At least one shipman would lose his life tonight.

Gunnel touched her hand lightly. A sign to move on. Swallowing the sickness that crawled up her throat, Reyna followed her to the captain's quarters, which took up the entire width of the stern. The room was far more richly appointed than hers. The massive oak bed could sleep six captains. A wire-fronted bookcase held years' worth of charts and logs. She started there, clearing the shelves and throwing everything into the water. Working fast. With every armful, she ran by the desk, where a taper flickered cheerfully beside an untouched supper and a full glass of red wine. The captain had not had time to eat.

Outside, it was as Gunnel had described. Two ships dwarfed their own, nearly impossible to distinguish in the night.

Gunnel beckoned Reyna over to another window. "Do you know where we are?" She moved aside so that Reyna could see.

Reyna tipped the last of the charts overboard before peering out. The lights of a city glimmered in the distance. A large city, and to its west . . . *Oh. So that's where we are.* She could not fail to recognize that particular lighthouse. It was the brightest beam in the known world.

"That's Selene." Capital city of the kingdom of Lunes. They were only a four-day journey from del Mar.

Gunnel nodded, eyes traveling upward as the sea raider's voice rose. He issued what sounded like a command. Another man answered.

Reyna asked, "Do you recognize them?"

Gunnel listened a bit more. She looked confounded. "I don't believe it. I think they're —" A loud thump from the deck. The sound of a man falling. Whatever Gunnel might have said remained unspoken. "Never mind that now. Pay attention. Ginés says you're a fine swimmer. A strong one?"

Reyna met her eyes and understood what was intended for her. Gunnel had not led her to the captain's quarters to destroy his maps. Gunnel was a Coronad; she would not care too deeply about protecting del Marian trade routes. Unlike the other cabins, this one had windows large enough for a person to climb through. Reyna stuck her head out one of them and looked down. It was good it was so dark, for if there were sea monsters below, she could not see them. And if she happened upon one, well. Too late to do anything about it then. She would have lived a short life, but an interesting one. At least the water would be warm.

Reyna pulled her head back in. "I can swim," she answered quietly. Jaime had taught her. "What about you?"

"I never learned," Gunnel said. Deep lines bracketed her mouth. "We both know what's in these waters. I think you're safer out there than in here. But it's your life. Your choice."

Reyna was a young female on a captured ship. It was not really a choice.

"I'll go." Before she could change her mind, she swung onto the ledge, arms braced by her sides, bare feet dangling over nothing. Her heart thundered in her chest. She looked back at Gunnel. They had known each other weeks only, but in that time Reyna had come to consider this woman her friend. "And I'll bring help. I swear it."

"Use the worms if you can." Grim-faced, Gunnel checked the seal on Reyna's carrier. "Best to avoid the castle if you want to keep those maps."

"I will." She would find a del Marian ship. In a harbor of that size, there was bound to be one.

Gunnel's gnarled hand covered Reyna's own. She squeezed hard. "I promised Ginés I'd keep you safe. Do not dare make a liar out of—"

A shout. A dark figure stood on the hatch steps, looking

beyond the passageway directly at them. He scrambled down the rest of the way, yelling. From above came the sound of many running feet.

Reyna said, "Gunnel!"

Gunnel shoved her. Reyna pointed her toes downward and tucked her arms in tight, making herself small, and when she entered the water, it was without a whisper; it was without a sound.

TWO

DEAR PAPA,

Greetings from Caffa. I hope this letter finds you
well and in fair spirits. You will be pleased to know I am in good
health, wholly devoted to study, and ever mindful of Carpus:
"If a man neglects his education, he walks lame to the end of
his life." The university is near the great libraries where I have
spent many hours in diligent scholarship. You will tell Levi this?
I know my dear brother has his doubts. Perhaps you will also tell
him he would not find fault with the friends I have made here.
There is not a loafer or drunkard among them. These are men
of noble virtue, equally devoted to learning and upholding their
families' good names.

I send my affections, as always, to Vashti and Sara. The
enclosed drawing is for Sara. The parrot belongs to a friend. It
is a prickly, ill-mannered beast, but I have taught it how to say,
"Princess Sara is a lovely girl, the loveliest in the land." I hope it
pleases her.

Regretfully, Papa, the matter of money stands in the way of

my studies. Caffa is expensive and makes continuous demands on my purse. Lord Kish has severely underestimated the costs extorted by the parchment sellers and the booksellers, as well as numerous other places I cannot now specify. Please do not blame him, for few could comprehend the speed at which prices rise here. The truth is, I have not a penny to my name, and I respectfully beg your paternity and discretion in this matter. You will not share this portion with Levi?

The message bearer has been instructed to await a response. Please send with all possible haste sufficient coin as well as the items I have listed below. I fear any delay will lead to me being tossed from my chambers or mistaken for a beggar. Levi will claim I exaggerate, but truly, I say this in all seriousness.

I remain your devoted son and servant,

Asher

(From Asher, third child of Lunes, to his father, Lamech, king of Lunes)

Asher,

I write this letter with great sorrow, knowing it will break your heart, as it does mine. I will say it plain — Papa is dead. He was found at his desk this morning. The physicians blame his heart. It was a quiet passing, a peaceful one. But that offers no comfort, does it? We are orphans, you and I and Vashti, and though we are no longer children, his loss is as bitterly felt as Mother's.

The councilors swarm around Vashti now, demanding father's funeral take place without delay as tradition dictates. We cannot fight them on this, Asher, though I deeply regret you will not be here to bid him farewell.

Master Hiram accompanies this letter. He has arranged for your passage home and will settle your debts. "Do not tell Levi" indeed. But we will speak of it later. With fair winds behind you, you should arrive in time for Vashti to accept her crown. It is the one beacon in this darkness. I will be glad to have you near.

Sail home swiftly, brother.

Levi

(From Levi, second child of Lunes, to his younger brother, Asher)

Instinct drove Reyna deep beneath the surface, trying to outswim the arrows that chased her to the sea floor. She felt them rather than saw them, deadly bolts of iron slicing past her arms, legs, and head. None pierced her. A miracle. The water was warm, the silence heavy. She swam toward shore, blinded by nightfall and seawater, surfacing only when her lungs could no longer bear the strain.

The raiders did not see her or hear her gasping breaths. By

then she was well out of arrow shot. Torchlight roamed the deck of the *Simona* as they searched, pacing to and fro along the rails. Their features were indistinct, shadow puppets against open flame. But sound carried over water: great snarling voices raised in anger and frustration. One voice louder and angrier than the rest. There was no more singing.

A quick inspection assured her that the map carrier's seal had held. A heartbeat later, a sharp squeak erupted by her ear. Reyna flailed in a panic, then remembered abruptly that sea serpents did not squeak.

"Hello there," she said as a sea worm — no, two worms — nudged against her, curious and playful. "You gave me a fright. The pair of you."

There were more friendly peeps in response. She treaded water and considered them. The stars were bright enough for her to see that both worms were infants, roughly fifteen feet long, their width spindly as a child's arm. Skin a pinkish gray, lidless eyes bright as polished onyx. One had been recently injured: a crusty scab ran a third of its length. The wound explained the creature's movements, slower, more tentative than its companion's.

She grabbed the end of the uninjured sea worm with both hands. Irked, it flicked its tail in an attempt to shake her off. When she tightened her grip, the worm spun in a circle, once, twice, then shot off, thankfully toward Lunes and not away from it. The sea spray blinded her momentarily. She looked back to see the three ships growing smaller. In no time at all, the shouting faded. All that remained was the water rushing past and the fear drumming deep in her heart.

Sea worms could not be steered in the right direction. Unlike sea horses, worms were largely content to gnaw on seaweed or kelp and chase after their own tails, wherever their tails led them. But horses were rare in these parts, and the worms had their uses. When they chose to, they could be very, very fast.

Fortune was on her side once again, at least when it came to her worm. This one pulled her a full quarter of the way to Lunes before it reversed direction and headed back out to sea. When she felt the shift, she let go, taking a moment to catch her breath and check the seal on her map carrier, before continuing on her own to shore. As her arms sluiced through the water and her legs propelled her toward land, she focused her mind. *Do not think of what is behind you. Do not imagine what may have already happened to Gunnel and your shipmates. Forget also what might be swimming beneath, lurking and hungry and watchful.* Her task was to think ahead, to the harbor and a del Marian ship. Sailors from home, who would help her.

Her eyes grew accustomed to the darkness. Gradually, the lighthouse took shape behind its beam, tall and regal atop a rocky promontory. She swam in that direction. The sea was calm, with the occasional ripple and splash of worms too far away to be of any use. A school of lightning fish darted by. She did not know what made her stop swimming and tread water, scanning her surroundings.

There it was. Some distance away, between her and Lunes, a dark shape. It looked like a large triangular rock jutting from the sea, but seconds after she spotted it, the rock disappeared beneath the water. It reappeared minutes later, a short distance east, closer to her than it had been before. There were no more squeaks from the worms. Only a terrible, menacing silence.

The finned lion was no small threat. A fully grown male could measure twice the length of a man. Spikes edged the fin on its back, and its mane, a grand, golden halo, never flattened in the water, for it was not hair, but thousands of stiff, needle-thin quills, poisoned at the tips. If the lion's teeth did not finish you off, the stab of a single quill would.

Like most predators, the finned lion was attracted to movement and to blood. She would offer neither. Tipping her head back, she loosened her limbs, floating upon the surface with her arms and legs extended and looking straight up at the sky. Outwardly calm. But inside? That was another story.

Bargaining with herself offered a distraction. If she survived this night, she would do things differently. Better. Go to church sometimes, like a normal, God-fearing del Marian. Wear more dresses. Her Uncle Ginés cared nothing about the former, but had grown increasingly persistent on the latter. *You are seventeen now, my dear. No longer a child. You should wear more dresses.* She had laughed when he said these things. Kissed him on the cheek and asked what one had to do with the other. Thinking of him hardened her resolve. She would *not* die tonight, for the simple reason that it would break his heart. Her uncle had not had an easy life. His heart had been broken enough already.

A growl in the distance sent her thoughts scattering.

After a time, a worm brushed her hand and squeaked cheerfully at her. She took it as a sign the lion was a safe distance away and grabbed the worm's tail. This one pulled her straight toward the sea floor. Releasing it, she fought her way back to the surface. Once again she checked the carrier seal and set off on her own, eventually latching on to a third worm. One that took her the rest of the way into the vast harbor of Selene on the island kingdom of Lunes.

No torches burned; no lanterns flickered. Starlight only lit her way. The harbor was at its quietest in the small hours before dawn. Even the cogs, the caravels, and the fishing boats appeared to have nodded off, bobbing gently alongside one another.

She kept low to the water, eyes and nose exposed, like a crocodile. Despite the hour, there would be guards patrolling the seafront. Guards meant questions, along with endless delay and a thorough search of her carrier. She must avoid them.

Lunes and St. John del Mar were not enemies, and they were not friends. Too many centuries of scheming and envy lay between them. Mercedes had once compared their relationship to that of two women who had lived as neighbors for many years.

Always pleasant at the annual harvest picnic, but each secretly vying for the grandest manor, the choicest furnishings, the brilliant marriages for their pretty daughters. For the two kingdoms, however, the prizes were not houses or unions for their offspring. They were the trade routes, jealously guarded pathways that showed where and how a kingdom supplied its wealth.

If she arrived at the castle and explained what had happened, and who she was, the royal family would help her. As any good neighbor would. She would be offered fine clothes and excellent food, escorted home on a royal vessel. But hospitality came with a price. A peek into her carrier. Her maps "borrowed" while Lunesian artists copied her work and claimed it for their own. It did not bear thinking about.

Reyna navigated between two caravels and hauled herself, gasping, onto the landing. That was as far as she made it. Even as she told herself she must hurry, she sprawled face-down onto wood that stank of damp and gutted fish. It smelled beautiful. Her laugh was more of a whimper. She had done it. Made it all this way without an arrow in her back or a single gnawed-off limb. She took a moment to marvel at that before she froze. Somewhere close, under cover of night, came the sound of flint striking stone.

She scrambled off the ground as a lantern sparked a dozen feet away. A lone figure sat directly across from her, his back against a waist-high coil of rope and his legs splayed before him. A young man, not many years older than she. He wore a white shirt and dark trousers. Leather boots came to his knees. Beside one leg, the lantern. Beside the other, a discarded dagger and belt. She took all this in at a glance before lifting her gaze, and from there, wariness turned to confusion.

He was weeping, this stranger. His was a narrow, handsome face. Sharp edges and strong black brows. His cheeks were wet with tears he made no effort to brush away, and a smudge like a dirty thumbprint marred the center of his forehead. She knew what the mark represented. A symbol of mourning in a hundred kingdoms, including her own. He had lost someone he loved not too long ago.

They regarded each other quietly across the landing. Reaching up, he knuckled away his tears and studied her own bedraggled appearance: hair and clothing plastered to her skin, seawater pooling around bare feet. Her shirt was also white, and she was glad now of the vest that kept her as decent as circumstances permitted.

He was the first to break the silence. In Lunesian, in a voice that rolled deep and pleasant into the dark. "Between the two of us, I wonder who's had the worse night of it."

The answer was clear. In Lunesian, she said, "I have."

The smallest of smiles touched his lips. There was little humor in it. "I doubt that very much." A glass bottle rested on his leg, gripped around the neck. He brought it close and peered into the opening. "Do you know, I'm not certain what this is, but it's stronger than I thought. I can't feel my legs."

That was welcome news to her. She heard the liquid slosh around within. The bottle was nearly empty, and she could smell its contents from where she stood. Mandarin and lemon masking a far more potent ingredient.

"It's called kudzu." She shifted a half foot or so, prepared to run if she must. Though he did not *feel* threatening, there was the matter of his dagger. Her arm brushed her belt to ensure her own weapon had completed the journey with her. It was there, Papa's old dagger, comforting in its deadliness. "People drink too much of it because it's sweet, but it's quite strong."

"Kudzu?"

A second small step. "Yes, it's from the Bushidos. You'll have a rough time of it in the morning."

"I think I knew that already" came his rueful answer, followed by "It's a fine night for a swim. Warm."

This time she did not move. She found herself wishing the lantern burned brighter, to better show his face. Something warned her he was not as inebriated as she had first imagined. Cautiously she said, "I thought so too."

"Not very safe, however. Monsters of all sorts in these waters."

"There are monsters everywhere."

The bottle stopped halfway to his lips. He lowered it. "Indeed," he said. And, with barely a pause: "That's quite a large dagger you have there."

"It's smaller than yours." She thought quickly. It was unlikely she could outrun him. He would know this harbor better than she. Better to end this conversation, dive back into the water, and try her luck there.

"So it is." The bottle came up. When he finished drinking, he wiped his mouth with the back of his hand. "Are you an assassin? If you are, I hope you're not going to the castle. It has excellent guards, you know."

The castle was the last place she wanted to be. "I'm no threat to your king, or to anyone on this island. I swear it."

Her words were meant as a reassurance. Instead he flinched, and his voice turned flat. "No one is a threat to him, not anymore."

The reason behind his ash mark became clear. Shocked, she said, "Your king is dead?"

"My . . . king is dead." He looked away, toward the blackness of sea, and in a distant voice said, "I'm no danger to you, whoever you are. I won't ask what papers you carry, or why a del Marian female is swimming this harbor in boys' trousers." He flung the bottle into the water, and Reyna tensed. A splash followed. "You're on some dark mission, I'm sure. I can't bring myself to care."

He thought her some sort of courier, a spy. Yet he was letting her go. Why, then, was she still here? It did not feel right leaving him alone in his grief.

Yet now was not the time to question this reprieve. There were others to consider. She backed away. "I am sorry," she said, and when he did not answer, she turned on her heel and ran.

THREE

REYNA KEPT CLOSE to the water's edge, eyes peeled for skulkers in the shadows. Her feet slapped against stone and dirt and far worse. Her clothing dried stiff and itchy against her skin. She tried not to think about it. Harder to ignore was the exhaustion that threatened to envelop her. Even with the help of the worms, that swim, this night, had taken its toll.

The sky remained the deepest indigo. But Selene was at its most striking in the daylight hours, she remembered: a city painted entirely in blue. She had visited a number of times with her uncle. Walls, doors, steps, all washed in blue, from the humblest tenements in the Old City to the royal castle, stone and crenellation nestled up against the base of Mount Abraham.

The harbor slithered along the waterfront like a snake. To her left, great bearlike snores erupted from the anchored ships. Sailors preferred to sleep on deck whenever possible, rather than in the dank, smelly confines of a hold. To her right were shuttered shop fronts and warehouses. Even with sunlight, it would have been difficult to locate one ship among so many others. She peered up at the pennants hanging limp from their masts, then at the names painted along the hulls. The *Guardian*, the *Peacekeeper*, the *Flying Stag*. It felt as though every kingdom was represented here, save hers. There were Coronad junks aplenty. Lunesian carracks? One could take one's pick. Along with galleys from Caffa, cogs from Oslaw, caravels from Pillard. Not one ship bearing the flag of St. John del Mar: two serpents entwined and hissing against the backdrop of a rogue wave. Trying not to give in to panic, she ran on.

Though she stopped twice. Once to wring out her hair like a rag and tie it back at her nape. The second time before a church, unexpectedly nestled between two warehouses. *Sanctuary*, she thought, reaching back to touch her carrier. She spotted candlelight in a stained-glass window and, rattling the door, found it unlocked. Not surprising during the formal mourning of a king. The interior was dimly lit and nearly empty. More rumbling snores arose from the front of the church. A priest having nodded off behind the altar, or a mourner curled up in a pew. Whoever it was, it would be better if she did not wake him. She lingered for minutes only, after the hastiest of prayers, careful to note the church's location so that she would be able to find her way back.

By the time she left the church and returned to the water's edge, dawn crept along the horizon. She was scowling up at yet another Caffeesh galley when footsteps intruded on her search. She spun around.

The stranger from the pier stood mere feet away. The lantern was nowhere to be seen, but he wore his belt and dagger and a hard-eyed expression. He said, "I'm curious after all. Who are you?"

She might have been back in the sea waiting for the finned lion to pounce. He'd followed her here? Had he seen her enter the church? "My name is Reyna."

Two men appeared at the railing of a nearby ship. The Caffeesh galley. They looked down upon Reyna and her nameless companion with bleary eyes, scratching their armpits and yawning.

"Reyna, is it? Well, Reyna, what business do you have in Selene?" When she shifted, he matched her movements, warning softly, "Don't try it. You can answer me now, or later, after a night in a crowded cell. It's your choice."

She gave him a withering look. Some choice. Gunnel had given her one as well: remain on the ship, or swim with the lions. She was growing sick to death of choices.

"What happened to not caring who I was? Or what I was doing here? You said —"

"I changed my mind."

The sun had risen high enough for her to see that his eyes were blue. The blue of sapphires shot through with red. She suspected she looked just as battered. They were both in a bad place. She said, "I'm looking for a del Marian ship."

"Your ship?"

"No. Mine was attacked by raiders. My captain and crew are still there. I was sent here . . ." She scuffed one foot on top of the other to dislodge a sharp pebble. "I'm here to find help."

"Sent?" His eyes had widened, and he looked at her clothing in a whole new light. "You're saying you *swam* here? All the way from the shipping lanes?"

"Where else?" He had seen her, hadn't he? Lying on the pier and gasping for breath.

Dark brows shot up. His answer was to sweep an arm along the harbor front with its endless row of ships. He thought she'd snuck off one of the anchored vessels. If only.

"Well, I didn't." Reyna tried to step around him, and this time when he moved to stop her, her dagger was in her hand. She pointed it at him, ignoring the startled shouts of "*Whoa, whoa!*" coming from the galley's deck.

"Don't," she warned. "You're wasting my time here. I don't want to hurt you."

"I don't want to hurt you, either" was his quiet, ominous reply. He did not look in the least afraid of the dagger twitching by his nose. "What's in your carrier?"

"Paintings."

"You're a *painter?*" Skepticism laced his words.

"It's true." And it was, partially. "Not a courier. Not an assassin. Will you go *away?* Find someone else to use your thumbscrews on? I don't have time for you."

There was a short silence during which they exchanged scowls and suspicious looks. She had thought him to be a regular shipman. A closer look at his clothing changed her opinion. His linen shirt was of a finer quality than that worn by most sailors, as were his boots, the leather soft and supple.

He said, finally, "I don't know any man who could make that swim."

"As you see, I'm not a man."

Someone laughed. Though she did not turn to look, she knew more sailors had gathered at the railing to watch their exchange. She could hear them, amused at this morning's unexpected entertainment.

The stranger said, "Come with me."

"No."

He reached out, slowly, pushing her hand down until the dagger pointed straight into the dirt. She let him and she did not know why she did. He said, "You need ships? Soldiers? Then come with me."

Who was he, that he could offer such help? And why would he do so? Nothing about his stony expression reassured her. She would not have thought him capable of weeping, for his king or anyone else, had she not seen it with her own eyes. But he held out his hand to her and kept it there even as the silence ticked on.

Another set of choices. Trust this stranger? Or . . . only there was no other choice, was there? Time was running short. Even as the realization came to her, she reached out and placed her hand in his.

Reyna snatched her hand back almost immediately. He led her down the harbor, demanding answers to his questions along the way. That her name was Reyna, that she was from del Mar, her parents long dead, were the only truths she told him. The rest were variations on the truth. She was a painter, like her guardian and uncle, Ginés. They spent much of the year traveling throughout the Sea of Magdalen, fulfilling commissions and accepting new ones as they came. Her uncle had decided to extend his stay abroad to visit with friends, but he'd sent Reyna ahead to del Mar to prepare their home, which had been closed these many months. It was on this journey that her ship had been attacked. It was a plausible collection of half-truths, given how tired she was. She only hoped she could recall the details for later.

When she was done, he said, "What is your ship's name?"

"The *Simona*." He had shortened his stride to match hers, she'd noticed. He kept frowning down at her bare feet in the muck.

"What sort of ship is it?"

She opened her mouth to say a cog, a del Marian merchant-man with a crew of thirty, but caught herself in time. A painter would not necessarily know these things. She said, "Who knows? It's the one that looks like a floating banana."

That earned her a quick, unreadable glance. "You were on a cog," he said after a moment.

"All right." Inwardly, she shrugged. He thought she was dim. It couldn't be helped.

The harbor woke slowly around them. Fishing vessels headed out toward the rising sun; trinket and food sellers prepared their booths. Within the hour, the waterfront would be a cramped, lively place, best navigated by using sharp elbows and slipping through gaps in the crowd.

The questions did not stop. "Who were you traveling with?"

"My uncle hired a woman named Gunnel to escort me home." What would they do to Gunnel if she tried to fight them? *When* she tried? With Gunnel, there was no *if*.

Incredulous, he said, "He sent two women on a ship without a guard?"

"Gunnel *was* my guard. She's a Coronad." The women of Coronado were as big and strong as their men. Both frequently offered their services as armed escorts to anyone willing to pay their price.

"Ah." He rubbed his temple, dropping his hand when he caught her looking. The kudzu was taking its toll. His next words were brusque. "Tell me what happened, and don't leave anything out."

She started with Gunnel waking her in her cabin. He listened intently, interrupting once, when she came to the part about the singing from the deck. "Were you and this Gunnel the only females aboard?"

"Yes."

"And you're thinking what? That some sort of pied piper for sailors captured your ship?"

Reyna's ears turned hot. It really did sound preposterous. "You asked me to tell you what I knew."

"So I did."

They passed a stone church. One painted the same blue

as the warehouses beside it. She was careful not to look in its direction.

"Why did you go into the church?" he said, then caught her elbow when she stumbled.

She yanked her arm free, annoyed with herself and with him. He had meant to surprise her with his question and had succeeded. "Why does anyone?"

"Confession?" he answered, and there was something sardonic in his tone.

Which required a curt response. "Prayer."

"A short one. You weren't in there long."

"I was in a hurry. An efficient prayer is still a prayer."

Another skeptical look, but he eased off his role as grand inquisitor. He brought her to the far end of the harbor, where a fleet of carracks and galleys were anchored below the sweeping scope of the lighthouse. Unlike the rest of the waterfront, this area was heavily guarded. Soldiers roamed the docks. Others stood upon decks and forecastles. An ash mark on every forehead.

They were met by a guard who wore a blue tunic with a silver crescent moon and star emblazoned across his chest. "Captain Levi. Has something happened? We weren't expecting you."

A captain. That would explain much. She could almost hear the soldiers' spines snapping to attention around them.

"Some pirates in our shipping lanes again, Matthew," her companion said. "I thought we'd have a look. Is Caleb up there?"

There being a handsome carrack, the name *Truthsayer*

painted in white along the hull. Two eyes had also been drawn on each side of the prow. Great, bulging orbs big as a cart wheel, glaring down at Reyna.

"No, sir." The soldier cast a quick, curious glance in her direction. "He slept in town last night. Should I fetch him?"

"Yes. Tell him to hurry."

The soldier rushed off. At the same time, Reyna's knowledge of Lunesian royalty came rushing back to her. The widowed King Lamech had three children. The eldest a daughter named Vashti. Now queen. And two sons. The younger a boy Reyna's age, Asher. The older was Levi, a captain in the royal navy.

Horrified, she looked up, found his eyes on hers already. "The king was your *father?*"

"Yes."

She pictured him huddled in the dark, seeking privacy so that he could grieve for his father. Not just his king. Her tears alarmed them both.

Panic flared in his blue eyes. He glanced around at the soldiers watching with great interest. Under his breath, he ordered, "*Don't.*"

"I'm not." She scrubbed away at her tears using a shirtsleeve. Her lower lip trembled.

"Reyna," the captain said, softly, "please don't. If you start weeping, then I'll start weeping, and I'll never be able to captain this ship again."

To her he felt like two different people. The boy on the pier. And this captain, a royal prince, trying to keep a brave face in front of his men. She nodded to show she understood. "Captain," she began.

"My name is Levi."

"Levi. I'm sorry I pointed a dagger at you."

His smile was unexpected. Before either of them could say another word, they were interrupted.

"Captain!"

A boy came bounding down the *Truthsayer*'s gangplank. Ten years old, she guessed, all arms and legs, with a cowlick that waved about his head like a rooster's crown. The ash mark on his forehead had been freshly applied. Levi caught him by the shoulders before he could crash into them.

He kept the introductions brief. "Benjamin, this is Reyna. She's your responsibility. Find her some clothes. Food. Mind her feet. We sail shortly."

"Yes, sir!" Benjamin turned to Reyna. His face was sunburned and covered in freckles. "Come with me, miss."

Reyna followed Benjamin up the ramp. She did not look back, not once, though she could feel the weight of the captain's gaze on her. On her neck, her shoulders. On her map carrier. A Lunesian prince had offered desperately needed help.

What, she wondered, would it cost her?

FOUR

THE CABIN WAS like any other. A narrow berth set against one wall, a small round window, a chair but no table. Travelers were expected to provide their own in the form of sea chests. Hers had been abandoned on the *Simona*.

She crawled into the berth and rested the back of her head against the wall, mumbling in agreement when Benjamin said something about finding her fresh clothes. She had only meant to close her eyes for a minute, but when she woke, he had already returned. And he had been busy. A tub filled with steaming water took up most of the cabin. He'd dragged in a chest and set it beside the chair. On its closed lid was a stack of neatly folded clothing and a silver dish that held a comb, a square of soap, and two corked bottles. A plate of food rested beside this bounty, clearly taken from the captain's stores and not the crew's. There was fish, freshly caught, alongside sliced melon and biscuits soaked in butter and honey.

Benjamin occupied the chair, fingers thrumming along the armrest as he waited for her to wake. He jumped to his feet when she said, "Oh! How long have I been asleep?"

"Not long," he assured her. "We're just leaving the harbor." He spoke in a rush of Lunesian, and her tired mind struggled to keep up. "The captain wants you to join him as soon as you're able. These clothes are clean. The captain says it's fine if you wear boys' clothes, since we didn't have time to send for a dress. This bottle's for your feet. Do you need help with your . . . ?" He glanced at the tub; his face flushed a bright mottled red. "I can close my eyes," he offered gamely. "I have sisters."

Reyna smiled. "I'll manage, I think. Benjamin," she said, stopping him at the door, "what happened to your king? Did someone hurt him? I don't mean to pry," she added quietly, when his face fell. "Only I don't want to say something wrong in front of the others, out of ignorance."

Benjamin's shoulders curved inward. Even his cowlick drooped. "They found him two days ago. At his desk. He was writing a letter to Prince Asher and just . . . No one hurt him. He was old."

"I see." Had the king finished the letter to his son? Poor Prince Asher. "I'm sorry."

The boy nodded. "I'll be right outside, miss. No one will come in here," he said, and closed the door behind him.

She would have to take him at his word. The door had no bolt. She listened. Her young guard paced back and forth in the passageway, while above, the familiar sounds of a ship in motion reached her ears: sailcloth unfurling in the wind, the drag of rope across the deck, a shouted order, a piercing whistle.

She left her carrier on the berth and hopped off. It was a

relief to shed her clothing and submerge herself in the tub. Her feet stung from cuts and scrapes, but upon further inspection, she discovered no splinters. Excellent. Uncorking a bottle, she sniffed. It was filled with scent. Jasmine, the last thing she would have expected to find on a Lunesian warship. She poured a liberal amount into the bathwater and used it to scrub the rank seaweed smell from her skin and hair.

When that was done, she applied the ointment to the soles of her feet. It helped tremendously. She dressed in a hurry: an undershirt, a cream-colored linen shirt with lace at the cuffs, brown trousers that were tighter than she preferred tucked into high boots, which, to her surprise, fit well. She attacked the knots in her hair with the comb, eventually managing a damp braid that fell to her waist. The map carrier took up its usual place on her back. As for breakfast, it would be coming with her.

When she flung open the door, she had a biscuit in her mouth and the plate in her hand. Benjamin stopped mid-pace and exclaimed, "That was fast! For a girl!"

Conversation dropped off the moment she appeared on deck. Not that the work actually stopped. The deck continued to be swabbed, the ropes inspected, the metal greased. By the rails, a dozen archers readied their bows and arrows. But Reyna saw the furtive glances and frank stares. Low whistles made their way to her ears. In her heart, she heard Uncle Ginés sigh: *It is* the trousers, Reyna. They will not do any longer. We will take time at the next port. Find you more dresses. There was no help for it today. The men could only be ignored, and so she walked on, plate in hand, finishing her biscuit.

Her resolve lasted a full three seconds until a pair of mariners snickered as she passed. Benjamin, seeing her spine stiffen, was quick to offer reassurance that they were not laughing at *her*.

"It's not you, miss. Honest. It's just that you're a girl wearing Seth's things, and they already give him grief for the lace."

She glanced at her frothy sleeves, then at the red-faced boy by the cookstove having his ribs poked by his shipmates. He was about her age, delicate-looking — a natural target on a ship — and dressed in clothes nearly identical to hers. She offered a tentative smile to show her gratitude for the loan, but he whirled away and stomped off in the opposite direction.

Benjamin watched him go, frowning. "Nothing else fit," he said, defensively.

"Seth's a sailor?" she asked. He looked more like what she claimed to be: a painter. Or a poet, even.

"Our cook. They don't tease him too much, really. He's in charge of our food."

Reyna looked down at her plate. Seth was a good cook. And he had fine taste in clothing. She hoped he would not suffer too much on her behalf.

She followed Benjamin up the steps to the sterncastle. On most ships, the sterncastle was the pilot's domain. It was there he plotted each course, surrounded by his charts and compass and sandglass turned on the half hour. Before they reached the top, voices drifted their way from within. Two men. One was Levi.

"Six ships, Levi! On her word alone. You don't really believe she made that swim."

"No, that part I believe," Levi said. "But if she's a painter I'll eat that compass. And anyway, since when do we turn our backs on our neighbors?"

"Del Marians don't count."

"Caleb."

"Have it your way. But I saw your pretty feather. Don't tell me we'd be here — with six ships! — if she looked like a horse."

Benjamin coughed, loudly, and sent an apologetic look in her direction. By then they stood side by side in the doorway. Levi and another man had their backs to the door, studying something on a chart table. They turned at Benjamin's cough.

Levi had changed into the same blue tunic and light chain mail worn by the archers. Tall black boots gleamed. He was still pale, reflecting the weariness of someone who had not seen his bed in many hours. But his eyes were no longer red, and the scruff that had darkened his jaw was gone. He looked like a proper ship's captain, stern and formidable.

The other man, the one who had called her a pretty feather, folded his arms and regarded her with a distrustful expression. He was the same height as Levi, with softer features and curly hair. He reminded her of the cherub carvings one saw in churches. Only this cherub was all grown up and surly-looking.

Unlike Levi, he was not dressed in royal colors, but in the white shirt and rough linen trousers of a professional shipman.

"Good work, Master Benjamin," Levi said after taking in this cleaner version of Reyna, and, when the boy grinned, added, "You're up in the nest this morning. Off you go."

"Yes, Captain!" Benjamin gave her a quick smile before leaving. There was a small silence while they, obviously, wondered how much she had overheard.

Levi said, "The food's good?"

Reyna nodded, quite unable to speak now that she understood what had been meant by *six ships*. The sterncastle was circular with wooden shutters. On a fair day such as today, the shutters had been left open, letting in the air and sun and offering an unfettered view of the harbor. Five ships sailed behind the *Truthsayer* in a V-shaped pattern. Six ships in total to hunt down two, readied in no time at all.

"Captain," she said, the only word she could manage. *You need ships? Soldiers? Then come with me.*

Levi had followed her gaze. "I don't want anyone thinking they can raid our lanes so easily. Best to nip this before they grow too comfortable here." He turned to his companion, made the introductions. As she had already guessed, Caleb was the *Truthsayer*'s pilot.

"Sir." Frost layered her greeting. She was no one's pretty feather.

Caleb's lips twitched. "Well, come in. Look at this chart for me, would you?"

They made room for her at the table. She slipped into the space between them. They towered over her. When she set her plate down, Levi glanced at her fish, swallowed, and looked away.

"Sorry." She'd forgotten about the bottle of kudzu. The sight and smell of her fish could not be helping. "I'll take it outside."

"No, it's fine. Leave it."

"You're certain?"

Levi said, "I'll live, I think."

Caleb studied the chart before them with both palms flat on the table. He kept an orderly space. Blank parchment stacked neatly beside sticks of charcoal. A handsome compass secured within an ivory box. The chart itself was a dull one, a rendering of Selene's harbor and the sea beyond it. No secret Lunesian trade routes here. He asked her, "Do you remember where you last saw the *Simona*? Was it south of the harbor? North?"

She stifled the urge to point and say *It was right there*, instead looking from the chart to the window, where she could see the lighthouse high atop the rocky promontory. "I could see the lighthouse when I jumped. It was directly ahead, but small." She held up a thumb and index finger to indicate size.

Levi leaned in to give the chart a closer look. "You said the men looked like Coronads?"

"Yes. Sort of."

Levi turned to her. "What does that mean?"

"Here," Reyna answered. "I can show you. May I?" She indicated the parchment, the sticks of charcoal.

Obliging, Caleb reached across the table. He paused when Levi said quietly, "Don't you have any?"

Caleb glanced back and forth between the two. Levi waiting, Reyna silent. Straightening, Caleb left the parchment where it was.

"You said you were a painter," Levi reminded her. "Don't painters usually carry parchment with them? Charcoal?" Deliberately, he looked at her carrier.

Without saying a word, Reyna pulled the strap over her head. She twisted the cap free and upended the contents of her carrier onto the table. Parchment scattered across the surface. Levi looked down, surprise replacing suspicion.

Caleb was the first to respond. "These are good. For a del Marian." He riffled through the loose sheets of parchment. Portraits and landscapes, not a single map among them.

Reyna spooned up a large portion of fish and took her time chewing. Levi's nostrils flared slightly. She licked her spoon, both sides, then repeated politely, "May I?"

A flush rose up Levi's neck. He reached for the parchment and charcoal himself. But he never quite lost that puzzled look, as though there was something about her he could not quite decipher.

The *Truthsayer* drew closer to the mouth of the harbor. While she sketched the raider from memory, Levi watched her work. Caleb swept up her paintings and looked through them one by one. After a time, she dropped the charcoal onto the table, satisfied. It was a good likeness.

"He's a Coronad, for certain," Caleb announced. "Though I don't know about that lady hair. You're sure you drew it right?"

"I'm sure," Reyna said.

"Huh. Look at that axe, Levi! . . . Levi?"

The captain had been staring intently at the new drawing. He lifted his head to find both Reyna and Caleb watching him. He looked dazed, she noticed, and a muscle ticked along his jawline. He really should have let her take the fish away. He said, "What? Yes. It's a good axe."

Reyna had sketched the raider from topknot to boots. The axe he carried was not the sort of weapon that would have been made in large quantities. The jade handle was too dear, the chrysanthemum carving the work of a master. A weapon that had cost someone a fortune, once. She had caught the briefest glimpse of it back on the *Simona*.

Levi said to her, "You speak Coronad?"

"Yes."

"And you understood what was said?"

"Only a little," she answered. "I think it might have been some sort of dialect." She repeated what she had heard. *Yes. Lame. No.*

"It isn't much," Caleb said, unimpressed.

Reyna shoved another biscuit into her mouth so that she would not have to respond.

Levi picked up one of her drawings. A bearded man in his middle years, somber and handsome. "Is this your uncle?"

"Yes."

"And this?" He used her uncle's portrait to point at another.

It was a drawing of Jaime. She had captured him sitting on the beach, strumming a guitar and smiling. "A friend."

Both Levi and Caleb took a closer look. Frowning, Levi tossed the drawing of her uncle onto the table, where it covered Jaime completely.

"Captain?" An archer leaned in the doorway. "A word?"

Levi followed the archer outside. When Caleb turned back to his chart, Reyna took the hint. She repacked her carrier, gathered her plate, and found a spot on the deck out of everyone's way. The sun was pleasant upon her face and neck. There was little else to do but finish her breakfast and wait.

They had reached the mouth of the harbor. From her vantage point, she could see Levi deep in conversation with the archer. Caleb stood outside the sterncastle, calling down orders to the helmsman. She had taken her last bite of melon when a shout came from high up in the crow's nest.

Benjamin pointed into the distance. Levi yelled something to the boy, his words lost to her. Benjamin pointed again and held up one finger. She understood. He saw one ship, no more. Minutes later, they sailed around the hills. And there it was, the *Simona*, exactly where she remembered leaving it. It was only as they drew closer that she saw the gulls circling above and the two lions, enormous finned beasts, clawing at the hull and growling, ravenous for whatever had been left aboard.

FIVE

NEVER SEEN A SACKED SHIP look like that before."

The observation came from a shipman named Samuel, a dubious expression on his face. There were murmurs of agreement. No one appeared on the *Simona*'s main deck as the Lunesian flotilla circled, archers watchful, arrows nocked. Not a soul stirred when Levi took up his horn and called out over the water, ordering everyone aboard to show themselves. From where Reyna stood, white-knuckled at the railing between Levi and Caleb, the ship looked abandoned, not destroyed. Absent were the usual signs of struggle: a cracked mast, splintered railings, blood splattered across the rigging. The men might have merely disembarked and gone off to the taverns for some ale and good company.

Where was everyone?

"You think they were fed to the lions?" Caleb asked, then grimaced at the frown Levi sent him and the look on Reyna's face. "Sorry," he offered.

Levi squinted up at the circling gulls. "Something on the

ship is setting them off." He called out, "Let's get rid of those birds, Master Ram."

A "Yes, Captain!" was followed by a lone arrow shot through the sky. Not striking the gulls, only frightening them away, flapping and screeching, toward shore.

The same archer asked, "Ah, what about them?"

The ship tilted slightly as everyone looked down at the lions trying to grapple their way aboard the *Simona*. Jaime had once told her of a finned lion that had clawed aboard a ship and eaten every man sleeping on the open deck. He had sworn it was true, but with Jaime, one could never be certain.

Levi said, "Shoot them only if someone falls in. Or they climb to mid-rudder. Otherwise let them be." He turned to Reyna with a distracted air. His thoughts were elsewhere. "I'll send someone back with news. Soon as I can."

"What?" She could not have heard right. "No, I'm coming with you."

"You're not," Levi said, his tone flat. The men had fallen silent, listening.

She jabbed a finger toward the *Simona*. "That's my ship!"

"And this is mine. It's too dangerous. Stay here. Wait." He walked off, calling out orders in that calm, measured way he had and sending men scurrying to do his bidding.

Fuming, Reyna watched him go. Stay here? *Wait?* Farther down, a ramp was hauled into place, connecting the *Truthsayer* and the *Simona* at their rails. The ramp was a pace wide, a mere two feet of rough planking. Her heart dropped to her stomach when she saw Levi swing onto the rail in one graceful move and step onto the plank.

Caleb had remained by her side. She turned to him in disbelief. "He'll go first?"

"Every time," Caleb confirmed.

Levi bent his knees, testing it for balance. A queue of ten or so men formed behind him.

Reyna gripped the railing with both hands. The lions paddled beneath the ramp, eyes gleaming as they tracked Levi's progress over open water. One actually licked its lips.

"He's mad!" she said under her breath.

Caleb surprised her with a grin. Twin dimples appeared, further reminding her of a cherub. "A little. But you were the one swimming with them. Who's the mad one?" He jogged off to the queue, where they made room for him at the front. If Levi was to cross over first, then his friend and pilot, it seemed, would be second. Levi took small, measured steps, arms extended slightly for balance. He looked straight ahead. Reyna could barely bring herself to watch. Endless moments ticked by before he reached the *Simona*, jumping onto the deck with his sword drawn. Caleb followed. And so on. Even young Benjamin.

Conversation was muted so as not to startle the men crossing. Archers kept the lions in their sights. Several men flailed. One lost his balance completely and tumbled off, hollering, only to catch the ramp with one hand and haul himself back up, and on. Thwarted, the lions roared.

Reyna knew how they felt. The *Simona* was a del Marian ship. She should be onboard where she might be needed. Not here, *waiting*. By the time the third shipman had crossed safely, her mind was made up.

She edged her way toward the ramp as the men crossed, curious-like, as though she merely intended to get a closer look. But as soon as the last man in the queue jumped onto the *Simona*, she hopped onto the ramp, scuttling forward to avoid grasping hands. The shouting started immediately, from both ships.

She paused a fifth of the way across. "Stop shouting, please," she called out, arms windmilling until she steadied. "Or I will be their breakfast."

Silence fell instantaneously. After that there was only the sea lapping against the hulls, and the creak of the ramp, and the lions below, growling deep and hungry. Best not to look down. She kept her gaze firmly on Levi at the other end. He looked like he wanted to kill her. No way to reassure him she had crossed many ramps, equally narrow, though admittedly never with the lions. They were an added touch. He watched as she made her way closer, and she sensed that, like her, he was holding his breath. For the second time in as many hours, he held out his hand. She took it; the moment she landed on the deck, braced for his anger, he said, "There are bodies."

Her hand fell away from his. "How many? Gunnel?"

"No. Eight men."

The dead had been left against the bulkhead, where they would not have been easily seen from the *Truthsayer*. She sank to her knees before them. They were men from home, every last one of them stabbed. It was their blood the lions had smelled.

Levi crouched beside her, grim-faced. "I'm sorry."

Reyna barely heard him. This man had been the ship's scribe. He had always been kind to her. The fingers on his left hand were stained black with ink, while his right sleeve remained neatly pinned at the elbow. She'd never learned how he had lost his arm.

Levi said, "Reyna, I need to go below. Will you stay here? Until we clear the hold?"

This man had served as helmsman. Old scars crisscrossed his face. He had told her how he had come by them. Impaled by pieces of flying, splintered wood — a cracked mast — during a storm. Reyna reached down and closed his eyes.

"Reyna."

"I'll stay," she said.

Levi had to lean close to hear, so softly were her words spoken. "Do I have your word?"

That brought her head up. She had grown accustomed to seeing suspicion in his eyes, not this concern. "Is my word good enough?"

"It's good enough."

"Then I'll stay."

Reassured, he left her and knelt by the closed hatchway where his men waited. On Levi's signal, Caleb pulled the door open. They cocked their ears, listening. A moment later, Levi disappeared through the opening, followed by the others.

Reyna did not think they would find anyone alive down there, enemy or otherwise. This ship felt empty. She wrapped her arms around herself, hands curled into fists and tucked beneath the pits of her arms. It did not help. She could not stop trembling.

"We should cover them, miss. It's getting warm out." Benjamin stood before her, subdued. He held up a bolt of sailcloth.

The flies were feasting. Seeing them jolted Reyna to her feet. She shooed them away, and together she and Benjamin laid the canvas over the men. When they were done, she dashed away a solitary tear and said, "Thank you." Benjamin settled beside her, keeping her company while they waited to hear from below. A shipman appeared halfway out of the hatchway. Big and muscular, with a shag of black hair. She thought his name might be Hamish. He beckoned her over. "Captain wants you."

She hurried to his side. "Is anyone else down there?"

"No." His eyes flicked past her to the covered bodies. "Come see for yourself."

She followed him down to the captain's quarters. The cabin was as she remembered, save for the candle burned to its nub and the flies buzzing around the captain's uneaten supper. The rice and fish had gone foul; the air reeked of spoil and rot.

Levi stood by an open window. The one she had jumped from. Caleb crouched by the bookcase, riffling through scrolls and grumbling. He would not find any charts or logs here. She had made sure of it.

"There's no one here," Levi said to her.

"You're certain?" There were a thousand places to hide on a ship.

"The men are going through one more time, to be sure."

One level down, Hamish's voice mingled with others, along with muffled thuds as doors were opened and closed.

Levi said, "The cabins are mostly undisturbed. They didn't take anything other than the men."

"And the charts." Caleb snapped the bookcase door shut. On any other day, his disappointment would have cheered her.

Levi watched Reyna with an odd expression on his face. "And the charts."

She dropped onto a chair by the desk. The flies on the plate paid her no attention. "Why would they leave the ship but take the men?" *And woman,* she amended inwardly. She could not think of Gunnel now. If there was anyone on this earth who could take care of herself, it would be her.

"It's a good ship," Caleb said in agreement. "Can't be more than ten years old. Worth quite a bit of silver."

Levi leaned against the wall, one leg slightly bent. "What do you know about the captain? Is he a wealthy man?"

She understood why he asked. "No. He's a working captain and this is a courier ship. It's worth more than any ransom his family could pay."

Levi nodded, as though his thoughts had been confirmed. "No matter how good the ship, it would take time to sell. There's the risk it would be recognized. Men, on the other hand . . ."

"Are easier to sell," Reyna finished, sickened as his meaning became clear.

"Slave catchers?" Caleb said. "This close to Lunes?"

"Perhaps." Levi rubbed both hands down his face. He looked as weary as she felt. "Perhaps not. Who knows? Not one thing about these raiders makes sense."

Of the six Lunesian ships, only two sailed back to harbor, the *Truthsayer* and the *Silver Moon*. The others continued along the shipping lanes, patrolling the waters and searching for any sign of the vanished del Marian crew. The dead went with them. Reyna wondered if this had been done for her sake. Not to spare her from the bodies being buried at sea, but for what came afterward, when any creature swimming nearby caught their scent. As for the *Simona*, it trailed behind the *Silver Moon*, abandoned, forlorn, secured by grappling lines.

Reyna found herself back in the *Truthsayer's* sterncastle, trying desperately to keep her eyes open. It felt wrong somehow to want to sleep after such a horrific discovery.

"You should go below. Get some rest."

Reyna's head snapped upright. Levi stood looking down at her on the bench. They had sailed into harbor while she had nodded off, and they would be dropping anchor shortly.

"I'm not tired," she said, the last word drawn out in a yawn.

Levi smiled. It transformed his face, made him look

younger. "Stay here, then, if you insist. No one will bother you." He aimed a pointed look over his shoulder at Caleb, hunched over the chart table. The pilot did not look up, only raised a hand in acknowledgment.

"Yes, yes. I won't bother her."

Levi turned to Reyna. "I'll write a letter to your king, tell him what happened here. He'll want to conduct his own search. It will be sent" — he looked out the window, calculating — "later today, while the wind is still good."

A ship sailing for del Mar today. The news brought her to her feet. "I'd like to go with it."

Silence. "I thought you might stay here while you recovered. As my guest. You've been through an ordeal."

"I'm not hurt," she reminded him. "All I need is sleep, and I can do that just as easily on a ship."

The request did not please him. "You're in a hurry to leave."

"To get home," she corrected, aware of Caleb watching and listening, chin propped on his fist.

Levi's frown deepened. "Who will you go home to? You said yourself your uncle isn't there, and your parents are gone. Do you have other family?"

None who mattered. She could not tell Levi the truth, that her school was her home, its students and instructors her family. He would want to know what sort of school it was.

Fortunately, she was saved from having to respond by Benjamin, who stuck his head in the door. "Soldiers on the dock, Captain."

They looked out a window to see four soldiers on horseback, waiting on the dock. Their features were indistinct at this distance, but the men wore blue and silver, and the horses were the rich brown of ancient mahogany. Both men and beasts were strangely motionless against the waterfront's clamor. A fifth horse stood by the others, riderless. Levi sighed.

Reyna said, "Are you in trouble?"

"No." Levi's smile held little humor. "Only I won't have time to write that letter today after all. You'll stay until I do."

Reyna was dismayed. "You can't —"

"See her to the castle, won't you?" Levi spoke over her protest, to Caleb. "Get her settled."

"If that's what you want," Caleb said, his tone neutral.

Not neutral enough for Levi, who frowned at him. "A guest chamber, Caleb," he added in warning. "I don't want to hear of her in the attic with the servants."

Caleb grinned, and Reyna suspected the attic was exactly where he'd planned on tossing her. She must have missed a gesture on Levi's part, because Caleb left them alone without saying another word, taking Benjamin with him. They did not go far, but loitered just outside on the sterncastle's top step. Like guards.

Reyna had to work to keep her voice even. "Am I your guest? Or your prisoner?"

"You'll tell me." Levi untied the leather pouch at his belt and emptied its contents onto his palm.

She couldn't have prevented her small intake of breath. His

blue eyes flickered at her reaction. He had deliberately caught her off guard.

In his palm were three leading stones, each roughly the size of a walnut. Spare stones for her compass. She had last seen them at the bottom of her sea chest, alongside her divider, needles, cross-staff, and astrolabe. Uncommon possessions for a painter, perfectly normal for a geographer, an explorer, a mapmaker. Even worse was what lay beneath the stones: a thin sheet of gold reminiscent of a playing card. Only *this* card had been stamped with the image of her king, Ulises, in profile, and below him was del Mar's royal symbol — the two serpents, the rogue wave. A royal passport given to few. It met every possible need while away from home. Shelter, transport, food. Silver from the counting houses scattered throughout the Sea of Magdalen, her account to be settled directly by Lord Isidore, del Mar's lord exchequer. She stared at the passport in horror. She had forgotten all about it.

Levi said, "We didn't find a single chart or logbook in your captain's quarters. Or in yours. Someone was careful about removing them. Likely not the captain, if what your Gunnel saw was true. And I don't think your raiders were interested in world geography. At least not last night." He paused, expectant. When Reyna said nothing, he continued, "Your carrier is similar to those used by our own royal explorers. Watertight. Worth far more than most artists can pay. And not only can you swim, but you walk a plank in such a way that I wonder if you were raised aboard a ship." Another pause, longer this time, followed by an exasperated "Say something, Reyna."

She said, "I'm a painter. Nothing more."

"Common painters are not given royal passports. Which begs the question — is this truly yours? Nothing? You'll stay until I find out the truth, then. As my guest."

Reyna tried hard not to gnash her teeth. Passport and stones were returned to his belt. The *Truthsayer* rocked slightly as its anchor dropped. When she glanced out the window this time, the soldiers were directly below on the pier, looking up at them. One raised his hand to Levi, who did the same.

He said to her, "You are no mere painter. You are no mere anything." And he was gone, stopping briefly to speak with Caleb before disembarking. He swung onto his own horse and rode off, the soldiers following behind him.

In the end, it was a simple thing to lose Caleb. In fact, it was he who lost her. She stuck close to his side as they wound their way through the crowded port. He had to shout at her in order to be heard.

"I don't know where Levi thinks I should put you," he shouted. "The castle is filled to the tower tops as it is. Everyone is here for the funeral."

"When will it be?"

"Tomorrow." Caleb edged them out of the path of a little

old lady driving an ass and cart. Others were not so quick, if the yelps and curses behind them were any indication. "Don't expect to see him anytime soon," he added. "He'll be keeping vigil over his father."

"I did not expect it," she muttered, determined not to let him needle her. And, louder: "He'll keep vigil today?"

"And through the night."

Reyna stopped, forcing Caleb to do the same and to look down at her in annoyance. She said, "He hasn't slept."

"I know." For a brief moment in time, they shared a common interest, united in their concern for his captain. "It can't be helped. He has to relieve the queen. There's no one else."

She knew the custom. Tradition dictated that, until his burial, King Lamech must be watched over by a blood member of his immediate family. Queen Vashti or Levi. The queen's husband could not do it, and her daughter was far too young for vigils. But Vashti had another brother . . .

She said, "Where is Prince Asher?"

"In Caffa. At university. A messenger was sent, but he won't be home in time."

Reyna no longer heard him. They were nearing the opposite end of the harbor, where a familiar flag flew high above a galley. A del Marian galley, still too far away for her to tell what ship it was, or which captain sailed it. She looked away quickly, but Caleb did not see. He was frowning, not in the direction of the del Marian ship, but back where they had come from.

Reyna glanced around to see the ass and cart that had

passed them earlier. A man had grabbed hold of the donkey's reins and was engaged in some sort of tirade against the little old lady who drove it. She was no timid thing. As the man growled at her — he might have objected to having his toes nearly trodden on by the donkey — she shook her fist at him and yelled right back. Onlookers tittered. When her fist came too close to his face, he grabbed it and yanked her high off the cart. Reyna heard a squawk, caught a glimpse of raggedy underskirts, before the woman was lost from view.

"Oy!" Caleb shouted. He ordered Reyna to "Wait here" and shoved off through the crowd. The titters had turned to outrage. Pickpocketing was a way of life by the harbor, brawling was tolerated, but to abuse a granny?

Reyna followed Caleb, keeping to the outskirts. A break in the crowd showed him kneeling beside the old lady, who clutched her ankle and grimaced in pain. Her attacker was face-down in the dirt. Another man kept him there by digging a knee in his back. Reyna looked at the del Marian galley. She looked at Caleb, gathering the woman in his arms. *He will be a while,* she thought, taking a step back, and another, losing herself in the crowd.

Reyna slipped into the church for the second time that day. Sunlight poured in through stained-glass windows. The pews were filled with parishioners deep in prayer. Incense hung in the air, along with the dust motes and smoke wisps trailing upward from a hundred lit tapers. She ventured up a back stairwell, which led her to a balcony overlooking the pews and altar. This was where the choir normally sang. Today she was relieved to find it empty.

Niches lined the wall, each home to a stone statue about four feet high. Like the del Marians, the Lunesians had a patron saint for everything. The more important ones were displayed on pedestals below — saints for war and peace and trade. The lesser ones had been relegated here. She walked past saints protecting gravediggers, shepherds, and orphans, and another cluster for cobblers and beekeepers, before she found the saint she was looking for. A robed figure holding a book in one hand and an empty money purse in the other.

Jeremiah, patron saint of poor students.

A quick look over her shoulder confirmed that no one had followed her. Carefully, she nudged the statue aside and reached for the rolled parchment she had hidden hours before. No harm had come to her maps; they remained neatly secured with twine. She kissed them, tucked them into her carrier, and, after shifting the statue back into place, left the church the same way she had entered.

Reyna raced across the harbor just as the del Marian galley, the *Violetta*, prepared to sail off. The last of its mooring lines had fallen away.

"Wait!" she cried, waving her arms above her head. "Stop!"

Passersby chuckled, and someone commented that time

and tide wait for no man. To her immense relief, they were wrong. A shipman halfway up the *Violetta*'s rigging spotted her first. He whistled down to the deck and pointed at her, and a moment later a row of faces peered over the rails. She recognized every one of them, including the bald, portly man formally dressed in del Marian green and silver. Captain Eustache. The recognition was mutual. Baffled surprise passed over his face before he shouted something across the deck. When the gangplank hit the dock, Reyna was waiting. Captain Eustache met her at the top, exclaiming, "Why, Lady Reyna! Where on earth did you come from?"

"Captain Eustache." Reyna paused to catch her breath, then beamed at him. "Sir, I am very happy to see you."

"And I you, my dear. But . . ." He looked past her to the harbor. "Who has come with you? Surely you're not alone?" His men had gathered around him. One offered a waterskin, which she took with thanks.

"There's no one with me," she answered after she'd drunk her fill and returned the skin. "I have news. Are you sailing home?"

"We are," Captain Eustache confirmed, his normally amiable expression turned sober at her words.

"Do you have room for one more?"

"As if you need ask. Come with me, my dear. We'll have you settled, and you can tell me what's happened."

The *Violetta* sailed from the harbor without incident. Reyna need not have feared Master Caleb coming after her; his

SIX

THE *VIOLETTA* SAILED into Cortes early in the day, though Del Mar's capital city had been awake for hours. Reyna stood alone at the railing, where she could hear the clamor of harborside life. Merchants, food sellers, and street thieves earning their living. The harbor was shaped like a half-moon. Ships moored along docks that extended from the waterfront like long wooden fingers. From there, the streets wound their way, ribbon-like, up to the castle high on the hill. A round castle, not square, it had always reminded her of an immense white cake.

A pleasant breeze blew tendrils free from her braid. If she inhaled deeply, she could smell the aromas coming from the food stalls. Mussels, clams, and scallops. Delicate, flaky pastry bursting with pork and raisins. Sea serpent cooked over an open fire, and juice from the pomegranate, fresh and sweet. The anticipation of it all made her mouth water. There was nothing like the food from del Mar. She had been a year away from it.

Captain Eustache joined her at the rails. "It's good to be back?"

Behind them, the crew busied themselves in preparation for the customs inspector who approached, puttering closer in a smaller boat.

"I've missed the food" was her honest reply. Abruptly she remembered her captured shipmates on the *Simona*, who might not be eating anything at all. Her dreams of food and drink felt frivolous. Thoughtless.

The captain did not see her shame. He chuckled. "Yes, the food is what brings us home again and again," he agreed, then sobered. "How may I help you, Lady? You'll have to make a report to Admiral Maira, I imagine. I could escort you?"

Reyna grimaced at the thought of the admiral. "I need to go home first."

A moment of confusion on his part. "To Alfonse?"

"To the tower." Her gaze was drawn northward, where the Tower of Winds, home to the School of Navigation, loomed high as part of the castle. Some would think it strange. Her family owned a grand estate in the southern city of Alfonse. But she considered the tower her home, and her small chamber within held everything she most needed in the world.

The captain said, "I suppose Lord Braga will take care of matters. Well. Our ship is in port for the next two weeks. You'll tell him I'm at his service?"

Reyna smiled. "I will. I'm grateful for your help, Captain."

"I've not done much."

"You saved my maps," she reminded him.

"*You* saved your maps, and they were well worth saving,"

the captain said with a glance at her carrier. "It stops my heart to think of what you went through to bring them here. Finned lions indeed."

The customs boat pulled up beside them. Not long after, the inspector appeared on deck, a humorless-looking man clutching an oversize ledger to his chest. Captain Eustache sighed. He went to attend to his unwelcome visitor, grumbling about death and taxes.

After refusing the captain's offer of a carriage, or even a horse, Reyna set across the harbor on foot. She brought nothing with her except her map carrier. There was nothing *to* bring. She slowed her steps to watch a fish seller who had attracted a crowd by tossing a large carp to his son a dozen feet away. Back and forth the poor fish went, passed overhead and underhand, each successful catch met with a rousing cheer. Briefly, she wondered what acrobatics had to do with the selling of fish. Both father and son were strapping men with big grins and no shirts, and on closer inspection, Reyna realized the onlookers consisted mostly of women, young and old. She smiled to herself and walked on. Moments later, she passed another seller, whose shellfish and eels were displayed in neat, attractive rows, but who had no customers. The stooped old merchant gazed morosely across the way at his competitor. This merchant still wore his shirt. Reyna continued on, no longer smiling and vaguely indignant on the poor man's behalf. It was not enough anymore to simply catch your fish and bring it to market. The competition was too great. You must also have an *act*. And a muscled chest never hurt.

She stopped when she saw the queue of men and women by the geographers' booth. An unexpected lump formed in her throat. What she had told Captain Eustache wasn't the complete truth. Food was not all that she had missed while she'd been away.

Master Luca manned the booth this morning, a gruff-looking man nearing thirty, spectacles perched on his nose. He was similarly dressed to the people standing in the queue, more like a common shipman than a royal geographer, one of del Mar's finest. Jaime sat next to him, recording figures in an open ledger. A woman attempted to sell them a globe she claimed had once belonged to the first Bushido king, who had ruled to the east a thousand years ago. Master Luca was having none of it.

"... must think I'm an idiot. A thousand years? More like a week. Look, the paste is still wet. What say you, Jaime? Jaime!"

Jaime's head snapped around. He'd been caught blowing a kiss to the fruit seller's daughter two booths over, a pretty girl whose father's back was turned as he helped a customer. Reyna could not prevent a lifetime habit; she rolled her eyes. Jaime gave Master Luca a sheepish grin and looked past him ... and that was when he saw Reyna.

Jaime's eyes widened. Brown eyes, heavily lashed. They were the envy of his sisters. He startled those nearest him with a shout and vaulted over the booth. The queue scattered out of his way.

"Jaime!" She flung her arms around his neck and laughed as he swung her around in dizzying circles. Nothing about him had changed. His arms were strong. His hair needed trimming. A ruby, a speck only, glinted at his ear. He smelled of paint and parchment and home.

"We weren't expecting you!" Jaime exclaimed, his grin as wide and as silly as hers. "You didn't send word!"

"I wanted to surprise you!"

Master Luca cleared his throat. He had remained by the booth. Someone had to; a significant amount of coin lay behind it in a locked box. In his arms was the ledger Jaime had thrust at him.

She walked up to him. "Sir," she said.

Master Luca smiled. "Reyna. Welcome home." He handed the ledger back to Jaime and opened his arms wide. She walked into them. He held her tight for a moment, then asked quietly, "What's wrong?" He had seen something in her expression that told him all was not well.

She stepped away and, conscious of those listening all around them, said, "Uncle is well. He sends his greetings. But I have other news. None of it good."

"How much of this work is your own?" Lord Braga said after studying her maps and reading her reports.

Offended, Reyna answered, "All of it," and when the royal navigator glanced across the desk, one eyebrow raised, insisted, "Uncle Ginés didn't lift a finger to help. I wouldn't even let him sharpen the quills. This is my work entirely."

She was back in the Tower of Winds, her work spread out upon Lord Braga's massive, cluttered desk. Too restless to take the chair he had offered, she stood opposite him. He was a big man — tall, not fat — with a bald head and a black, broomy mustache. As royal navigator, he oversaw the kingdom's network of geographers, mapmakers, pilots, instrument makers, and apprentices. Reyna, at seventeen, was no longer an apprentice and not quite a master, but occupied that small space in between, accepting any task given to her. A general Tower of Winds dogsbody. Until this man decided she was deserving of something more.

Her work was only a small part of an ambitious project, the first of its kind. The humbly titled *Braga's Geography*, when it was completed, would be a massive tome, a compilation of maps of every del Marian possession, near and far. And not only maps, but studies of the people inhabiting those possessions, societies living under del Mar's rule. Who they were, how they lived, their customs, their traditions. Anything that could be gleaned from a year living among them. Reyna had been assigned the province of Aux-en-villes, a territory famous for the pearls that blanketed its riverbeds and lakebeds.

Lord Braga had moved on to another map. Without looking up, he said absently, "How is your uncle?"

"Very well." Reyna passed him a letter sealed with red wax.

It had been tucked in with her maps behind the statue of St. Jeremiah. "He sends his regards."

Lord Braga set aside the map. Wax crumbled to the desk as he broke the seal. He read the letter, chuckling once, snorting twice. Reyna waited and tried not to let her discomfort show. She never entered this chamber unless summoned. It made her sad. It picked at the stitches that kept her grief contained.

She had passed her childhood in this room while her grandfather worked. Learning by listening and watching. Occasionally permitted to help. After Lord Silva's death, Lord Braga had been named royal navigator. He had transformed the space so that it bore little resemblance to her grandfather's neat, tidy work chamber. The furniture was different, the chairs and desk grander to accommodate Lord Braga's frame. The maps on the walls had been exchanged for others. But Lord Braga smoked the same sort of pipe her grandfather had once favored, and the aroma of cloves and cinnamon permeated the air. Invoking memories she'd tried very hard to forget.

Lord Braga finished reading and said, "He makes no mention of returning home."

Her Uncle Ginés never did, though Lord Braga brought it up every time he read one of his letters. "I don't think he will."

A frown. "He has responsibilities here."

"He doesn't neglect them. The estate is looked after," she reminded him. There was a steward in Alfonse, and an army of servants. "So am I. Del Mar is not his home any longer, Lord Braga."

Sighing, Lord Braga tossed the letter aside and propped his boots onto the desk. He was handsomely turned out in a quilted brocade tunic as black as his boots. Sunlight poured through an open window, glinting off the two small gold hoops that pierced one ear. A single gold chain looped around his neck, at the end of which hung a miniature sandglass the length of her thumb. He said, "It was fortuitous, Elias finding Ginés when he did. We hadn't heard from him in years. I confess I didn't think he was still among the living."

It was the first time Lord Braga had said these things to her, in this mystified way. Perhaps he sensed he was missing a part of some untold story. Which he was, but her uncle's tale was not hers to tell. When she did not answer, Lord Braga said, "Has he been good to you?"

"Yes." At Lord Braga's doubtful expression, she gestured toward the maps. "I would not have been able to do this if he had not taught me how. I couldn't have asked for a better teacher."

"Are we speaking of the same man? The Ginés I knew would never have had the patience to take on an apprentice." Lord Braga folded his hands across his middle. Still a geographer's hands despite his lofty title. No rings in sight, only ink splotches and stubborn flecks of green paint. "Especially a girl." He spoke as though he were trying to work through some complicated puzzle.

Reyna offered a feeble "People change."

"That much?" Lord Braga's boots thumped back to the floor. "I don't mean to insult the man. Maybe I'm envious. I didn't expect Ginés, of all people, to turn out one of my best students."

Reyna smiled. "Better than Jaime?"

Lord Braga laughed. Jaime was his son. "Safer if I don't answer." He gathered her maps and notes into a crooked stack. "These are well done. A worthy addition for our book."

"I'm glad." Taking a deep breath, Reyna thought it was now or never. "I hoped we could discuss my masterwork."

His brows shot up. "You're seventeen only."

A masterwork was required before one could be elevated to master geographer. It could be anything: a map, a globe, a discovery, an invention. A final project for the current masters to examine and consider.

"Nearly eighteen," she countered. "Lord Elias and Master Luca were both eighteen when they began their masterworks. I'm not that far off."

"Only by six months," he said dryly. "Don't think I wouldn't remember. I was there when you were born."

Surprised, Reyna said, "I didn't know you were."

"I was with your father, anyway," he amended. "He paced holes in the rug outside your mother's chambers. It had to be replaced."

Reyna was quiet. She could barely remember her parents, gone these eleven years. What she did recall were the faintest wisps of memory. Her mother's laugh, the scent of jasmine, her father lifting her high in the air. Before she could think better of it, she asked, "Was he sorry? When he learned I was a girl?"

"No." Lord Braga was definite. "He wept when he first saw you, but it wasn't because he was sorry." He changed the subject entirely. "You were this close to being killed by those raiders. I can't help thinking that this is not the life your father, your grandfather, would have wanted for you."

Reyna lifted her chin. "I know it isn't. But they aren't here. And this is my life and no one else's."

"Don't you want a husband? A family?"

"I may want those things. Later."

"At your age there is always a later." Lord Braga's smile was rueful. "Today there are more pressing matters. Which reminds me . . ." He rummaged around before producing a key the length of her hand. He handed it to her.

She took it. "Where does it go?"

"To the storage vaults. I've been thinking they're overdue for a cleaning. And some inventory."

His meaning sank in. Her shoulders sagged. It was the opposite of a mastership. Punishment. She had hoped that if she presented her work on Aux-en-villes, he would be so dazzled by her skill he would forget the manner in which she had brought it home. She muttered, "I didn't lose a single map to the Lunesians."

"But for luck, and chance," Lord Braga countered. "It is the first thing you're taught in this school. These maps should have gone overboard."

"Would you really have done it in my place? After all this work?"

"I would have," Lord Braga said without hesitation. "But . . . I would also have taken the time to make copies and left them behind in my uncle's safekeeping."

Her shoulders sagged even more. She turned the brass key over in her hand. The storage chambers for the Tower of Winds were located several floors beneath the ground. Deeper than the dead were buried. A dusty room full of ancient books, abandoned furniture, and broken instruments. It was no small punishment he'd given her. This was to be her summer. *Welcome home, Reyna.*

"I understand," she said.

A knock sounded on the door. Lord Braga raised his voice. "Come."

A messenger poked his head in, informing them the king was ready to see them. The summons had been expected. Like Lord Braga, Reyna had taken care with her appearance. She'd had to make do with one of the dresses she'd left behind in her tower chamber. The green silk was not in the latest fashion, but it was better than the trousers she had grown accustomed to wearing while off island. King Ulises was a tolerant man, but not that tolerant.

When the messenger left, Lord Braga rounded the desk, offered an arm, and said, "No need to look so glum. Take the punishment. Learn from it. As for your masterwork, we can discuss it later. When you're *eighteen*."

SEVEN

"A STRANGE SINGING?" Admiral Maira repeated. "Do you expect us to believe the men were placed under some sort of *spell?*

Reyna felt her hackles rise. Three men gathered around a table in the king's chambers. King Ulises himself, Lord Braga, and Admiral Maira, stout and puffy-chested, like a well-dressed wine barrel. She knew his presence was required — he was responsible for all matters related to the sea — but she wished him far away. It was not his words that riled her — Levi had said something similar — but the man himself. It was his tone, which implied she was either hysterical or a liar. It was his demeanor, which said, quite clearly, she did not belong here. This was not her first encounter with Admiral Maira.

"I don't know what happened," she said evenly. "I only know what I heard and what Gunnel told me."

"Yes, Gunnel the Coronad. A trustworthy source." Admiral Maira smirked at her across the table. A wispy mustache drooped over his lips. In his hand was a second sketch she had drawn of the raider, the original having been left behind with Levi. "You are young, Lady Reyna. But this isn't a fairy tale."

Lord Braga's own mustache twitched, a warning sign recognized by those who knew him well. King Ulises watched her quietly, waiting for her response. Neither spoke for her. She could speak for herself.

"Why is it hard to believe?" She would not lose her temper. "We accept that there are monsters in the sea and ghosts in our forest. But the notion that some form of magic is being used to restrain our men, to silence them . . . how is that any less absurd?"

"There are no ghosts in our forest," the admiral dismissed. He did not see the glance exchanged between Reyna and the king. "You admit to being asleep before the attack."

Admit to? As though she'd done something wrong. She said, "I was."

"You would have been disoriented," Admiral Maira explained patiently. "Overwrought. Understandable — however, this is why we don't like women on our ships in the first place. Bad luck. You could have simply dreamt this . . . magical singing."

Reyna opened her mouth to respond. Lord Braga was quicker. He had had enough. "'Overwrought'?" he said coldly. "She was not too *overwrought* to escape from those raiders. Or too *overwrought* to use the worms, swim to shore, *and then* convince a Lunesian prince to help her. Show me any sailor under your command who could have done her better, Admiral. 'Overwrought.'"

An uncomfortable silence fell, long enough for the tips of Admiral Maira's ears to turn a bright, unbecoming red. Reyna kept her smile carefully hidden. Lord Braga would scold her for disobeying the rules; he would banish her to storage, where she just might die from inhaling centuries of dust. But he would never allow an outsider to criticize her. Beyond the Tower of Winds, they presented a united front, always.

Before them was a model of the Sea of Magdalen and its kingdoms — del Mar to the east, Lunes to the west, and Caffa, the ancient kingdom of scholars and learning, to the north. Their corner of the world had been brought to life with paint and clay: the tallest mountain ranges six inches high, the sea a swirl of green and blue and vicious whirlpools foaming white. Wooden ships marked del Mar's busy trade routes. The replica had been a gift from the royal explorer Lord Elias to his friend and king on his twenty-fifth name day. That had been two years ago.

The king spoke at last. He wore black from head to boot. Even his crown was black, a thin band of onyx with an emerald at its center. It sat upon dark hair, closely cropped, and framed a handsome, serious face. "No one here is questioning Lady Reyna's courage," he said mildly. "Or her hearing. Are we, Admiral?" Beneath the mildness lurked something less pleasant. A warning.

Admiral Maira heard it, and cleared his throat. "Your Grace, no insult was meant." He turned to Reyna, not quite meeting her eyes. "If I've caused offense, Lady, I apologize."

"Thank you," Reyna said quickly, because Lord Braga looked ready to reject the apology on her behalf.

The king said, "Good. Now, where do we go from here?"

"I'll send patrols at once," Admiral Maira said. "To Lunes and the surrounding waters. But we all know how common pirate attacks have become. A weekly occurrence sometimes."

To her surprise, Lord Braga agreed. "He's not wrong. A Bushido ship vanished two months ago. It was found on a sandbar near Caffa."

"Which ship?" Admiral Maira asked.

"The *Hishikawa*."

A shadow passed over the king's features. "Captain Yuri was your friend. I'm sorry, Braga."

"Thank you, Your Grace."

Something, *something*, had Reyna wondering. "Sir, was anyone left behind on the ship?"

A grunt. "One dead," Lord Braga said. "They didn't have the decency to bury him at sea. Do you remember Ryo, one of the officers? He had a —" He broke off, startled, and met Reyna's eyes across the table.

Admiral Maira looked from Lord Braga to Reyna. "What did he have?"

Lord Braga said, "The *Hishikawa* sailed into a storm two, no, three years ago. One of the younger boys was caught high up. Ryo climbed the rigging and rescued him, but he lost three fingers for his trouble."

Reyna said, "The men on the *Simona* had old injuries. Obvious ones." She described the helmsman with the scarred face. The scribe with the missing arm.

"All of them were hurt?" the king said. "You're certain?"

Reyna thought back. What else? A missing finger, a limp. "Most of them. The others were just old."

The king's expression hardened. "They're not wasting their time with imperfections, or men past their prime. Slave catchers?"

Reyna said, "Prince Levi thought the same."

Admiral Maira said, "I'll send men to inspect the markets closest to the shipping lanes."

"Do that," the king said. "I want it made clear, Admiral, that anyone who thinks to buy one of our men will face the same punishment as those who try to sell them. There will be no distinction."

"Yes, Your Grace."

The king turned to Lord Braga. "You're leaving for Coronado?"

Lord Braga nodded. "Before our next expedition sails east in a month. We have some business there. I leave in two days."

"Good. You'll speak to Frantz for me. Tell him what happened. I'll write a letter." Frantz was Coronado's king.

Lord Braga did not look hopeful. "He'll say he knows nothing."

"Of course he will," the king said. "It might even be true.

But I want him to know that we are unhappy. And unhappy neighbors are bad for trade. He might be able to do something about it."

Threatening the Coronad king without actually threatening him. Lord Braga agreed this was a sound idea.

King Ulises said, "Lord Elias will be sailing to Lunes for the coronation in my stead. You'll sail with him, Admiral. I want his ship well protected."

"Of course, Your Grace. It will be my honor."

Admiral Maira and Lord Braga departed soon thereafter. The king asked Reyna to stay behind.

"Walk with me, Reyna. I haven't been outside all day."

Obliging, she followed him, surprised when he strode right past the main doors, the only way out of the chamber if you didn't count the balcony. He said, "How many are out there?"

"A hundred, at least." She had passed them on the way in. There was always a crowd waiting outside the king's chambers, each person wanting something. To request a boon, or air a grievance. To present daughter after daughter in the hopes he would finally get around to choosing a bride. He was nearing thirty, after all.

"That's what I thought." He stopped at a wall where a magnificent tapestry hung, and flipped aside a corner, revealing a door. "We won't make it five feet if we go that way. Come on. Mind the spiders."

He led her into a gloomy corridor and down tight-winding

steps. Narrow slits had been carved into the walls. Enough light showed through for her to see the spiders tenanting the corners and the dust thick beneath their feet. At the bottom of the steps, he pushed open another door. The scent of blood oranges filled her senses before her eyes adjusted to the sun's presence. They had entered the royal orchards. The trees were arranged in perfect, angled rows enclosed by stone walls. One had to look carefully to see the guards among the leaves and fruit.

The king reached into his belt and pulled out a sheet of parchment, folded thrice. He handed it to her. "This arrived from Lunes. It's from your Prince Levi."

Her Prince Levi? She took the letter and unfolded it.

"He must have sent it right after you sailed to have it arrive so quickly," the king said. "The first part you know. The second . . . well. That might be of some interest."

They walked among the trees as Reyna read the letter. Levi wrote with a firm, bold stroke, his letters slanted heavily to the right. It began with:

To Ulises, king of St. John del Mar, esteemed friend of Lunes

"'Esteemed friend,' he writes," the king commented with a sardonic glance. "The letter must not have gone through Vashti's censors. It's far too polite."

Reyna thought it best to keep silent. There was no love lost between King Ulises and the new queen of Lunes. Years ago, there had been talk of a union between the two. Nothing had ever come of it, and Vashti, no older than Reyna's king, had married one of her father's friends, a doddering old man in his fifties. They had a young daughter.

Reyna read quickly. She could hear Levi's voice, the deep, serious timbre of it, as he described all that had happened, from Reyna appearing on the dock to the grisly discovery on the *Simona*. He wrote of the Lunesian ships searching for any evidence of the raiders and the missing del Marian crew. Offered also his kingdom's continued assistance should del Mar have need of it.

King Ulises reached up to pluck an orange from a tree. Orange peel littered the ground in their wake.

As for the girl, I have lost her. She vanished on her way to the castle, and we have been unable to find any trace of her. I am concerned, though she has proven more than capable of taking care of herself. Nevertheless, she has no money — because he had taken it from her — no friends here, only a courier's pack that survived the swim with her.

There is a chance she may have boarded a del Marian galley that departed the same day of her disappearance. The Violetta. If this is true, she may be on del Mar even now, or arriving soon.

Might I beg your assistance in this matter? Would it be possible to have inquiries made? She may have ties to one of your painters' guilds. The portraits and landscapes in her possession show extensive training and skill. Or I wonder if she might be the daughter of a shipping family. It is clear she has spent much time at sea, and knows her way around a ship as well as my own men.

I believe her to be an orphan raised by an uncle. The name she gave me was Reyna.

As for her appearance, she — here the stem of the *s* was heavy, suggesting the author had paused in thought without remembering to lift his quill — *is lovely. Slight of build, her hair the deepest brown, reaching to her waist, brown eyes, a tiny scar shaped like a crescent moon on her chin. You would not forget her face, once you had seen it.*

It would ease my mind greatly to know she is safe, and any help in this matter would be most welcome.

There was the usual cordial ending and a bold, hurried signature. When Reyna looked at her king, she knew her face was a terrible mottled red. There was no help for it. *You would not forget her face, once you had seen it.*

"I wouldn't have thought Prince Levi a romantic," the king remarked, offering her an orange. "In fairness, he was a boy when I last spoke with him, and far more interested in ships than young ladies."

"He's still interested in ships." Reyna nibbled on the orange. "I didn't know you had met him."

"He was nine or ten," the king said. "Quieter than his siblings, more serious, though I only spoke with him briefly. Mercedes knows him better."

"Does she?" Reyna said, surprised.

A nod. "Levi served as her page whenever she visited." Mercedes was the king's cousin, second in line to the throne, and for years now an emissary for the royal house of del Mar. It made sense they would know each other. The king tossed the rest of the peel away; his expression turned serious. "Did he behave honorably toward you?"

"Yes."

"Did you ever feel threatened in his company?"

She was adamant. "Never."

He nodded, unsurprised. "I'll write a reply to your prince, send it out with Elias when he leaves for Vashti's coronation."

Lord Elias, but not Lady Elias. Mercedes was with child, her second after Sabine, her pregnancy too far along for her to consider travel.

"When will he be home?" Lord Elias had gone to visit his mother in Esperanca, where she was recovering from an illness.

"Any day now. Commander Aimon had some business up north. They'll ride home together."

Reyna offered the king the letter. "You'll tell the captain I'm here? I didn't think he would notice I was gone."

"No? It sounds like you made an impression." He picked off a cobweb that clung to his sleeve and tossed it aside. "As for telling him you're safe, I thought you could write to him yourself."

Reyna was already shaking her head. "Oh, I don't think —"

"Reyna." He spoke firmly. "I know Levi's sister, and I will tell you I am certain, beyond certain, that she would not have been as kind to you as her brother was. Especially during these trying times. A personal letter is quite literally the *least* you can do."

What would she say in a letter? She'd never written to a boy before. Jaime did not count. This was different. Different in a way she did not fully understand.

"All right, yes. I'll think of something," she said.

The king looked amused, but said only, "Bring the letter to me. If it helps, you may seal it. No one will read your words, at least not in this kingdom." He plucked another orange from the tree and offered it to her. She took it.

They had reached the orchard gates. As the guards swung them open, King Ulises said, soft enough for her ears only, "The scar. Do others still ask of it?"

She reached up, touched the crescent moon, the size of a thumbnail, on her chin. "Everyone here knows what happened. But when I'm away, sometimes."

"What do you tell them?"

Reyna dropped her hand. "That I fell."

Her king was not one to show his feelings. In this way, he reminded her of Levi. But at her words she saw the anger that flared, bright and hot, in his eyes. On her behalf. She had not been hurt in a fall. The truth was far uglier.

They did not speak of it. The king leaned down, kissed the top of her head. "Welcome home, Lady," he said, and walked back into the grove, leaving her standing there alone.

EIGHT

EIGHT YEARS AGO, a stranger had tried to steal a map from the royal geographers' booth. Chance had placed Reyna directly in his path, leaving her with her ribs cracked, her fingers in splints, her face bruised and battered. It had hurt to eat, let alone descend the staircase within the Tower of Winds. When she had finally emerged from the castle, it had been at Lord Elias's urging.

"I won't go," she told him, near tears. "My face . . ." She had not wanted to leave the safety of her chamber. Her eye was no longer black, but the cut on her chin had grown worse. Red and itchy, oozing foulness, even with the doctor's endless potions and creams.

Lord Elias had knelt before her — gingerly, as he had his own hurts — so that he could look her in the eye. He was ten years older than she was. And he laughed a lot, at least until recently. Sometimes in her heart she pretended he was her brother. He said, "I think I know someone who can help, but he's a busy man. Or so he tells me. We must go to him."

She was not going anywhere. "People will stare."

"Wouldn't you? If you were them?" he said. "They stare because it is not *right* that a young girl was hurt as you were. You make them think of their daughters and their sisters, and if they look angry or shocked, it is because they are angry *for you*."

"Not everyone is good." A lesson she had learned curled up in the dirt, trying to protect her head as the kicks rained down upon her.

"Enough people are." Lord Elias's voice was gentle but firm. "Reyna, do you trust me?"

Of course she did. Where would she be without Lord Elias? Without Mercedes? Not everyone was good. But *they* were. And that was how she found herself in the parish of St. Soledad, outside the barber-surgeon's shop. A guitarist slouched by the door, strumming a soulful tune — which came to an abrupt halt when he caught a glimpse of Reyna's face. He started up again, hastily, but it was too late. The silver double-shell Lord Elias had fished out to give him was deliberately returned to the pouch at his belt. He scowled at the musician, wrapped a protective arm around Reyna's shoulders, and hustled her through the doorway. Humiliated, Reyna peeked over her shoulder. The musician looked dejected at his loss of income.

They entered a single chamber with low beams blackened with age, and Reyna promptly forgot all about the musician. She stared around in wonder. Shiny metal instruments had been arranged on a table in neat rows: shears, scalpels, three saws. Why would anyone need more than one? A staircase led to the upper floors. Bookcases lined the wall, filled with very few books and quite a number of small skeletons. She guessed they had once been rats, lizards, and owls — and what looked to be a cat, propped by itself in a corner. A man crouched before the shelves, searching for something. He looked over at their entrance and rose.

"What's happened here, Mori?" Lord Elias turned in a slow circle, a baffled expression on his face. "It's so clean."

"Too clean," Mori agreed with a grimace. He was not as young as Lord Elias. There was a sprinkling of gray in his dark hair. A white apron protected his shirt and trousers, but the neat condition of his clothing did not extend to his person. His hair was a wild mop, and the bristles on his face were more scruff than beard. Reyna did not understand. Was he not a barber as well as a surgeon?

"My niece has come to live with me. She's . . . particular about such things." Mori smiled at Reyna and bowed. "I am Master Mori. And you must be Lady Reyna, geographer in training."

The description delighted her. She startled herself — and Lord Elias, she suspected — by smiling tentatively at the barber. "I'm just Reyna."

"A pleasure." Master Mori eyed her chin, then said, "Lord Elias told me about your injury. How it's slow to heal. Will you sit here?" He offered a chair beside the table and all the shiny, sharp instruments. Seeing her hesitation, he added with a smile, "None of these is for you. You have my word."

Lord Elias was still looking around the chamber, bemused.

"What is that smell? Is it" — he sniffed the air delicately — "lavender?"

"Chamomile, if you must know." Mori frowned at him. "It's supposed to calm a patient's nerves. Or so I'm told."

"If you say so," Lord Elias said.

Reyna perched on the edge of the chair and held herself still as Master Mori bent to inspect her chin. He seemed like a nice man, and he smelled pleasantly of pipe smoke and chamomile. But he was too close. Close enough for her to see the individual hairs sprouting from his face. Close enough to hear his breath, slow and steady. When he reached for her chin, she cringed. Immediately Master Mori straightened and stepped away.

"I'm sorry," Reyna whispered, mortified. Lord Elias stood a little way behind Master Mori, watching quietly.

"You've nothing to apologize for." Master Mori's smile assured her he meant what he said. "How old are you, Reyna?"

"Nine, sir."

"My niece just turned ten," Master Mori informed her. "She doesn't know a soul in town, and I wonder if I might introduce her to you?"

Reyna did not know any girls her age. At least not well. There were only boys in the geographers' school. Intrigued despite herself, she nodded.

"Good." Mori hollered up at the ceiling with its blackened beams. "Blaise! Come down here!"

There was a loud thump from above, followed by the sound

of feet clattering down the stairs. A girl appeared in the doorway, wearing a white apron over her dress. Unlike Reyna's straight, waist-length braid, Blaise's hair was cut short: big, black, loopy curls circled her head like a halo. A red bow kept the hair off a cheerful round-cheeked face.

"You've been sampling the tarts again," Master Mori said to her. "Before supper."

"How can you know?" The girl came to stand before her uncle.

Master Mori, using a clean rag from the table, wiped what looked to be a lemon smudge from the corner of her mouth. "A hunch," he said with some dryness, adding over her laugh, "This is Lord Elias and Lady Reyna, from the Tower of Winds. My sister's eldest, Blaise."

Blaise and Lord Elias greeted each other; the latter looked charmed by the barber-surgeon's niece. And then Blaise turned to her.

"Lady Reyna." Her gaze did not stray to Reyna's chin once.

Even so, Reyna was tempted to cover it up with her hand. "I'm just Reyna," she said, and, remembering Master Mori's words, added, "You're new to town?"

"Two weeks only," Blaise confirmed. "I'm from Montserrat. My *maman* thinks Uncle Mori is turning into a curmudgeon, though he's only thirty, and so she sent me here to provide 'a necessary female presence.'" She spoke as though repeating another's words.

Master Mori sighed.

Lord Elias, smiling, said, "You've done a fine job of it. I hardly recognize the place."

"It was like a cave before," Blaise said. "Filthy."

"You don't have to tell me," Lord Elias said. "Speaking of which, what happened to the fire leech?" On a shelf, a glass cage lay on its side, empty.

Master Mori cast a dark look at his niece, who wore a guilty expression. "An accident" was all he said. He turned to Reyna, his face softening. "My sister is a midwife. But we've both been trained as healers. Blaise used to help her. I wonder if she might have a look at your injury?"

Reyna did not know what Master Mori's niece could do that the royal doctors could not, but she agreed. Blaise came to stand before her. The smile had gone from her face, replaced by a look of complete seriousness.

Master Mori addressed his niece. "The wound is a month old but has not yet closed. You've seen similar?"

"Yes, sir." Blaise asked Reyna, "May I touch you?" At Reyna's slight indrawn breath, she added, "I won't hurt you. Not ever. I swear it."

And Reyna believed her. She nodded. Blaise's fingers were gentle as she tipped Reyna's chin toward the light pouring in through the window. The guitarist had softened his tune to something even slower and more tragic, perhaps in response to his lost silver.

Blaise said, "Does it itch?"

"Very much," Reyna said.

"Does the wound start to close, then open again when you scratch it?"

"Yes."

"Hmm. You live in the castle, so you must have a fancy doctor. What did he give you?"

Blank, Reyna turned to Lord Elias, who answered, "Some sort of tonic-water compress. I don't know the name of it. It smells like dead roses." He shrugged at the reproachful glance Reyna sent his way. "It's true."

"Rosemead," Blaise and Master Mori said at the same time. They smiled at each other.

Master Mori explained, "Rosemead usually works well, but some people don't take to it. It can itch terribly, or cause a rash, and does more harm than good."

"It's been a month, Mori," Lord Elias said with a rare snap in his voice. "She's been in misery. How could he not have realized it was the rosemead?"

"We don't always get what we pay for, friend," Master Mori said. "We'll take care of it this instant. What do you suggest, Niece?"

Blaise thought it over. "Aloe for the itching, and then an aloe-mint compress?"

"Good girl. Come help mix it, and you can see to Reyna."

Master Mori and Blaise went to rummage about another shelf, this one lined with stone jars, and soon after, Blaise returned to apply the compress and bandaging. Lord Elias leaned against the table and rubbed absently at his leg. He had nearly lost it, not too long ago. Master Mori fetched another chair from across the chamber, plunked it down beside him, and ordered, "Sit." Lord Elias sat.

Blaise said, "The aloe will help with any scarring. A few months from now and you'll barely see a thing." She met Reyna's eyes and said softly, "I'm very sorry you were hurt."

Something in Blaise's expression told her that, however new to Cortes she was, she had heard of Reyna's attack. The public beating of a royal navigator's granddaughter was no common occurrence. She *hated* that people knew what had happened to her. She loathed the pity she saw in their eyes. Her fists clenched in her lap. She drew back, creating an invisible wall around herself, and said, formally, "I owe you a favor."

"Oh!" Blaise's eyes widened. "Do you? I accept!"

Startled, Reyna said, "What? Now?" In her experience, favors were something tucked away for use when you truly needed them. They were not something squandered on a whim. In the Tower of Winds, favors were serious business.

"Why not?" Blaise said. "I could use a friend here. You look like you would be a good one. Will you show me the city? I have a whole list of places I want to see, but Uncle Mori is very busy."

Reyna was vaguely aware of the two men listening to their exchange. She said, to be certain, "You want me to be your friend, as a favor?"

"Yes, I . . ." Blaise's smile faded. "Is it too big of one?"

"It's not one at all," Reyna assured her, and felt the wall crack open. "I'll be your friend anyway. Keep this favor. You should save it for when you really need it."

"Oh." Blaise's smile returned. She stepped back from Reyna, eyed her handiwork. "All done. A few months only and you'll be as good as new. I promise."

Reyna returned to her chamber after speaking with the king, her mind so preoccupied with Levi and the letter she must write that she did not hear the feminine voices coming from within until she opened the door. By then it was too late for escape.

Her chamber wasn't large to begin with. It held the usual furniture: a bed and table, pillows heaped about a window seat. A small sitting area for visitors. No desk, but in its place a chart table, scarred and scratched. The rugs were the same midnight blue as her bedspread, and the stone walls were painted to mimic the night sky with its myriad of twinkling stars.

Now the chamber was made even smaller by six women and one monkey. Mercedes, Lady Elias, occupied one of the chairs, surrounded by colorful bolts of fabric. The royal seamstress hovered by her side. Galena, mistress of the royal household, oversaw the two serving girls pouring steaming water into a tub. By the chart table, Blaise sharpened her shears with a leather strop. And Jorge, Galena's pet monkey, sat by Blaise's elbow, peeling a banana. Reyna took all of this in, then glanced quickly over her shoulder.

"Don't try to run," Mercedes warned her.

Reyna laughed. "What is happening here? Those aren't for me, are they?" She indicated the bolts of fabric: cotton and linen and impractical silk. "I have plenty of dresses."

"You have plenty of *old* dresses," Mercedes corrected. Hers was a pale green that flared out beneath her breasts to accommodate her six months of pregnancy. The king's cousin was beautiful, with long black hair and clear green eyes that missed nothing. "And far too many trousers."

Reyna went to her side, examined a bolt of crimson silk. It would not last five minutes on a ship. "I'm not wearing that. Trousers are practical."

"They have their place," Mercedes said. "We're perfectly capable of doing what men can do. It does not mean we have to *look* like them." She held up a hand when Reyna would have spoken. "Before you say anything more, I must tell you my physician says I am in a delicate stage and must not be distressed in any way."

That silenced Reyna. Momentarily. "You're shameless," she said.

Mercedes's lips curved. "I think this red silk is just what you need. What is your opinion, Madame Julián?" She sought the seamstress's advice, and the two women put their heads together.

Wary, Reyna eyed Blaise and her newly sharpened shears. "What do you plan on cutting with that?"

"At least four . . . no, six inches from your hair." Blaise had spent the last eight years living with her uncle. Her skills were numerous, from setting broken arms to grooming sailors — as well as old friends who were away at sea for months at a time. "The ends are split and nearly white, Reyna. I can't bear to look at it."

Reyna flipped her braid over her shoulder and examined the ends. Now that Blaise mentioned it, the tips *were* looking a little broomlike.

"Let me see your hands, child." Mistress Galena took Reyna's hands into her own plump ones, turning them over and clucking. "It's as I suspected. Your hair first, and then every stitch off and into the tub."

"I don't need dresses," Reyna groused, even as she flopped onto the chair in front of Blaise. "I don't need soft skin. Lord Braga has me cleaning the storage vaults until I turn eighty. No, thank you, Jorgie," she added when the monkey shoved his banana in front of her nose.

"Storage?" Mercedes looked up from examining a square of black lace. "Make sure you wear your trousers for that, won't you?"

Reyna sighed. Blaise laughed behind her, and Jorge, his banana consumed in no time at all, hopped onto the window seat and pitched the yellow skin out the open window.

It was late in the evening when Reyna forced herself to sit at her chart table and pen her letter to Levi. A candle burned bright next to a vial of ink and a stack of fresh parchment. She would only need one sheet. The polite note she had turned over in her mind would take up a quarter page, no more. She dipped her quill in the vial and wrote, then chewed her lip, staring at the parchment in an agony of doubt and indecision.

"You've sighed a hundred times in the last five minutes," Blaise commented. "How difficult is it to write a letter?" She had stayed for supper and afterward made herself at home on Reyna's bed with her own sketchbook and charcoal. A love of drawing was something they shared, though Blaise's subjects were of a different sort entirely.

"It's harder than I thought," Reyna admitted.

Blaise slid off the bed and came to stand beside Reyna. She looked at the parchment. There was one word written:

Captain.

Blaise met Reyna's gaze. A full five seconds of silence passed before they burst into laughter.

When they finally caught their breath, Blaise said, "Prince Levi isn't very old, is he?"

"No. Nineteen — twenty, maybe." She had told Blaise about her time in Lunes, leaving out a few details. Levi's tears she had kept to herself; the same with the bottle of kudzu. It would have felt like a horrible betrayal of privacy to share these things with others. Even Blaise.

"What does he look like?" her friend said.

"Why?"

Blaise pressed. "Is he handsome? Hideous?"

"He's . . . tallish," Reyna said vaguely, waving a hand in the air to indicate height. "Not hideous. He has black hair. He looks like a Lunesian."

Blaise was studying Reyna in a way that made her realize she was drumming her fingers along the table. She forced them still.

Without saying a word, Blaise retrieved the charcoal from Reyna's bed. She dropped it onto the table and ordered, "Draw him."

Reyna protested, "I hardly remember what he looks like . . ." Blaise folded her arms. "Fine. Tyrant." She took up the charcoal and sketched quickly.

"Oh," Blaise said when Reyna had finished. "Look at his ash mark. Poor boy." She swept up the parchment for a closer look. "This is very sad and romantic."

"It is not romantic," Reyna said.

She had drawn Levi aboard the *Simona*, watching as she crossed the plank over open sea and finned lion. He wore light chain mail. A breeze had left his hair windswept, and his expression managed to convey both anxiety and a jaw-clenching aggravation. His hand was outstretched, toward her.

"You're right," Blaise said. "He's not hideous. And you're going to have to do better than this," she said of Reyna's letter. "Here, I'll write it for you."

Reyna laughed, digging her heels in as Blaise tried to nudge her off the chair and take her place. "What were you drawing over there?" She indicated the sketchbook on the bed, hoping to change the topic.

Blaise, mercifully, let her. Returning to the bed, she held up the book so Reyna could see its open pages. Reyna recoiled.

There was a dead man, completely naked, his torso dissected to show his innards: ribs, lungs, heart, liver, intestines. The detail was gruesome, but neatly labeled.

"Isn't he beautiful?" Blaise said, beaming.

"No!" Reyna exclaimed. "You should warn me before you show me these things!"

Blaise laughed. She leafed through several pages before commenting, "Do you know there are only eight physicians in Cortes? Eight, Reyna. For a city this size."

Reyna kept her eyes on her parchment, waiting for inspiration to strike. "That can't be correct."

"It is. And most of them serve the castle. Or St. Medina Parish. Tell me, who helps the people who are not rich?"

Reyna pointed out the obvious. "Master Mori?"

"Yes, he's the exception," Blaise conceded. "But for every Uncle Mori, there are fifty charlatans out there. Or midwives who can't birth kittens properly, let alone a human baby. We need more doctors."

The laughter had gone from her friend's voice. Reyna looked over her shoulder. "How much do you have saved?"

Blaise closed her book with a snap. "Enough for a year."

The medical school at Caffa required three years of early study, followed by a more rigorous five years, and finally a year under the supervision of an experienced physician. Nine years total. Reyna had more gold than she would ever need in twenty lifetimes.

"Blaise —"

"No, Reyna." Her expression was set in a way that had Reyna biting her tongue. It was an old argument, one she had yet to win.

There was a knock on the door. Jaime stuck his head in before Reyna could answer, and addressed Blaise.

"Did you bring a horse?"

Blaise smiled, because girls could never help smiling at Jaime. "I walked."

"Too dark for that now," Jaime said. "I have to talk to your uncle anyway. I'll take you home."

They agreed to meet downstairs momentarily. Before Jaime could duck out of the chamber, Reyna asked, "What do you have to see Master Mori about?"

A dull flush worked its way up Jaime's neck. He frowned at her. "Men . . . things. Honestly, Reyna."

"What sort of —" Reyna began, but the door closed before she could finish her question. She grinned at Blaise, pleased with herself. "It never grows old, needling . . . What's wrong?"

Blaise, no longer smiling, sat on the edge of the bed. "I'm glad I saw you today. We nearly missed each other."

"What do you mean?"

"I'm going home tomorrow. First thing. Uncle Mori's taking me."

Blaise did not mean down the hill to St. Soledad. She meant home to Montserrat. Reyna stifled her disappointment. She could not expect her friends to always be around when she returned. She was lucky Jaime was here and not off on expedition. Still . . .

"You'll give your *maman* my love? When are you coming back?"

Blaise dropped her head into her hands.

Panicked, Reyna shot to her feet and hurried to her friend's side. She put an arm around her. "What is it?" Was someone sick? Had someone *died*?

Blaise spoke into her hands, her words muffled. Reyna heard this: "I'm never coming back Maman wants me to stay in Montserrat and be a midwife like her and I'm going to deliver a thousand babies and marry a goat herder and then I'll grow old and die and that will be it that is my life forever and ever."

"Oh no!" Dismayed, Reyna pulled Blaise up by the shoulders so that she could see her face. No tears, but Blaise's eyes were full of misery. "Why didn't you tell me earlier?"

"I didn't want to ruin your homecoming" was her glum confession.

This was terrible news. Despite her village roots, Blaise was a city dweller. She loved Cortes: the immensity of it, the people, the noise. Even, strangely, the smells. But that was Blaise. How could this have happened? "What did your uncle say? Can't he help?"

"He tried. She's put her foot down." Blaise pressed her palm to her forehead. "I love babies. You know I do. It's just . . . there's so much else I *don't* know, and I want to *know* it. When there's plague in a city, why do some fall ill and not others? Why do some die and not others? Or . . . how do I cut off a leg without killing someone? How do I sew it back on? I know it's been done before. Uncle Mori was starting to teach me. Then Maman sent her letter and . . ."

"Have you said these things to her?" Reyna said.

"I sent her a letter. So did Uncle Mori. It's no use. I wasn't supposed to stay in Cortes this long to begin with."

They sat side by side on the edge of the bed. Reyna said quietly, "What can I do?"

"Nothing." Blaise leaned sideways, rested her head on Reyna's shoulder. "I can't think of a single way out of this. She needs the help, Reyna. And she is my mother."

It was much later, and with a far heavier heart, that Reyna picked up her quill. Knowing strangers would read her words, she wrote this:

Captain,

I am safe at home on del Mar. I'm sorry I worried you. It was not my intent, given your many kindnesses, to add to your burden. My deepest apologies.

She signed the letter *Reyna, Tower of Winds, Kingdom of St. John del Mar.*

NINE

THIS IS IMPOSSIBLE, Master Sabas. How am I supposed to clean this?" Reyna spoke to the old explorer whose cobwebbed domain she had been assigned to tidy. She had thought she'd come prepared this morning. Dressed in her oldest shirt and trousers and with a sack full of rags. Braced for a day of drudgery, of boredom.

There was no tidying this. It couldn't be done, not if she lived twenty lifetimes. This chamber was one of the tower's three storage vaults. The farthest underground and the least visited, if the thickness of the dust was any indication. Centuries' worth of discards filled the space: books, instruments, furniture. Heaps of furniture. Mountains of furniture. Odd bits of statuary loomed around every corner. Paintings moldered in their frames. The only light came from candles spiked onto iron floor stands. Reyna's mind shied away from what would happen if one of those stands fell over in a place like this.

Master Sabas did not look overwhelmed by the task ahead. But then, it was not his task to complete. "Clean?" he repeated.

"Oh no, I wouldn't waste your skills on something so mindless. That I will save for . . . ah. There you are. Late again, boy."

Jaime strolled toward them, yawning. He was also dressed for labor, his white shirt so thin from use and repeated washings that she could see through it to his skin. Jaime had brought a broom, carried over his shoulder like a fishing pole. He stopped when he saw her. "What are *you* doing here?" he said.

"Being persecuted," she informed him. "What are *you* doing here?"

Jaime shifted his broom to the other shoulder. "Same."

Master Sabas snorted. "Jaime is here because he cannot be trusted around Lord Fausto's daughter."

"Lord Fausto? But Ellisande is twelve."

"Not Ellisande!" Jaime glared at her.

Reyna made a face. "Beatrice is married." And older. At least twenty-five. What was Jaime thinking?

"Don't you start." Jaime turned to the older man, face full of resignation. "Where do you want me?"

Master Sabas pointed to a far corner. "And no napping," he warned.

Jaime lifted a hand in a *yes, yes* gesture and trudged off, disappearing around a stack of broken chairs.

"As for you, my dear," Master Sabas continued, "today will be more of a treasure hunt. There are quite a number of instruments lying about. A complete waste. Find what you can: astrolabes, cross-staffs, sextants. Anything that might still be used.

God's blessings to you," he said when Reyna sneezed twice in quick succession. "Once you've completed that, we'll decide what can be repaired and what must be discarded permanently. The repairs are your responsibility."

"Yes, sir" was all she said. What use complaining?

Master Sabas explained that she was to spend her mornings here until he said otherwise. The remainder of her day was not his business. He took himself off, but not before informing her that Jaime, too, was her responsibility.

Reyna had already spotted her first astrolabe. It lay half concealed behind a looking glass: a brass disk two feet in diameter with intricate engraving. Numbers and scales and symbols. Before its banishment to the vaults, it might have been among an explorer's prized possessions, helping him find his way by measuring the distance between the land and the stars. It did not appear broken. Only dusty and forgotten. *How did you come to be here?* Reyna wondered, blowing away the first layers of dirt. When Jaime appeared, she said without looking at him, "Back to work, you. It's my head if he finds you loafing."

"I could sweep in here for a hundred years and no one would tell the difference."

It was so close to her own opinion that she smiled at him. There was no sign of his broom. "I've never been in here before. Have you?"

"No, the doors are always locked." He eyed the astrolabe. "What are you doing?"

When she told him, he decided to help her instead. They cleared away a space. Then Jaime, easily distracted, happened upon a rug. He could use a new rug, he told her. The one in his chamber was covered in paint. He unrolled it, snapped it in the air three times — the dust that emerged sent them both into coughing fits — and spread it onto the floor. They knelt at the edge and studied the images before them.

"Is she a siren or a harpy?" Jaime asked. "I can never remember the difference."

A naked woman sat on a rock playing a lyre. The rock rose from the sea; among the waves were sailors trying desperately to swim to her, lured by her beautiful music. A ship, anchored and abandoned, drifted in the background.

"A siren," Reyna decided.

"But she has legs. And . . . you know. Lady parts. No fish tail."

"They're not always painted with tails. Sometimes they look like humans. Sometimes they have feathers. I don't think you want this rug. It has a hole." She showed him a small tear by the ship.

Jaime's gaze went from the tear back to the siren. He shook his head. "You're the only one who would notice. Wait. Don't harpies have feathers?"

"I suppose so," Reyna acknowledged. That part *was* confusing. "But a harpy never has a lyre. The siren lures the sailors with her music and pretty face. The harpy is a hideous bird-woman who swoops from the sky and snatches people up."

She remembered the stories from their childhood: *When a man vanishes so completely, it's said he's been carried off by the harpies.*

"Huh. So the siren is a beauty and the harpy is a hag."

"If that makes it simpler for you." Reyna rose and dusted her hands on her trousers. "Quit ogling the rugs. We have work."

The instruments they found were placed in three rapidly growing piles. The first, perfectly usable items that only needed a cleaning and polish. The second, instruments requiring mending. And the last, instruments beyond repair.

Reyna thought she saw a cross-staff on top of a bookshelf packed tight with scrolls. "Lift me up," she said.

Gamely, Jaime grabbed her around her knees and raised her high, long enough for her to grab the cross-staff. He set her down. "Didn't they feed you at Aux-en-villes? Carrying you is like carrying air."

"I eat plenty," she informed him. "What are you doing with Lord Fausto's daughter?"

"Not one thing." Jaime snatched the cross-staff from her and stomped off toward their clearing.

She followed him. "Jaime, her husband is scary." She pictured him, a fat man with a loud voice and a quick temper. "You could get hurt if he finds out —"

"I said I've done nothing!" Jaime burst out. "I don't try to see her. I don't even like her. She follows me everywhere, leaves me these letters. And she doesn't care who sees. No one believes me, and when I try to explain to Father, he throws a broom at me and sends me here!"

There had always been ladies coming out of Jaime's ears, out of his pockets, falling from the cuffs of his trousers. Females around every corner with their batting eyelashes and tinkling laughter. But Reyna had known him a long time. Knew when he was genuinely upset. He gripped the cross-staff in both hands. It looked a breath away from being snapped in half.

She took it from him. "I believe you."

"What?" He scowled down at her.

"I believe you," she said again, and then, "You shouldn't look so surprised when people say they believe you. It doesn't help."

Some of the tension eased from his shoulders. Jaime managed a half smile.

After closer scrutiny, she tossed the cross-staff onto the beyond-repair pile. Its pole was soft with rot. She asked, "Where is her husband?"

"Off island somewhere." Jaime sat on a chest beside his rug. "He's been gone a month."

Which was likely why Jaime's head remained on his shoulders.

"What are you going to do? He's a mean one."

A dejected shrug. "I dunno. Hide out here, I suppose. Hope she goes away."

"The trouble is you're too pretty." She had told him this before. His hair flopped over his brows just so. His smile was full of mischief and invitation. A full-length looking glass propped up a corner of Reyna's chambers. She had seen Jaime using it to practice that smile, many times.

His lips turned up at the corners. There it was. "Not as pretty as you," he said.

She was not even a little flattered. With Jaime, sweet words were as common as fresh fish at the harbor. "Maybe that's why Lord Braga sent you down here," she suggested. "To hide. Your father's protecting you."

"Ha. You wouldn't believe that if you'd heard his shouting." He eyed her curiously as she inspected a mountain of moldering furniture. "*Why* do you believe me? No one else does."

"I already know all the bad things about you." She plucked a small statue off a table, examined it, put it back. "Why bother lying to me?"

There was a silence. Then, in a perfectly serious voice, he said, "I've missed you, Reyna."

She glanced over and they smiled at each other. Something glinted in the corner of her eye. Brass? She backed up a step for a better look . . . and tripped, landing hard on the stone floor.

"Ow!"

Jaime was there in a thrice, pulling her to her feet. She rubbed her backside, and they stood looking down at what she had tripped on.

"Huh," Jaime said. "That's not unsettling."

A life-size statue lay on its back. A soldier in armor, made of clay. The sculptor had not captured a traditional soldier pose: a man standing tall and proud as he gazed off into the distance, or a man with his sword at the ready. This man was in a crouch, arms flung up to shield his face . . . which someone had covered with a handkerchief. The way one would cover the newly dead, on a battlefield. Reyna tugged off the handkerchief and felt the hairs prickle at her nape.

"Jaime." She knelt before the statue.

Jaime crouched beside her. "What's wrong?"

"He looks like the raider on the *Simona*." The same gathered knot above his head. The same wide face and sharp cheekbones. "And look at his sword," she said. It hung from the statue's belt without a scabbard to protect it. "Have you ever seen anything like it?"

"No." Jaime was certain. "Pretty fancy for a Coronad."

The men of Coronado favored function over beauty. Their swords and daggers were as lethal as their neighbors', but they did not bother with engravings or jewel-encrusted hilts. Or elaborate chrysanthemum carvings, like on this sword here.

Not too far off, a door creaked open. Master Sabas come to check on them.

Jaime sprinted off, back to his broom. Reyna stayed where she was. There was another difference between this statue and the living raider. The raider had looked cold, commanding, a man who inspired fear. This statue . . . he looked frightened. Eyes wide with horror, mouth opened in a scream.

The shuffling footsteps grew louder. Reyna shook out the handkerchief. It was more grayish yellow than its original white, but it would have to do. She draped it carefully over the statue's face, so that she would not have to see his terror.

TEN

REYNA'S MORNINGS WERE SPENT in the storage vaults, her afternoons in the humble parish churches of St. Soledad. Eight funerals over two days without a single body to bury. She dressed plainly, in black, a lace veil concealing her features, and kept to herself in a back pew. Some would say she was hiding. There was truth there. She did not want to make her presence known, to see the anger and bewilderment on the faces of grief-stricken mothers, wives, daughters, sons. Why are *you* here and not them? She had asked herself the same question with no answers. Halfway through the first funeral, someone slid into the pew beside her. She jumped slightly when a hand covered hers. Warm. Familiar.

Jaime.

Soberly dressed, hair neatly brushed, he said not a word. Only took her hand in his and held on tight. Through all eight funerals.

Reyna returned again and again to the statue. It was like a compulsion. She would gather up an instrument or two, then find herself back before the Coronad. Studying him. Studying his sword. How had he come to be here? Which explorer had brought him home? Had the sculptor used a muse? Or was this terrified man created purely from someone's imagination?

With Jaime's help she had pulled the statue upright. It had taken some doing, even with the two of them. The clay was solid, not hollow. There was much heaving and grunting involved. But leaving him on the floor had felt like an indignity to her. She ignored Jaime when he pointed out that the statue was not real.

"You've never shown this much interest in a boy before," Jaime commented. He had found a bench in some far-off corner and dragged it over. It still had its cushion. Tufts of wool poked through faded red velvet. The bench was too short for Jaime's tall frame, but he looked perfectly content sprawled across it, legs hanging over the edge. In one hand he held a small book bound in leather. It had been unearthed beneath some tapestries, the title obscured with dust. Jaime had scrubbed it free of grime with the statue's ratty handkerchief, the only bit of tidying he'd done all morning. In his other hand was an apple. "Never thought your first love would be made of clay."

"Very funny," she said absently. "Jaime, do you remember your Coronad history?"

"No." He spoke with a mouth full of apple.

"Neither do I," she admitted. "What a pair we are."

"What's to remember? They're thieves and cutthroats."

"Not all of them." Her words fell on deaf ears. The last time Jaime had visited Coronado, he had been robbed in an alley and relieved of his prized dagger. The loss smarted still.

"Pfft. Name one good thing about a Coronad."

"Gunnel saved my life."

"And the rest of them tried to take it," Jaime said, unimpressed. "I'm telling you, Reyna. Never trust a Coronad."

A voice interrupted. "Hard at work, I see."

Reyna whirled around with a squeal, hand at her throat. Jaime flailed and leaped to his feet. His half-eaten apple rolled across the stone.

"What are you two up to, besides loafing?" Lord Elias had returned from Esperanca the night before, riding with Commander Aimon, his *maman* thankfully on the mend. The look in his eye suggested he had meant to creep up on them and was enjoying their reaction immensely. He was dressed formally, in black and silver, something he usually tried to avoid.

"Where did you come from?" Reyna looked past him. They had not heard the creak of the door or footsteps to warn them that they were not alone. Was there another way into the vaults?

Jaime pointed his book at the statue. "We were discussing him. Reyna thinks this Coronad looks like her raider."

"He isn't *mine*." She threw a dark look Jaime's way. "The hair is the same. And the design on his sword."

Lord Elias walked up to the statue. He was no longer smiling. "The same design? You're sure?"

"Yes. I remember the chrysanthemum."

Lord Elias circled the statue. Black boots kicked up the dust. Jaime fetched his apple from the floor, brushed it off against his sleeve, and took another bite. He grinned at Reyna's expression.

Lord Elias said, "This man is no Coronad. He's Miranese."

Reyna wasn't *that* ignorant of Coronad history. "Miramar? Aren't the Coronads their descendants?"

Lord Elias nodded. "The Miranese kingdom exiled its criminals four — no, five hundred years ago. Murderers, rapists, thieves. They were sent to colonize one of their island possessions."

This bit of information interested Jaime. "Coronado was a prison colony?"

"Yes."

"That explains many things," Jaime said with a sour expression.

"What happened to Miramar?" Reyna said. "It's barely mentioned in the history books."

Lord Elias ran a hand along the statue's sword hilt. "It's still there, as far as I know," he said. "They're isolationists. Completely self-sufficient. Foreigners are rarely admitted. You must have a good reason for going there. And few Miranese leave."

"I've never seen a Miranese in person," Jaime said.

"You might have once or twice," Lord Elias assured him, "and thought he was a Coronad. There are a few in Cortes."

"Who?" Reyna said.

"There's an old woman in the Coronad parish. Her name

is Niemi-si." Lord Elias circled the statue once more, frowning. "Miranese ships in the Sea of Magdalen. That is not normal."

"Do you know who brought it here?" Reyna gestured to the statue.

"Could have been anyone." Lord Elias peered behind its neck, inspected its wrists, licked his finger and scrubbed some of the dust from its sword. Searching for something. "Let's have a look underneath. See if there's a sculptor's mark."

Obliging, Jaime went behind the statue and tipped it back while Lord Elias and Reyna knelt and looked beneath its boots.

"Nothing." Reyna's sigh was a long one.

Lord Elias said, "Don't give up just —"

Jaime yelped. Reyna and Lord Elias jumped aside as the statue toppled onto the floor with a sickening crack. A snake slithered by: four feet long, speckled green and gold. It disappeared around a floor globe.

"Bloody snake!" Jaime cried. "Where did it come from?"

Unfazed, Lord Elias said, "Who knows in this place?"

Dismayed, Reyna picked up the statue's head. It had snapped clean off its body. She held it away from her as an ashy substance poured from within onto the floor. In her arms, the head became hollow and light. She glared at Jaime. "You broke him," she accused.

"Don't look at me like that! You saw the snake."

"It was a *baby*."

Lord Elias said, in placating tones, "Come, the damage is done." He took the head from her and tossed it to Jaime, who caught it with one hand. "I almost forgot why I was here in the first place. Pack your chest. You're coming with me to Lunes."

Jaime looked startled and delighted. "For the coronation? Why?"

Lord Elias was blunt. "Because Beatrice's husband returns in two days, and your father wants you off island before then. He left me a detailed letter. We leave tomorrow."

It was all Jaime needed to hear. He hurried off, compounding Reyna's aggravation by taking the soldier's head with him, cradled beneath one arm like a ball.

Lord Elias sat beside the apple Jaime had abandoned on the bench. "I didn't have a chance to ask you . . . How is your uncle?"

"Very well." She settled beside him, Jaime's apple between them. Before yesterday, it had been six months since she had last seen Lord Elias, when he and his family had visited Aux-en-villes. "He has an admirer."

"Does he?" A sideways glance. "Who?"

"Her name is Lise. She owns the cottage we rent by the river. You met her."

"I remember. A widow?"

"Yes."

"Does he admire her back?"

Her uncle did not speak of such things to her. Reyna said only, "She makes him laugh."

Candles sputtered in their iron stands, the wax nearly melted away. She would have to remember to bring fresh ones tomorrow, or risk being trapped here in the dark.

When Lord Elias spoke again, his voice was carefully neutral. "I'm glad." Silence followed, then, "I need a favor."

Reyna looked over, waiting.

"Mercedes is . . . The baby is harder on her than Sabine was."

"What's wrong?" she demanded.

"Nothing," Lord Elias was quick to reassure her. "Only, she tires more easily and . . . Will you keep an eye on her while I'm gone? Make sure she doesn't do too much?"

"Sir." *What was he not telling her?*

"Nothing's wrong," he said again. "I would not lie to you. I just need someone around her who can't be browbeaten."

He meant for her to smile, so she did. They both knew Mercedes could be scary when she wished.

Lord Elias had never asked her for a favor before, though his own kindnesses toward her were many. He had found her uncle. He had championed her as a geographer in the earliest days, when few others would. He championed her still.

She spoke her thoughts aloud. "I would do anything for you."

Another smile. "Then do this." He stood, ruffled her hair as if she were still nine, and made to leave. A look at the statue stopped him. It was a macabre sight, lying there without its head. "The Miranese don't have a history of piracy, Reyna. I can't imagine what they're doing this far east. Let me think on it while I'm gone. If Admiral Maira hasn't found our men by the time I get back, we'll figure out what the Miranese have to do with any of this."

ELEVEN

WEEKS LATER, Reyna consulted the scrap of parchment in her hand, then studied the building before her. A narrow structure, three stories tall, and painted a green so dark it reminded her of seaweed. The color was not important. Every home in this corner of St. Mark's Parish bore the same depressing shade — the Coronads did not favor bright colors — but this door was different from the rest. At eye level, where there would have been a knocker, or nothing at all, someone had carved a chrysanthemum the size of a fist. The same chrysanthemum she had seen on the raider's axe. On the clay soldier's sword. It was no coincidence. She knocked.

The door was opened by a boy her own age. In a gathering of Coronads, he would have earned no special attention. Not with the broad face and hulking figure that distinguished the men of Coronado from their neighbors. His expression was neither friendly nor unfriendly.

"You're lost?" He spoke the del Marian of someone born and raised here.

"I don't think so." She had to tip her head back to meet his eyes. "I'm looking for a woman named Niemi-si. I was told she lived here."

Reyna's original plan had been to visit her with Lord Elias, but as the days passed, she had grown impatient.

His look shifted distinctly toward the unfriendly. "What for?"

"I was hoping to ask her a few questions. About her . . . childhood."

"Wrong house. You're lost." He stepped back. The door swung toward her.

"I can pay," Reyna said quickly.

The door stopped, caught in his hand with inches to spare.

Reyna held up a silver double-shell. A calculating look came into his eyes, prompting her to add, "It's yours when I'm done. There are people nearby to make sure I leave here in one piece." She made a show of looking up and down the street.

He scanned the busy parish road full of people and horses and stray dogs. Impossible to say who, if anyone, was paying them any particular attention. His scowl deepened. "Wait here." The door shut in her face.

She turned around, careful to keep her back against the door. The windows above were open. She had no wish to have the contents of someone's chamber pot flung onto her head. This lesson she had learned the hard way, long ago. The boy returned in no time at all. He jerked his head — *In!* — and walked off. Following, Reyna discovered the children of the household taking their afternoon nap. A chamber opened off to the right, shuttered and dim. Straw mats covered the floor, and on them slept four children dressed in long white shirts. An older girl knelt close by, fanning the young ones with a large palm frond. She looked over curiously as Reyna walked by.

The boy led her straight through to the back of the house and out into a garden. High stone walls separated them from their neighbors. A stunted palm dominated the space, and beneath its leaves was a miniature house, no bigger than an out-house, really, painted a glorious shade of amber. It would have stood out in any parish, on any island, and was like discovering a sparkling jewel by her feet in the mud and rain.

The boy knocked. A female voice said, "Enter, boy."

He reached for the latch, said in a low voice, "If you're cruel to her, it will be unpleasant for you," and opened the door.

With that threat hanging over her head, they entered a single chamber, large enough to hold three floor cushions the color of sunset. Red and gold hangings decorated the walls, the burnished shades heightened by lit candles. Reyna saw that the voice belonged to an old woman. Small and hunched. White hair gathered into thin braids so long they brushed the cushion she sat upon. Niemi-si wore an amber robe with a black sash. Her face sent a jolt of horror through Reyna. Someone had gouged her eyes from their sockets, leaving two scarred black-ened holes in their wake.

The boy loomed over Reyna in warning. She gave him an offended look. What cruel thing did he imagine she would do to this poor woman?

"Madame," Reyna said. "Thank you for speaking with me."

"Don't thank me yet." Niemi-si spoke in heavily accented del Marian. The chamber smelled vaguely of ginger root and candle smoke. "What interest could a del Marian painter possibly have with me?"

Reyna's fingertips bore faint traces of black ink and blue paint. The boy had surprised her, observing more than she had credited him. "I wondered if I might ask you about Miramar."

The boy started to speak. Niemi-si said, "Be silent, boy. Sit there." She pointed to a cushion. He sat, muttering under his breath.

"And you," Niemi-si said to Reyna. As soon as Reyna knelt on the third cushion, she demanded, "What is your name?"

"Reyna."

"Ray-nah. Named for the sun goddess?" In front of Niemi-si was a black lacquered tray, not covered with food or tea, but with paper tortoises the size of a thumb. Exquisite little creatures, created by a woman who could not see.

"No, madame. There are no goddesses on del Mar."

Niemi-si looked amused. "I forget. Del Marians worship one god. And a hundred saints. Pray, what is the difference?" And before Reyna could think of a response to that: "You're not a painter?"

"I do paint, mostly maps. I'm a geographer for the royal house."

A snort from the boy, which Reyna ignored.

"A girl explorer?" Niemi-si mused. "How very strange."

Reyna smiled. "You're not the first to say so."

Niemi-si picked up a half-completed tortoise and resumed folding. "There's a nice boy in the Tower of Winds. I met him years ago. Lord Elvin."

"Elias," Reyna corrected. "Yes, he told me where to find you."

"Why? Why do you ask questions about Miramar?"

Reyna had thought carefully about what to say. "My apprenticeship with the tower is finished, and I'm required to begin a masterwork . . ."

"And you chose *Miramar*?" Skepticism coated each word.

"It interests me," Reyna insisted. "The kingdom exists still, yet little is known about it. I could only find two books on it in the tower, both hundreds of years old, and one is unreadable." Parchment crumbling to dust, ink fading, it had been of no use to her.

Niemi-si said, "What sort of masterwork do you intend? A history?"

"Perhaps," Reyna answered. "I thought I would learn what I could first and go from there. When Lord Elias mentioned you lived here, I wondered if you might be able to help."

Niemi-si had finished her tortoise. She set it aside and began another. "The boy says you have silver."

"Yes."

Niemi-si cocked her head, listening as Reyna's double-shell clinked onto her tray. "One more" was her suggestion. The boy smirked.

Reyna placed another double-shell on the tray and asked, "What is Miramar like?"

The coins disappeared within the folds of Niemi-si's robe. "It is lovely," she said. "Clean and bright. The people as well as the buildings. Do you know Coronado?"

"Very well."

"Then I'm sorry for you," Niemi-si remarked, and Reyna found herself smiling. It wasn't just Jaime. Coronado wasn't to everyone's taste. It was a rough, illiterate kingdom with little interest in art, music, or literature. Reyna thought Coronado was not so different from other kingdoms. If you looked hard enough, beneath the surface, you would find both the ugly and the beautiful.

Niemi-si continued, "Take everything you've seen and heard and smelled on Coronado and picture the exact opposite. *That* is Miramar."

"How long have you lived here?" Reyna said.

"On del Mar? Since I was fifteen. And before then I lived on Coronado for three years."

Only a girl when she had left home. "It was my understanding that leaving Miramar was forbidden."

"It was," Niemi-si acknowledged. "Do you know the meaning of *tutto mortise*?"

"I do." Reyna leaned forward, repulsed and fascinated. "Is it a Miranese custom?"

"When I was a girl, yes."

Tutto mortise was an ancient, barbaric custom once practiced in kingdoms such as Pillard and Caffa. But that was so long ago. Reyna did not know of a single kingdom that still honored it. It meant that when a king died, he did not die alone. To offer him comfort in the afterlife, scores of men and women were sacrificed and buried with him, sealed alive in his tomb until they too succumbed from lack of food and air. Who was sacrificed varied, though usually included were the king's trusted councilors and their families, his favorite wives, his top generals and soldiers. Dancing girls and musicians were occasionally granted the honor. She had even read of an entire menagerie being sacrificed once. War elephants and colorful, exotic birds. *Tutto mortise* cleared the way for the new king to begin his reign with advisors of his own choosing, and to not have to face opposition and discord from meddling, older statesmen.

"My father was a councilor to the king," Niemi-si said. "And then the king died. In life and death we serve."

"Did you escape?" If Reyna understood correctly, Niemi-si should not be here. Or anywhere. She should have been sacrificed in that tomb, along with her family.

"I did not have to. The royal family of Miramar values beauty and strength above all else. My father made it so I was no longer valuable."

The boy sat so quietly Reyna had almost forgotten he was there. She shared a brief glance with him, united in their unspoken horror, then looked into the woman's ruined eyes. "Your father did this to you?"

Niemi-si nodded. "I sailed from there with one servant and two silver candlesticks. All I had left in the world."

"And your parents?"

"Remained with the king." There was an awful finality to the answer. She turned to the boy. "What does she look like?"

The question startled him. "Grandmother?"

"Is she plain? Pretty? What does she look like? Paint a picture for me, boy."

He turned an assessing eye on Reyna, who gave him a baleful look and held her tongue.

"She has brown hair and brown eyes," he said finally. "She's small. She would not birth strong boys."

"Yes, what else?" Niemi-si said.

"Her skin is golden, like this chamber, and her nose is peeling. She does not care for her skin."

Self-conscious, Reyna scratched her nose.

"Not beautiful, then," Niemi-si said.

"She's beautiful," her grandson said reluctantly. "For a del Marian."

A dozen more questions Reyna wished to ask, but the boy rose. Reyna knew when she had overstayed her welcome. "Thank you for seeing me, madame. I'm grateful."

"Yes?" Niemi-si held out a palm. "How grateful?"

Reyna pressed a third double-shell into her hand, and nearly jumped when the old woman grabbed her wrist and held tight. "A word of warning, Reyna of the Tower." Niemi-si pulled her closer. "You don't even have to pay me for it." Her grip tightened.

"I'm old but I'm not foolish. A masterwork will require more than speaking to me. Geographers are not known for staying home and minding their business. You will dig deeper, I think. And deeper is not safe."

Reyna did not bother to deny it. "I'm always careful."

"Are you?" Niemi-si released her hand, straightened. "My grandson says you are beautiful. Beauty will open many doors, but it can also be a prison. Have a care. I was beautiful once."

Reyna wanted to ask what she meant, but the boy jerked his head — *Out!* — and she had no choice but to follow.

The bells rang as Reyna left St. Mark's Parish and made for home. A great clamoring coming from the harbor. Like those around her, she stopped in the street, one lined with palms, and turned her head toward the waterfront. Not frightened, only curious. What they heard was not the alarm that signaled attack. Those bells were distinct: three peals followed by a count of ten, the pattern repeating until the threat had gone or the bell ringer had been forced to flee. What, then, had happened?

Thundering hooves joined the bells as a company of soldiers bore down from the castle. Having no desire to be trampled, Reyna scurried off the street with the rest of the crowd. The men were led by a grim-faced King Ulises. Clothing as black as his horse, a cape billowing behind him. A fearsome sight. When he saw her, his hand shot up, signaling the men to stop. The horse came to a halt directly in front of her.

"What's wrong?" she cried. All around them, men and women swept low in deference.

King Ulises reached down, ordered, "Come with me."

Automatically, Reyna placed her hand in his and found herself hauled up behind him.

"Something's happened to the *Amaris*," he said over his shoulder, and raced on toward the docks, leaving onlookers wide-eyed in their wake.

Confusion swung to dread. The *Amaris* was Lord Elias's ship. Jaime would be with him.

When they reached the waterfront, she saw what had caused the alarm. Five ships from the royal fleet had sailed into the harbor, the same five that had gone to Lunes for Queen Vashti's coronation. Four appeared undamaged, but the fifth vessel, the *Amaris*, flew the royal flag of del Mar at half-mast, and below that pennant was another. A plain red flag that signaled a ship in extreme distress.

TWELVE

THE CREW OF THE *AMARIS* had vanished. Not a soul had been left behind, alive or dead. To Reyna, perched on the railing, the scene took on a terrible familiarity.

Admiral Maira and King Ulises exchanged tense words beneath the mainmast. The deck swarmed with people hanging on their every word.

"The storm came from nowhere," Admiral Maira told the king. Sweat beaded his forehead and soaked his mustache, which hung limp around his mouth. "Two days after we started home from Lunes. It lasted hours only, but it turned the sky black and we could not see our sister ships. When the storm cleared . . ." He trailed off, his voice full of trepidation. *And no wonder,* Reyna thought bitterly. The king had sent him specifically to command this flotilla. Lord Elias's safety was his responsibility. And he had *lost* the king's oldest friend and cousin by marriage. "When it cleared, the *Amaris* was as you see. There was no one here, Your Grace. Not one man."

King Ulises demanded, "How far did you search?"

"In every direction, for a day. When we saw nothing, I

ordered our return to Cortes. For reinforcements. I don't know how they managed to take our men without a fight —"

Didn't he? Reyna wanted to choke him. She remembered his smirking words. *A strange singing? Do you expect us to believe the men were placed under some sort of* spell?

Towering beside the king was a man with kohl-rimmed eyes, silver-black hair pulled into a queue, and a face that smiled rarely and scowled often. Aimon was commander of the king's armies. On land, and at sea, when necessary. He said, "It's the same as the *Simona*. And the Bushido ship near Caffa. Just as Lady Reyna said."

Upon hearing her name, Admiral Maira's lips thinned. The look he sent her was full of venom, as if she were the root of all his troubles. She returned his poisonous glare with one of her own. What had she done, except live to tell what she'd seen? He said, "There were no bodies left this time . . ."

Every part of Reyna was strung tight as the rigging. She was afraid she knew why. The shipmen aboard the *Amaris* were not strangers to her. She had known them since she was a young girl. Not one of them had a physical defect, at least none that could be seen. No missing limbs or burns. The oldest shipman was in his forties, hale and hearty despite his years. There had been no reason to leave anyone behind. They were all strong men. Men who would fetch good prices at the slave markets.

Lord Elias.

Jaime.

Slave markets.

Reyna did not realize how hitched her breathing had become until she saw the king watching her. Even from where she sat, she could see the vein pulsing at his temple. The admiral babbled on, his words trailing off only when a cry emerged from the docks.

A woman calling for help. Reyna, at the opposite rail, could not see who it was, but one of the men peered overboard, then swung around in shocked dismay. "Your Grace, it's Lady Elias!"

The *Amaris* tipped alarmingly as everyone hurried to the side. Reyna jumped off the railing and ran across the deck. Horrified, she saw Mercedes on the dock, in a heap of yellow silk. One of her ladies knelt by her in a panic. Dita. It was her voice Reyna had heard. King Ulises was the first over the hull and down the rope. Then Commander Aimon. Reyna fought her way toward the ladder but was repeatedly shoved aside. Not deliberately — the men simply did not see her. An elbow connected with her cheekbone and sent her teeth rattling. She heard a snarl. "Get out of the way! You're hurting her!" Reyna found herself yanked high by the collar, like a kitten from a litter. Pulled out of harm's way. She looked straight into Levi's eyes, blue as the sea at its deepest.

Levi set her down. His hand brushed her smarting cheek. "Are you hurt?"

Reyna could only stare, mute. How was he here?

"Reyna! Are you hurt?"

She managed a "No!"

"Then hold on." Once again, she found herself lifted high, sailing over the side of the ship onto the ladder. Levi held tight to her forearms, demanding, "Do you have it?"

Reyna grabbed on to the rope. "Yes." When he let go, she put him out of her mind. She had to. Because there was Mercedes. She climbed down as fast as she could, sliding in some parts, nearly burning her hands in the process, and almost fell over Commander Aimon at the bottom. He righted her.

The king knelt with Mercedes in his arms. She clutched his shoulders, crying, "I'm not going anywhere! Where is Elias?"

Blood soaked her yellow skirts. It pooled onto the dock. Reyna had never seen so much blood, nearly black against the wood. Dita tried helplessly to mop it up with her shawl, as though that would help in some way. King Ulises said, "There's no one on the *Amaris*. We don't know where he is."

Green eyes had turned glassy with shock. "What do you mean?"

He cupped her face in his hands. They were trembling. "Listen to me. I promise I'll find out more, but for now we must get you help. *Do you hear me, Cousin?* You must think of the child."

At the word *child* Mercedes at last focused on the blood around her. "Oh," she said with some surprise. To Reyna it looked as if her breath stopped before her eyes rolled back in her head and she slumped into the king's arms.

"Mother and child are safe, Your Grace. For now," the midwife said.

"What do you mean, for now?" King Ulises kept his voice low, careful not to disturb Mercedes sleeping in her bed. He glared across the expanse of blankets and pillows. "Spit it out, woman."

That he was so discourteous showed how anxious he was. Though his appearance would have already given him away; he must have run his hand through his hair a hundred times. Lord Elias was missing, and Mercedes had yet to open her eyes.

The bedchamber was decorated in green and gold. Sunlight and fresh air drifted in through open balcony doors. Reyna hovered by the foot of the bed, not trusting completely the midwife's pronouncement. She watched the rise and fall beneath the blankets, counted each beat in between. Where there was breath, there was life. But for how long? Dita took Reyna's hand in hers and gave it a reassuring squeeze. This would be devastating for Dita as well. Lord Elias was her cousin. And her betrothed had also been lost at sea. Years ago, after a storm.

Despite being hissed at by the king, the midwife remained calm. "She cannot be moved for the remainder of her pregnancy."

An appalled silence filled the chamber. The king said, "For three months?"

Commander Aimon had slipped into the chamber, listening by the door.

"It's necessary," the midwife insisted. "She's had a more

difficult time of it than before. And with Lord Elias . . . away, she must rest and be kept as free from worry as possible."

"You ask the impossible. Her husband has vanished." The king looked agonized.

"Nevertheless," the midwife said quietly.

King Ulises rubbed both palms down his face, then spotted his commander near the door. "What is it?"

Commander Aimon said, "The queen of Lunes requests an audience. She says it's urgent."

Reyna's hand slipped free of Dita's. Another strange, inexplicable occurrence: the del Marian flotilla had returned with Lunesian ships carrying important guests, Queen Vashti and her brother, Prince Levi.

Why would the queen leave her home so soon after a parent's death, as well as her own coronation? What was Levi doing here?

A thundercloud descended over the king's expression. "I don't have time to trade insults with her today. I didn't invite her here. She can wait. Forever is my preference."

"She thought you might say that," Commander Aimon acknowledged. "I'm to tell you she has information on our missing shipmen. All of them." He paused, long enough for his words to register. All eyes were riveted on him. "She sailed here at Lord Elias's request."

The king looked down at his clothing — sweat-stained, bloodstained — and grimaced. Urgent or not, one did not meet a visiting queen in such conditions. He said to the commander, "One hour."

"I'll tell her," the commander said. "She asked for Lady Reyna as well."

"Me?" Reyna asked. At the same time, the king said, "Why?"

"She did not say."

King Ulises looked a hairsbreadth away from gnashing his teeth. Instead he circled the bed, leaned over Mercedes, and kissed her on the cheek. He said to Reyna, "One hour."

"Your Grace." Before Reyna had risen from her curtsy, he was gone, taking the commander with him. The midwife moved off to the small adjoining bedchamber. Normally reserved for a lady's maid, it would be her sleeping quarters for the foreseeable future. The king wanted her nearby at all times.

Reyna and Dita remained at the foot of the bed. Softly, in case her suspicions were wrong, Reyna asked, "Are you asleep?"

"No." Green eyes snapped open. Mercedes's expression said she'd heard everything. "Why would Vashti ask for you?" Awake, but her voice was thready and weak.

"I know as much as you." Reyna came to stand beside Mercedes, placed her hand in hers. Dita followed. "I'll find out in an hour."

"You'll tell me everything?"

The glance Reyna exchanged with Dita held both worry and resignation. They knew that trying to keep anything from Mercedes would likely cause more harm than telling her the truth.

"I promise," Reyna said.

Mercedes's breathing eased. "Thank you." Her eyes shifted to Dita. "She has less than an hour. You'll put her in the red dress? It should have been delivered this morning."

"I will," Dita said. "Don't worry."

At Reyna's bewildered look — why were they speaking of *dresses?* — Mercedes said, "You'll need armor for a meeting with Vashti, dear heart. Clothing can be its own kind of mail. Keep your chin high. Don't let her scare you."

"Is she scary?"

"When she chooses to be." Mercedes struggled to sit up. The force of two glares sent her flat again. "Reyna. Ulises and Vashti . . . apart they are rational people. But when they are together, it is something else entirely."

"What do you mean?" Reyna asked.

"A long story, and not mine to tell. Someone must keep a cool head during that meeting." Her friend placed a hand over her belly. "Do you understand? Someone will have to remember Elias."

Reyna did not understand a thing. She said, "I understand."

The midwife returned, clucking and shooing them away when she saw Mercedes was awake. Reyna had time enough to kiss her friend's cheek before Dita dragged her off to prepare for a royal summons.

The dress was the most exquisite Reyna had ever owned: made of silk the color of garnets, it was cut off the shoulder to reveal her bare throat and collarbone. Black lace trimmed the hem and sleeves. As far removed from trousers as was possible.

"My goodness," Dita said. "I've never seen such a transformation." They stood by a full-length looking glass in Reyna's chamber, Dita expertly weaving strips of gold wire into her hair. It had been left loose; there was no time for anything more elaborate, and the strands fell like liquid onyx to her waist. "You're like a chameleon. So much beauty under that scruff and paint."

"I'm scared to death, Dita."

Dita's hands stilled. She met Reyna's gaze in the looking glass. "Of Queen Vashti?"

"Of everything. What if Mercedes doesn't get better? What if we can't find Lord Eli —"

"Don't borrow trouble." Dita resumed her weaving, this time with more vigor. "What we choose to believe is powerful, Reyna. Mercedes and the babe will be fine. Elias will come home safe. He always does. *This* I believe." Her reflection showed busy hands and a solitary teardrop on her cheek.

Reyna did not flinch when Dita pulled too hard. She said, "And so will Jaime."

A black lace fan lay on a high chest. Dita took the fan, offered it to Reyna. "And so will Jaime."

King Ulises looked splendid and bad-tempered. Reyna had arrived at his chambers before the appointed time. So far, there were only the three of them present: Reyna, the king, and Commander Aimon. The commander with his ceremonial weapons, sword and dagger as deadly as they were beautiful. The king in pale green and silver, robes lined in ermine. Diamonds studded a crown made of hammered gold and silver, more elaborate than the black onyx he usually wore. This crown was fit for a visit from a queen.

The balcony doors had been left open, a dozen of them, allowing the salt air to drift in, along with the cry of the gulls and a ship's horn, blasting long and low from the harbor.

"Sit, Reyna," the king invited. "If I know Vashti, she'll have us waiting half the day before —"

The doors opened. A steward announced the arrival of Queen Vashti and Prince Levi.

"*Early?*" King Ulises said, flummoxed. "What is happening here, Aimon?"

"A strange day," the commander agreed, before their guests walked through the door.

The family resemblance was impossible to miss. Queen Vashti was close to thirty, the same age as Reyna's king. She shared Levi's dark hair and blue eyes, his masculine features softened only slightly upon her smaller frame. Her dress, as blue as her eyes, draped a figure that made Reyna feel like a young boy in comparison. Flat and formless. A black ribbon circled the queen's neck, and a sapphire rested in the hollow of her throat. She was striking, in the way that enormous sapphire was striking. Reyna heard the king's breath catch and pretended she heard nothing.

Levi found Reyna the moment he stepped into the chamber. His steps faltered, resuming only after his sister's nearly imperceptible glance. He was not accustomed to this version of Reyna — all smoke and mirrors, black lace and red silk — and she decided not to be offended by it. She had been shocked herself, standing before the looking glass.

King Ulises spoke first. "Queen Vashti, Prince Levi, welcome to del Mar." His words were correct, but his tone was curt, hardly welcoming. It was not lost on Levi, who bristled.

Queen Vashti was not put off by the cold formality. She swept up to the king, took his hand in both of hers. He went completely and perfectly still.

"Ulises." Every inch of Queen Vashti radiated concern. "Your poor, *dear* cousin. How is Mercedes?"

"Not well."

"No! And the child?"

"The same." Carefully, the king peeled her hands from his and stepped back. "My house is burning around me, Vashti. Your prayers have been answered."

And just like that, all pretense of civility was gone. Reyna thought she heard Commander Aimon sigh.

"You cannot think I would wish this on you!" Queen Vashti burst out.

"I don't think it," King Ulises retorted. "I'm certain of it. 'A pox on you, Ulises.' Isn't that what you said? 'A pox on your whole kingdom —'"

"You would throw that in my face?" Temper sparked in the queen's eyes. "After what you did to —"

"I did what was best for —"

"Oh, you are ever so self-righteous —"

Slack-jawed, Reyna listened as the two rulers bickered like a couple married far too long. Centuries. Even more amazing was that she appeared to be the only one who was astounded. Commander Aimon merely studied the frescoes on the ceiling. Levi moved closer to Reyna so that their shoulders nearly touched. His words were quiet, for her alone.

"Lady. I was glad to hear you were safe."

Seconds passed before her tongue untied itself. "Captain. Welcome to del Mar."

"I —" Levi stopped. Commander Aimon's attention had shifted from the ceiling down to Levi, standing too close. Levi turned back to Reyna and spoke urgently. "Don't hate me for this. Not forever."

Commander Aimon raised one eyebrow. Levi heeded the warning, steping away before she could ask what he meant. Of course she did not hate him. Why would he think so? Because he had taken her royal passport? It was nothing compared to his many kindnesses. Even if she could ask, this was not the time. The two rulers were still sniping at each other.

Ulises and Vashti . . . apart they are rational people. But when they are together, it is something else entirely. This was what Mercedes had meant, and it was where she would have stepped in.

Smoothing everything over with words and a smile. She had once told Reyna that diplomacy was the true power behind any throne. That flies were more easily caught with honey than vinegar. It was not a simple thing to learn. It meant biting one's tongue and thinking hard before one spoke. It meant swallowing one bitter pill after another in the hopes that small compromises could be agreed upon. Diplomacy kept neighbors from becoming enemies. It saved lives. And just now, many lives Reyna cared about hung in the balance. Both Levi and Commander Aimon showed no signs of entering the fray. And Mercedes could not be here.

So Reyna stepped forward and curtsied, low and formal, bringing the quarrel to a halt. She held her position through the silence until Queen Vashti spoke above her.

"You must be Lady Reyna."

Grateful, Reyna rose. Her legs had begun to tremble. "I am, Queen Vashti. Prince Levi was kind enough to come to my aid on Lunes. I regret not being able to pay my respects to you then. I'm grateful to do so now."

Vashti's irritation lingered. She said, crisply, "No one stopped you from paying your respects. You chose to leave Selene of your own free will. Without a word to my poor brother, who worried greatly."

Reyna had left because if she had not, Levi would have found her maps and kept them for Lunes. Everyone here knew it. *Hold your tongue, Reyna. Vinegar. Honey.*

Ignoring her king's slightly flaring nostrils, Reyna said, "The opportunity to leave on a del Marian ship presented itself.

Rather suddenly." Now she felt another sardonic gaze on her, this time coming from Levi's direction. "And I did not wish to impose on your family any more than necessary during such a time. If I've caused offense, I am sorry."

"Hmm." Queen Vashti took Reyna's chin in her hand and studied her. Reyna did not look away. "I am not offended," Queen Vashti announced at last. The tension in the chamber eased. She turned Reyna's chin slightly left, then right. "Such a face," she murmured, with a glance at her brother. "Some things are clearer now."

"Vashti." Levi's expression was pained. Reyna was careful not to look at him.

Queen Vashti dropped her hand. She addressed the king with a scowl. "Your sea raiders aren't Coronads," she informed him.

"They're from Miramar," King Ulises said. At her startled expression, he pulled out a chair for her. "What do you know, Vashti?"

"A year ago," Queen Vashti said, "my father was approached by an emissary from Miramar. The son of the Miranese king. His name was Jian-so. It was the first contact we'd had with the kingdom since they closed their harbor to trade and foreigners."

"Five hundred years ago," Ulises said from the head of the table. Queen Vashti sat to his right, her brother beside her. Commander Aimon sat to the king's left, Reyna beside him.

"Yes," Queen Vashti said. "Naturally, my father was intrigued."

"What did he want, this prince?" Ulises asked.

"Our clay," Levi said.

There was a silence. Commander Aimon broke it, in his usual brusque fashion. "Your clay what?"

"Just the clay," Levi said. "We have quarries full of it, and Prince Jian-so offered a staggering sum. My father agreed."

"Why did he want it?" King Ulises asked him, perplexed.

"He would not say," Levi said.

"And you did not ask?"

"Ulises," Queen Vashti said, testily, "it was clay. Not sulfur or saltpeter. For what they offered, we did not care."

The king conceded grudgingly, "It's a fair point."

"I'm delighted you think so," Queen Vashti said.

Reyna's fan lay gathered on the table. With a fingertip, she spread it open, black lace on ancient, polished wood, and she thought, *Clay, sulfur, who cares? What does any of this have to do with Lord Elias?*

Levi said, "Prince Jian-so returned months later for the agreed-upon cargo and went on his way. We saw nothing of him afterward until . . ." He trailed off, glanced across the table at Reyna, glanced away.

Queen Vashti finished for him. "Until Lady Reyna drew his picture for Levi."

Reyna's fan snapped closed, impossibly loud in the silence. Stunned, she stared at Levi across the table, but he would not look her way. She could not have heard right. Levi had known who her attacker was then, many weeks ago, and he'd said nothing?

Don't hate me for this. Not forever.

Commander Aimon said, "You're certain it was him?"

"Yes," Levi said. "He had the same face. The same pock scars." He withdrew a folded sheet of parchment from his jacket, opened it, and placed it on the table for all to see. The *Simona's* attacker glared up at them from Reyna's original drawing. "The same axe."

The king brought the drawing close, then tossed it back onto the table. A different sort of anger settled over him. "So. These raiders are making slaves of my men. And you're their trading partner."

"Your Grace." Levi's words were cold, clipped. "With respect, we do not answer to you. My father chose to trade with the Miranese. My sister and I stand by that decision, as he is no longer here to stand by it himself." Both fists were clenched on the table. "We came here, at Lord Elias's request, so that we may work together. If you are in disagreement, we will leave. At once."

At the mention of Elias, the king's antagonism dimmed. "Work together in what way?"

Levi said, "We have an invitation to deliver more clay, when it's ready. I have the cargo on the *Truthsayer* now. I can get my ship into their harbor, and from there try to discover what has happened to your men. But from what Reyna — Lady Reyna," he amended, after a hasty glance in her direction, "has described, they are being restrained in some way. I may need help getting out."

It was a generous offer. King Ulises looked first at the commander, then Reyna, before he spoke. "What did Elias promise you in exchange?"

"Nothing." This from a more subdued Vashti. "Our brother has gone missing."

"Asher?" The king's gaze sharpened. At Vashti's nod: "We haven't heard of any missing Lunesian ships."

"There are none," Queen Vashti said. "Asher was attending university in Caffa. He was to return home for the coronation, but the Lunesian ship he was to sail home on needed repair."

"He would not wait," Levi said, "and instead booked passage on a Caffeesh messenger. He planned to travel as a common passenger, a student returning home. No one knew who he was."

"*Foolish* boy," Queen Vashti said. Levi's hand came up to brush his sister's shoulder, in comfort.

"How do you know this?" King Ulises asked.

Levi said, "He left a letter behind for Master Hiram, who was to have accompanied him home. No one has seen the ship, or any of its passengers, since."

Commander Aimon spoke. "You're on good terms with the Miranese, it sounds like. They are not targeting your ships. Why wouldn't your brother have told them who he was? They would have been lenient."

"He might not have been able to, Commander," Reyna said, and reminded him of the strange humming she had heard on the

Simona, and how the men had gone above deck without a fight. She did not look at Levi. He did not look at her.

A long silence filled the chamber.

King Ulises said, "Del Mar will give you all the men you need for a rescue. For my men and your brother. I have conditions."

Queen Vashti looked unsurprised. "Name them."

"We will not raise arms against them," King Ulises said. "Not one Miranese harmed, until we're certain this is their doing."

Levi frowned, "I'm quite certain —"

But King Ulises was adamant. "I'll have absolute certainty before I send in my men."

Queen Vashti spoke. "You said conditions. What else?"

Ulises said, "The proof will come from one of my own people. Someone who will sail with you, who can easily pass for a Lunesian . . ." He paused. "Someone who has an uncanny ability to remove herself from tricky situations."

The chamber went quiet once again. Everyone turned to Reyna. Beneath the table, she pressed a palm flat against her belly. It did nothing to calm the butterflies flapping around in a panic. When she saw that Commander Aimon's gaze was on her hand, she dropped it.

And said, "I understand. When do we go?"

THIRTEEN

REYNA, WAIT."

She ignored Levi, storming across the open courtyard of the Tower of Winds. An immense mosaic compass sparkled green and silver beneath her feet. He had known. He had known from the beginning who the raider was and had said nothing to her. Not one word.

A hand came down on her shoulder. She wheeled around, dislodging it, and jabbed her fan into his chest.

Levi did not flinch. "Listen to me —"

"I showed you his picture the first day I met you!" she cried. "And you stood there and you looked at it and you lied to my face!" There was no king or queen here to temper her words. *Honey. Vinegar. Ha!* She did not know how Mercedes did it.

"I didn't lie!" Levi looked as upset as she felt. *Good!* "Not exactly. I needed to think what to say —"

"*What* to say?" she repeated, aware they had attracted an audience along the covered passageway and not caring one bit. "How about the truth? What is so hard about that?"

"It's not that simple —"

"No?" Reyna spread her arms wide, scornful. "How is it, then? I'm listening."

They stood too close, breathing in the other's angry, fiery words. Levi inhaled so deeply she thought his lungs would burst. He said, with some difficulty, "Lunes has a trading relationship with the Miranese. It's not something easily set aside. When I saw your picture, it was my duty to speak to my sister first, to my *queen*, before I said anything to you. I did not lie."

"You said nothing because you didn't want to risk losing your precious Miranese gold. And now that your brother is missing, you've come here to beg for our help."

"You —" Levi's blue eyes widened in outrage. "This is what you think of me?"

"Do you know what you've done?" Reyna could feel the tears threatening. "If we'd known who they were, we could have done something sooner instead of —"

"What could you have done? There's nothing —"

"Something! *Before* Lord Elias and Jaime left here. Not *after*, when it's too late!"

Levi's face altered as if she had hit him. He lifted a hand toward her, dropped it. "Reyna . . . I didn't know you then."

"You still don't know me."

"What is this?" another voice demanded.

Master Luca. He pushed his way through the onlookers gawking in the passageway and stalked toward them. So many people watching. Even the first-years, still dripping from their lessons at the beach. Sensing disaster, she said, "Master Luca. This is Prince Levi."

"I know who he is." Master Luca was shorter than Levi, but broader, with enough muscle to give anyone pause. A bull with round spectacles. That was how Lord Elias had described him once. His hand rested on his sword hilt in a threatening manner. "I don't know how things are done on Lunes, but we do not *shout* at our ladies here on del Mar. In public or private. Step away!"

Levi's hand was also on his sword. A muscle twitched along his jaw, and for one horrible instant, Reyna could picture it: Master Luca's sword through Levi's gut, and Vashti's terrible rage. Wars had been started with less provocation. She stepped between them and raised both hands, palms out, the way one would when confronted with wild animals.

"We weren't shouting, Master Luca. We were just —"

"Don't speak for me." Levi's words were cold, clipped. He kept his eyes on Master Luca. "This is a private conversation."

"Is it?" Master Luca returned. "Yet half the castle is here, listening in."

Frustration lay upon him like a cloak. Levi turned to her. He wanted to stay, to finish what they had begun. She had heard enough. A step back, toward Master Luca, was all it took.

Levi's expression closed. He turned to Master Luca. "Well? Are you going to use that sword or not?"

Master Luca's eyes narrowed, but Reyna could see reason

returning. His hand dropped away from his hilt. "You're not welcome here. Prince." The last sounded more like a slur than an honorific.

Without a word, and without a glance at Reyna, Levi stalked off, his first visit to the Tower of Winds concluded.

After supper, a grim affair in which Vashti and Levi were guests of honor, Reyna dispatched a messenger to Blaise in Montserrat. She had promised to visit her friend the moment her work in the storage vault ended. That was no longer a possibility. The knowledge left her heartsick. Once that was done, Reyna returned to the king's chambers. There was much to be orchestrated and little time in which to do it all. The *Truthsayer* would be sailing for Miramar in two days.

Important people crowded the chamber: Lunesians, del Marians, none inclined to exchange more than a few terse pleasantries. They gathered around the table, standing, not sitting, as King Ulises and Levi laid out a plan of action. Reyna could not help noticing that Admiral Maira was nowhere to be found. No one explained why, and Reyna did not ask. She did not need to. It would be a long time before King Ulises forgave the admiral for allowing Lord Elias to be taken on his watch. Queen Vashti was present with her councilors, but she had ceded authority to her brother in all matters relating to the rescue. Beside Reyna was Master Luca, who, with Lord Braga away on Coronado, represented the Tower of Winds. Levi and Master Luca had exchanged frosty looks across the table and then ignored each other. From Levi, Reyna had received the stiffest of bows. He, in return, had earned the briefest of nods. And from there, they too had avoided each other.

It was decided that Reyna would act as a Lunesian scribe. The role meant she would be present whenever Levi met with the royal family of Miramar, as it would be her responsibility to record all that was discussed. And, as an upper servant, she would be able to go places a foreign prince could not. A translator would not be needed. From Levi they had learned that most Miranese spoke the language common to all their lands, ancient Caffeesh.

They would be in each other's company always, Reyna realized. There would be no avoiding him. She was so absorbed in her thoughts she nearly missed the king's question, for Levi.

"This Jian-so. He's a younger son?"

"No," Levi answered. "He's an only child. His father's heir."

King Ulises said, "Why would the heir to the Miranese kingdom be conducting sea raids? He could be killed. It seems a foolish move to me."

"To me as well, Your Grace," Levi said. "I don't have an answer."

"Hmm" was the king's response. "How long was this Prince Jian-so on Lunes?"

"Half a month," Levi answered.

"What did you think of him?" the king asked. "Lady

Reyna's experience was a grim one. A pirate, a murderer. Yet I can't imagine you would knowingly allow such a person in your home."

"We would not," Queen Vashti said.

"No." Levi glanced at Reyna before answering. "Prince Jian-so was on Lunes on trade business. He was prompt with his payments, amusing at supper, respectful of our customs. The clay was to be used for some sort of gift for his father, though he would not specify what. The way he spoke of King Botan-so . . . He was a man who loved his father."

King Ulises watched him closely. "You liked him."

"I had no reason to dislike him," Levi said.

"The feeling must have been mutual if he invited you to Miramar," King Ulises said.

"I think it was," Levi said, then stopped, frowning. "He was a little strange with his crew."

Queen Vashti said, "I'd forgotten about that."

"Strange how?" King Ulises asked.

"He would not allow them to leave the ship. Ever," Levi said.

"For half a month?" the king said in consternation.

Levi nodded. "They anchored mid-harbor. The only men who made it to shore were the prince and his guards."

Reyna addressed her king. "If the Miranese are like other hermit kingdoms, they would not want their people exposed to foreigners. To see how others live. It gives people ideas, sows discontent."

"Makes them want to leave," the king said.

"Sometimes, yes," Reyna said.

Queen Vashti tapped her finger on the table twice as if something had just occurred to her. "The guards' teeth were black."

King Ulises regarded her with puzzled irritation. "So the Miranese don't care for their teeth? That is interesting." His tone implied the opposite. The Lunesian stirred, prepared to take offense on their queen's behalf.

"It wasn't rot," Queen Vashti snapped. "It was paint. And I thought it very strange, that is all."

"Oh!" Reyna said. All eyes swung her way. "It's an old custom. Isn't it, Master Luca? Painting teeth black?"

"It is."

"It's like the Bushido women when they leave their mustaches untrimmed," Reyna explained. "Those men are looking for wives. It's their version of a mating call."

No one spoke. More than a few cleared their throats. Levi looked at her, looked away just as quickly. Master Luca spoke under his breath, but in the quiet his words were heard by all. "Reyna, we cannot say things like *mating* in such company."

Reyna, suitably chagrined, was made less so by the smile, wide and genuine, that Queen Vashti sent her way.

The discussion continued.

"Best not to do anything out of the ordinary," King Ulises said. "It will only make them suspicious. The *Truthsayer* will sail into Miramar's harbor alone. But we won't be too far away.

Del Mar's next expedition leaves in one week, once Lord Braga returns. The expedition is no secret." He turned to Levi. "You have heard of it?"

"Yes," Levi confirmed.

"Good," King Ulises said. "The ships will leave Cortes as scheduled. They'll stop here" — he pointed to Aux-en-villes on the large map unrolled before them — "presumably to take on additional fresh water. We've done this many times. No one will think it strange. This port is only a few days from Miramar. They'll wait to hear word from the *Truthsayer*. We'll proceed from there."

Levi leaned closer, frowning at the map. "Days? Do you mean weeks? There's no direct route from Aux-en-villes to Miramar."

The king said, "There is, by river, here . . ." He trailed off, his finger on a blank space on the map. "Where did this map come from?" he demanded.

Master Luca looked. "Not from us, Your Grace."

"It's ours." Instantly, Queen Vashti bristled. "What's wrong with it?"

"It's archaic." The king found Reyna, who had shifted halfway behind Master Luca, knowing what would be asked of her. A rueful smile emerged on the king's face as he said, "Under any other circumstance, I would not ask. I know what you risked to bring it home. But in this, we must show good faith."

"I understand," she said. Then, to be sure: "Aux-en-villes?"

"I'm afraid so."

Most of the others looked baffled by the exchange. Master Luca, however, massaged his chest as though his heart were in great pain.

Reyna knew how he felt. "I'll fetch it now."

She found her maps in Lord Braga's work chamber, on his desk, though she had to sift through dozens of other charts to find what she needed. It looked like a storm had passed through. Lord Braga had not tidied before he left, and he expressly forbade the servants from touching his desk, saying he could never find anything afterward. When she returned to the king's chambers, room was made for her. She unrolled the map on the table. It was clear hers was the more current, the empty space on the Lunesian map fully drawn in. They were all distracted for a time, noting the changes, admiring the skill.

Levi forgot he was not speaking to her. "You hid them in the church?" he asked.

Her nod was stiff, but civil.

Levi spoke as if to himself. "This is why you ran."

"I did not run," she said evenly, and saw the king's lips curve upward. "But yes, it's why I left."

"And you were right to do so." Queen Vashti eyed Reyna's rendering of Aux-en-villes and the rivers and roads surrounding it, previously unknown to Lunes. "I would have taken this from you with great pleasure. Clever girl."

Her words wiped away any trace of amusement from King

Ulises, who said in a sour tone, "As I was saying, from Aux-en-villes there is another way into Miramar . . ."

"This can't be what they meant by bed rest," Reyna said.

"I am in bed, and I am hardly moving. It's enough." Mercedes was sitting up, wearing a blue-and-silver dressing gown. Her color *did* look better. Reyna sat cross-legged on the covers, shoes kicked off onto the floor. They were alone in the bedchamber, but in the adjoining room, the ladies of the court had gathered. There was laughter and gossip. Many of them were knitting gowns and blankets for the baby. Reyna suspected Dita had had a hand in this. *What we choose to believe is powerful, Reyna.* If it proved true, the baby would be born in excellent health, with more clothing than he or she could possibly wear.

Mercedes worked as they spoke. A small table lay across her lap. On it was a dagger, as well as a flat piece of leather, the size and shape of an open book. It had once covered a book, in fact, but was now worn and faded. With quick, efficient hands, Mercedes sliced strips from the leather, each the width of a finger. One by one, the strips were wrapped around the dagger's grip and tied off. Mercedes snipped the excess away with a pair of shears.

"There." Mercedes held it up, satisfied. "Plain and simple. No one will look twice at this, but you won't find a sharper blade anywhere else. Keep it close."

"I will." Reyna took the dagger and turned it over in her hand. With its worn grip, it was exactly the sort of weapon a scribe would carry.

Mercedes took up a spare leather strip and tied it into a knot. Over and over again. She could not keep her hands still. "You're not to worry about me."

"If you say so." Reyna slid the dagger into its sheath.

Mercedes smiled. For the briefest of moments she looked like her old self, but then the shadows crept back behind her eyes. "I hate that I can't go with you," she admitted.

"I know."

"I *hate* that I can't keep you safe."

"I'm not nine any longer, remember?" Reyna reached out and squeezed her hand. "I can take care of myself."

"Yes. And Levi will be with you. I'm glad."

Reyna dropped her friend's hand.

"You've never been one to hold a grudge." Somewhere beneath the amusement, Reyna heard a scold. "Poor Levi."

Poor *Levi*? What about her? "I don't like being lied to."

"It's never pleasant," Mercedes conceded. "He was here earlier, your nemesis. That is from him."

A vase sat upon an open windowsill, its color Lunesian blue. It held a single peony as white as a swan's feather.

Reyna refused to be charmed. She showed the vase her back. "The king said he was your page on Lunes."

"He was." Mercedes smiled faintly. "He would meet me at the harbor. Always so sweet and serious. Being my page was not a task he took lightly." She tied another knot onto her strip. "Levi is different from his siblings. He doesn't like to have everyone's eyes on him, like Vashti. He doesn't befriend everyone he meets, like Asher. He has a few good friends, and they are all he needs."

Reyna heard the affection in her voice. "You admire him."

"Oh, very much."

Reyna could not help herself. She pointed out, "Because he reminds you of yourself."

Mercedes's laugh had the women in the outer chamber pausing to look in. She said to Reyna, "No need to be spiteful, even though it's true." Her smile faded as she placed both hands across her rounded belly. "If I could not look for Elias myself, then I would choose you to do it. You and Levi."

Reyna waited until she was sure her voice would not betray her. "I'll find him, Mercedes. I'll bring him home."

"Bring yourself home too, little sister. Do you swear it?"

Reyna smiled. She leaned close and kissed her friend, once on each cheek.

And made no promises.

FOURTEEN

REYNA RODE INTO THE HARBOR at dawn. She came with Master Luca only, for she had not wanted grand farewells from the tower, not for this particular journey. Master Luca was more than enough, suspiciously damp eyes masked behind strict orders to watch her back, keep her dagger close, and make sure she drank lots of water. Reyna, for her part, flung her arms around his neck and wept. Saying goodbye had never come easy to her, no matter how often she did it.

Her role as a scribe meant she had no use for the beautiful dresses Mercedes had ordered for her. They were left behind. Instead Reyna had packed clothing hastily fitted by Madame Julián: plain, serviceable frocks in Lunesian blue. Her sea chest had been delivered to the *Truthsayer* the night before. When she made her way up the gangplank, it was with nothing more than the clothes on her back. Trousers, boots, a white linen shirt. Also a cap on her head, faded and blue, her hair stuffed inside it.

Levi met her at the rails. Dressed formally in leather and mail, he offered a civil "Lady."

"Captain."

There was little he missed. He took in her red eyes and a nose that must be equally red. A glance over the side showed Master Luca, all alone by the mooring posts. Before he could say more, there was a shout from overhead.

"Lady!"

Halfway up the rigging, young Benjamin waved his cap at her, grinning. Seeing him lifted her spirits. Smiling, she removed her own cap and waved back. Her hair unfurled in the wind, like the sails, the ends whipping against Levi's face before she moved hastily away. All around her a familiar crew prepared to sail. Not all the faces were friendly. The pilot, Caleb, would have slunk past without a word if Levi had not said his name in that scary, warning tone he sometimes used.

Caleb's sigh was lengthy and put-upon. But he stopped and bowed. "Lady Reyna."

"Master Caleb."

And that was the extent of their conversation. Caleb looked at Levi as if to say, *There. Is that polite enough for you?* Levi nodded once, and with those niceties out of the way, Caleb marched off toward the sterncastle. Reyna watched him go and thought, *This is going to be a long voyage.*

"Ignore him," Levi advised. "The men haven't let him forget how easy it was for a girl to outsmart him."

Reyna felt a little bad. She had taken advantage of his concern for that injured old lady in Selene's harbor. "It wasn't his fault."

"Nevertheless."

A violent retching claimed their attention. The sound came from the rails opposite, where a shipman leaned over the side, quivering from the force of his sickness. The contents of his stomach rained onto the fish below.

"Poor man," Reyna murmured. The *Truthsayer* was still moored. How much worse would he be when they actually set sail? "Who is he?"

"My new doctor." Levi didn't look the least bit sympathetic to the shipman's plight. "Borrowed from my sister. He's temporary."

"Temporary? Where is your permanent one?"

"Back in Selene. His wife is ill. I told him to stay behind, that I would take one of the castle physicians instead."

More retching at the rails. Reyna guessed, "You're regretting that decision."

Levi's lips curved, rueful. "A little. He's an excellent doctor. But not on the water."

A wary truce had developed between them. They did not mention the argument at the tower, but left the words unsaid, simmering beneath the surface.

Three more shipmen hurried by, stopping long enough to greet her. *Lady. Lady. Lady.*

It would not do. Reyna said, "I can't be a lady on this ship."

Levi only looked at her.

She explained, "Someone will forget and call me *lady* when they're not supposed to. I'm your scribe. It's better to begin as we mean to go on."

Levi nodded, understanding. "So . . . Master Reyna?"

Master because women were considered bad luck on a ship. It was best to pretend there were none aboard. A silly rule, made by men. "Fine."

"I'll see to it," Levi said. Then: "You have the middle cabin by the stairs. Your maid slept here last night. Readied your things. We gave her the cabin next to yours."

"Maid?" Reyna said blankly.

"Mm. You'll have to do without her on Miramar. I don't know of any scribes with personal maids."

"What maid?"

A crease formed between his brows. "The one who came with your chest." He looked past her. "That maid."

"Reyna."

The voice — female, familiar — belonged to someone who should have been far away from here. In Montserrat, to be exact. Reyna spun around. Blaise stood by the open hatchway, nervously smoothing the white apron she wore over her dress.

Astounded, Reyna said, "What are you — oh no. No."

"Just listen," Blaise said. "I'm coming with you."

"*No.*" The fragile, unspoken truce Reyna had built with Levi crumbled. She turned on him. "You let anyone aboard who says they're my maid? She could have murdered you in your sleep!"

Levi didn't look any happier than she did. His tone was clipped. "Your Master Luca brought her here. He said you knew her well, since you were girls."

"Which is the truth," Blaise offered.

"What is your name?" Levi snapped. The crew had gone quiet around them.

"Blaise." She swallowed and tried not to look cowed. The wind sent her short curls in every direction despite the pretty clip of silver and pearls. "I went looking for Reyna yesterday. I found Master Luca first. He didn't feel she should be the only female here, and I agree..." The look on Levi's face sent her trailing off into silence.

"It's not for you to agree or disagree." Levi looked over the railing once again, but Master Luca and the horses had conveniently vanished.

Blaise said quickly, "I promise not to loaf. I can help your doctor there. He looks like he could use the help."

Levi's expression became one tiny bit less forbidding. "You're a healer?"

"Yes," Blaise said. "Well, almost."

"Which means what, exactly?"

"I've worked in my uncle's shop since I was ten. He's a barber-surgeon. I can fix broken things."

"Arms? Legs? Fingers?"

"All of it," Blaise said. "And fever, stomach ailments. I can deliver babies..." She stopped, ears reddening, realizing what she had said. More than one shipman snickered.

Levi's expression did not shift. "That won't be necessary."

Blaise sent Reyna a desperate glance. "And I can speak Lunesian and Caffeesh. Reyna can vouch for me."

Everyone turned to Reyna, who said, "She can, and she's an excellent barber. That isn't the point. It isn't safe, Blaise. I told you so in my letter."

"Then you shouldn't be going either." Blaise folded her arms.

Reyna did the same. Levi, standing between them, looked from one glaring female to the other. He took a step back.

"How are you here?" Reyna asked. "What did your *maman* say?"

At this, Blaise faltered. Her mumbled response sounded suspiciously like "I left her a note."

"You ran away!" Reyna cried, scandalized.

"You know I can't stay there, Reyna. Please. Let me come with you."

Reyna turned to Levi, who was eyeing his borrowed physician across the way. The man had lowered himself onto the deck, eyes closed. Sweat dripped from his temple. His face was the color of seashells bleached from the sun. Levi lowered his voice, addressed Reyna. "I can send him back to Vashti. Right now. We could use your friend, but this I'll leave up to you."

"You'll allow two females on your ship? What about bad luck?"

Levi shrugged. "We're not as superstitious as you del Marians. We'll call her Master Blaise and be done with it."

Reyna was torn. She knew how miserable Blaise was. She saw her desperation to get away. But the journey they were about to embark on was full of uncertainty and danger. She thought of her missing shipmates, the dead crew, the abandoned vessels. Master Luca! How could he have placed her in this wretched position? If she had to choose between Blaise's safety and her happiness, then there really was no choice to be made.

High above their heads, the seagulls greeted the new day. Heartsick, Reyna turned to Blaise, who saw the refusal in her eyes. And that was when Blaise lifted her chin and said, "You told me once that I should not waste my favors. That I should save them for when I truly needed them. Do you remember?"

"*You wouldn't,*" Reyna breathed. Eight years since she had first made the offer, and Blaise had never brought it up again. Until today.

"I would," Blaise said. "I would like to stay on this ship. And you owe me a favor."

"Don't be angry," Blaise said.

"Your *maman's* going to kill us both." Reyna sat in her berth, in a different cabin from when she had first boarded the *Truthsayer* all those weeks ago. This one was three times the size, with a window large enough to jump from. Was this how she was to judge cabins from now on? she wondered. Were the windows large enough for escape? "If your uncle doesn't beat her to it," she added.

"Yes," Blaise admitted. "But I'll worry about that later."

Reyna flopped onto her back, staring up at the ceiling.

"Reyna."

Reyna turned her head. Blaise sat on a chair beside Reyna's sea chest. There were two chairs, not one, and a small table where a platter displayed fruit, sugared almonds, even a cake. A thick rug covered most of the scarred wooden planks.

Blaise said, "Jaime's my friend too."

"I know." Reyna rolled onto her side, propped herself up on an elbow. "I think he's safe. He has to be. It doesn't make sense to hurt them. Levi's plan is a good one."

Blaise's eyebrows rose. "Levi?"

"Captain Levi," Reyna corrected.

"I like your captain."

Reyna did not bother to say he was not *her* anything. It would be pointless, anyway, with Blaise. She had seen the picture Reyna had drawn of him, all those weeks ago. And Blaise had known her a long time. "Why do you like him?" she asked. "He's done nothing but bark at you."

"He can be scary," Blaise admitted. "But he was kind last night. He wanted to make sure your room was comfortable. The rug is his. He had it moved from his cabin."

Reyna looked over the edge of her berth. It was a beautiful rug, with intricate blue-and-silver scrollwork. Why would he give it to her? She said, "He lied to me."

"True," Blaise said after a moment. Reyna had told her everything in her letter. "It's unforgivable, I suppose. Especially since you were so honest with him from the beginning."

Reyna scowled at her before flopping onto her back once again.

Unfazed, Blaise riffled through the contents of Reyna's sea chest: clothing and parchment and books. She pulled a leather-bound tome free and read its cover. "*A Complete and Concise History of Miramar?* This looks ancient."

"It's all I could find," Reyna said. "I don't want to be completely ignorant when we sail into that harbor."

"I'll help," Blaise offered. There was a knock on the door. Reyna hopped from her berth and answered it. It was young Master Benjamin, come for Blaise.

"The captain wants me to show you the infirmary, miss."

Blaise followed him to the door. She looked over her shoulder, smiled at Reyna. "Save me some of that cake, won't you?"

"You didn't get one?"

Blaise looked down at Benjamin. He looked up at her. They both laughed.

"I did not" was Blaise's response. "Go see for yourself."

Curious, Reyna went next door to Blaise's cabin. Now she understood her friend's amusement. This was what Reyna had been expecting for herself: a sliver of a room with a narrow berth. A round window smaller than her head. No extra table or chair, no colorful rug, and certainly no platter of food.

Levi had done this for her. Why would he bother? *Don't you know?* a voice asked. She lingered in the doorway, deep in thought, trying to hold on to her outrage, finding it impossible.

FIFTEEN

A S FAR AS REYNA KNEW, there were no rules for offering bribes. She would have to make an educated guess and hope it worked.

She opened her sea chest. There was more here than clothing and books. More even than parchment and ink. A rectangular box lay at the bottom, a tight fit, and Reyna had to ease it straight upward with her fingertips in order to remove it. The box was nearly flat; it would accommodate no more than a handful of maps. She had only needed it to hold one. Tucking the box under one arm, she went in search of Master Caleb.

From the deck, she could see him up in the sterncastle with two men, twin brothers named Samuel and Hamish. Not wanting to disturb them, she found a seat on a wide bit of railing and settled in to wait.

One could not have asked for a better day at sea. The sun was high, the sky clear, the wind brisk enough to move the *Truthsayer* along at a steady clip. Del Mar was long gone. There was no sign of land in any direction.

Eventually, the brothers left the sterncastle and strode past her. Reyna would have gone up then, but Caleb came down the steps before she had a chance. He paused when he saw her sitting on the railing, clutching her large, mysterious box.

"Careful." He looked past her to the sea swirling green below. "You don't want to fall in. Accidentally."

So this was how it would be. "I wouldn't bother with threats," she said evenly. "You'd be the first person the captain would suspect if I fell in. Accidentally."

Caleb smiled before he remembered he did not like her. A scowl dropped back into place. She hopped off the railing and held out the box before he could stomp away.

She might have been presenting a plate of rotten crab. His hands remained by his sides. "What is it?"

"A peace offering." Reyna held it out even further. "Take it. It's not poisonous."

Suspicion remained, but curiosity won out. He took the box, undid the clasp, and lifted the lid. His mouth fell open slightly.

It was a beautiful map of Lunes, one she had copied off a Tower of Winds original two years earlier during a storm that had kept her indoors and restless for a week. She had used blue paint for the harbor, gold for the land, green for the rolling hills surrounding Mount Abraham. An intricate pattern of gold leaf and lapis lazuli decorated the borders. It was the sort of map commissioned for a great lord or lady, or even a king and queen.

Someone with deep pockets. The obvious pleasure in Caleb's eyes was gratifying. As a bribe, she thought it would do.

"I'm not betraying any secrets giving it to you," she said. "It's your kingdom, after all."

Caleb reached to touch the map, then stopped at the last moment. "This is your work?"

"I didn't chart it. Only painted it."

"You're giving it to me?"

She nodded.

"Why?"

"This is a small ship, Master Caleb," she said. "I'd rather share it with a friend than an enemy."

His attention was drawn, once again, to her work. "You buy your friendships with maps?"

Reyna shrugged. "You tell me. It's the first time I've tried."

She knew from his expression that he would not be rejecting her gift. Sea water misted the deck. Quickly, Caleb closed the lid to protect the map. His map.

He said, "I wasn't angry about you running off. Well," he amended at her skeptical look, "that was embarrassing, and I will think twice before helping old ladies in distress from now on." They shared a brief smile, which disappeared when he said, "He looked everywhere for you. When I realized you were gone, I planned to say nothing until after the king's funeral. But Levi . . . he wanted to know where you were. Make sure I had not stuck you in some hovel." He leaned against the railing.

"When he should have been grieving his sire, when he should have been *sleeping*, he was riding his horse over every inch of Selene, searching for you. All this effort, for a girl he'd known for hours."

Caleb spoke to the top of her cap. She had lowered her head, studying the grain in the planks by her boots as he painted a picture for her.

As for the girl, I have lost her.

"I know it's not your fault," Caleb said, and her head lifted. "But he's my captain and . . ."

"Your friend," Reyna said quietly. "I understand, Master Caleb."

"Caleb," he corrected after a moment. He held up the box, smiled. "My thanks for this. It is the most spectacular bribe."

"You're welcome."

He left her and disappeared through the hatchway. Reyna scanned the deck until she found Levi up in the forecastle with Benjamin. The boy held a cross-staff at eye level, pointed northward. It looked as if Levi was showing him how to measure the angle of the sun. His captain's uniform was gone now that they were away from shore, and this afternoon he looked like any other shipman with his white shirt and rough linen trousers. She wished Caleb had not told her that story. She wished she hadn't seen how patient Levi was with Benjamin. It only complicated matters, in a world that was complicated enough.

An invitation had been relayed through Benjamin to dine in the captain's quarters. Reyna had passed along their regrets with the excuse that Blaise was weary after her first day at sea. Best if they shared a quiet meal in Reyna's cabin. Her friend, polishing a set of scalpels on the rug and looking perfectly *unweary*, had shaken her head. She departed after supper for the infirmary.

The thought of dining across from Levi had made Reyna's stomach queasy. As if she had eaten something off. Or maybe that was it. The food was to blame. Perhaps she truly was ill.

You're not ill. You're a coward.

Yes, well. What of it? Leave me alone.

She was arguing with herself, inside her head. This was not good. She fled the cabin.

It was late. On deck, the only light came from two lanterns. One in the sterncastle by the compass box, the other shared among the watch. The two guards nodded when they saw her. Each man carried a bow and arrows on his back. She climbed onto the railing and stretched her legs. A length of rope, pulled taut, offered a backrest.

The sky was a bolt of midnight-blue silk, the sea as calm as the night she had plunged beneath its depths. She closed her eyes, reliving her last minutes on the *Simona*. Remembering Gunnel, the arrows, the sea worms. Picturing Levi in the shadows of the dock, mourning his father.

"I'll go, if you'd rather."

Her eyes snapped open. Levi stood several feet away,

watching her. Almost as if she had conjured him with her thoughts. "It's your ship," she said.

"You're my guest." His white shirt glimmered faintly in the night. Like the guards, he carried bows and a quiver on his back. The necessity of it had her peering uneasily into the water.

When she did not answer, he stepped away, prepared to leave her. She did not want him to go. "Have you ever heard of *tutto mortise?*"

Levi stopped. "Yes. Why?"

Looking out at the water, she said, "When the Miranese king dies, he takes his best soldiers with him. The young ones, the strong ones. They're supposed to protect him in the afterlife."

Levi came closer. "Where do the old soldiers go?"

"Nowhere, I suppose. He has no use for them."

Levi came closer still, resting his forearms along the rail, only inches from her boots. "Just the soldiers?"

"It depends on the king," Reyna said. "Some chose the prettiest dancing girls. Others the finest musicians, poets . . . jugglers, even. One king had his portrait painted by the most famous artist in Miramar. And when he died, both the painting and the painter were buried with him."

Levi whistled low. "They can't have gone willingly."

Reyna thought of Niemi-si, who had escaped that fate. "The book I'm reading claims they did. The Miranese have a saying: 'In life and death we serve.' It's supposed to be a great honor, being chosen by the king."

"Is that so?" His sideways glance was full of skepticism. "Who wrote that book?"

"Ah . . ." Reyna tried to remember. "It's a del Marian translation of a Miranese history."

"That's what I thought."

The *Truthsayer* rocked slightly. Reyna grabbed on to the rope, having no interest in an evening swim. "What do you mean?"

"Well." Another sideways glance. "Most histories are written by the king's historians. Historians who serve at the pleasure of the king."

Reyna found herself wanting to smile. "You're saying they lied."

"Why bite the hand that feeds you?" he reasoned. "If Ulises said, 'Come along, Reyna, I would like you to suffocate alongside my cold, dead body; it will be a great honor for you,' what would you say?"

"I love my king," Reyna said immediately, knowing that was no answer.

"I love my queen. Very much. But . . ." Levi shrugged.

"Maybe not that much," she finished.

"No."

They shared a smile. Fleeting, fragile as spun silk. He exchanged words with the guards as they walked past before turning back to the water. "Can I ask you something?" he said.

"Yes."

"Where did you hide your maps? When you went into the church?"

"Behind St. Jeremiah."

Silence met her words. Then: "Patron saint of poor students."

An obscure saint. Unknown to most. Levi must have sensed her surprise because he said, "I used to tell Asher there was a saint for everyone. Jeremiah was his."

Reyna did not scoff, exactly. "Your brother's a Lunesian prince. How poor could he possibly be?"

"You haven't met Asher." His smile returned. "He left for university a year ago, and not a month has gone by without a letter pleading for funds. It's like he has a hole in his pocket and the silver pours right down his leg to the street."

Behind the amusement, she heard the disquiet. To have a brother go missing, right after losing his father.

"Captain," she said quietly. And, when he turned to her: "In five days, we'll see the Strait of Cain. After that, the Chrysanthemum River. We're on our way to find him now."

"Will we find him? Everything we're doing is based on a hunch. We don't even know if they're there. If we're lucky, Asher will be on Miramar. Or something there will tell us where to look next. If we're unlucky . . ."

There had been no sign of this uncertainty back on del Mar. Speaking before King Ulises and his sister, Levi had sounded so sure.

"What do you have against hunches?" she said.

He turned his head to her, perplexed. "Ah . . ."

"Every time a fleet leaves del Mar, it's because we're following a hunch," she said. "We go where our noses lead us, trust in what we feel *here*." She pressed a hand to her stomach, to her gut. "And that is why our explorers are vastly superior to yours."

Her teasing worked. Some of the darkness left his eyes. "You're not so superior."

"Of course you would never admit it."

A small laugh, holding little humor. "I hope my nose is right, Lady, because I won't return home without him."

A companionable silence fell between them, long enough for the guards to complete another turn. Levi said, "You're close to the royal family."

"They were good to me after my grandfather died. I had no one."

"No? Where was your uncle?" Levi asked.

"Abroad. I had never met him before. We weren't even sure he was still alive. Lord Elias tracked him down, and he sent for me."

"Do you get on with him?"

Reyna smiled. "Most of the time."

Would the news have reached Uncle Ginés by now? The king had promised to send him word. She would hate for him to hear about Lord Elias's ship by accident, in some casual manner, or to wonder why she did not write. He would worry greatly. She said, "Lord Elias . . . he was the first person to make me believe I could be a true member of the Tower of Winds. Not just an explorer's granddaughter. Or someone who stands at the docks and waves goodbye . . ."

He finished, "While everyone else sails off."

"Yes."

Levi was facing her now, listening intently. "Do people give you grief over it?"

Oh yes. "Sometimes."

Perhaps he heard what she'd left unspoken, because he said, "Has someone taught you how to fight? I know you have a dagger."

"Mercedes tried her best. So did Commander Aimon. It's not my strength." She shrugged. "Mostly I know how to run."

Silence. "Have you had to run often?"

"Once or twice." Adding, because even in the darkness she could see how her words upset him: "I can take care of myself, Captain."

"So you keep telling me."

Another silence fell, less companionable. Until Levi held out his hand, offering something to her. Gold, the size and shape of a playing card, stamped with an image of her king. Her royal passport. The one he had taken from her on Selene.

He said, "I never meant to keep it forever."

Reyna took it, her fingers brushing his. "No?"

"A few days only." He rubbed the back of his neck in a self-conscious gesture. "I wasn't ready to see you go."

The words had dried up for her. Just as well, for Levi was not finished. "About Jian-so." He stopped, looked away, forged on. "I should have told you. It was a mistake."

Levi was trying, and it sounded like it was costing him plenty. She said, "I'm sorry I let Master Luca yell at you."

Levi smiled. "I'm not afraid of your Master Luca." Some thought caught him, she could not say what, only he no longer met her eyes. "That first day," he said, "you had a drawing of your uncle and another man. A younger one. You said he was a friend."

She thought back to the drawing Levi spoke of. A portrait, drawn on the beach, a guitar. "His name is Jaime."

His smile was gone. "I recognized him at the coronation. He was with Lord Elias. A friendly sort."

Reyna smiled at the description. "That was him."

The hatch opened. Blaise's laughter drifted through the opening before she emerged, followed by Caleb. For some reason, Blaise held a large saw. Reyna squinted in the darkness as they approached. No, she was not mistaken.

"What are you doing with that saw?" Reyna slid down from the railing.

"It's a cranial incisor!" Blaise held up the saw with both hands, like a priest presenting a newly blessed infant at a baptism. "I've never seen one in person! It's for slicing through a person's —"

"Yes," Reyna said faintly. "I'm familiar with the cranium. Why are you carrying it around the deck?"

Levi, with a smile in his voice, said, "You'd get along well with our doctor, Master Blaise. No one else here appreciates Noah's collection of . . . fine instruments. Don't worry," he said to Reyna. "We haven't had to use it."

"It *has* been used, rather badly. Look." Blaise turned the saw over to show the teeth, several of which were bent.

"Hamish used it to repair some posts," Caleb responded to Levi's questioning look.

"Posts? Noah's going to saw *him* when he finds out."

"Aye, I warned him," Caleb said. "I told Master Blaise we might be able to fix —"

Levi's hand came up fast. A finger to his lips, for silence. Only then did Reyna hear it: the scrabble of claws against wood, accompanied by a long, low growl. There was no mistaking what it was. A finned lion scaling the hull. No. Not one lion.

Two.

Everyone froze. Even the guards standing by the cookstove. Levi looked to them; instantly their lantern was extinguished. A fire could not be risked. High in the sterncastle, a single lantern remained lit. Levi grabbed Reyna's arm. Before the terror of their situation fully sank in, she found herself shoved into a sliver of space between a water barrel and the curved interior of the hull. Blaise toppled in beside her. *"Don't move!"* Levi ordered; then he was gone.

"A lion?" Blaise hissed in her ear, her voice thin with fright.

"Two." Reyna heard men running. The growling grew louder. Holding tight to Blaise's hand, she peeked around the barrel, praying. *Please let them be smaller lions. Females. Cubs.*

The scene unfolded in shadows. First she spotted the cranium incisor on the deck. Blaise had dropped it. Directly opposite their hiding place, a pair of terrifying beasts appeared over the railing, manes full and bristling — adult males, twice the size of a man. Her prayers had gone unanswered. The lions slunk over the side and onto the deck, sleek and rumbling, each with a spiked fin on its back and a long, curving serpent's tail. Fearsome as the spikes were, it was the mane — a halo of sharp quills — that must be avoided. The quills were filled with poison. A single stab meant death.

Levi shot the first arrow. Reyna could see him halfway up the sterncastle steps. A pained roar followed — the arrow had found its target, but it was not enough. More arrows flew, from every direction. From Levi, from Caleb in the forecastle's doorway, from the guards hunkered down by the cookstove. At last one lion reeled, weakened by arrow shot, before managing to leap over the rails. A tremendous splash followed.

The second lion was furious, injured, and it had set its sights on Levi, bounding across the *Truthsayer* even as arrows struck a shoulder, an arm, its side. Reyna could not look away from Levi with his bow raised high, shooting faster than she had ever seen anyone shoot before. Raw panic filled her. The arrows were not working. Why did he still stand there? Why didn't he run?

Ignoring Blaise's shocked "What are you doing?" Reyna bolted from their hiding place. She waved her arms over her head and shouted, "Oy! Lion! Look here!"

The lion's head whipped around. Reyna saw the dumbstruck

horror on Levi's face before she turned and ran in the opposite direction. Her heart drummed like thunder in her ears. She felt the lion's roar, a hot, pulsing wind at her back, before something tripped her. She pitched forward, hitting the deck with outflung hands.

A deathly silence followed. In its wake, the familiar hiss of a lantern being lit. Reyna rolled over with a groan. She had been tripped by a mighty paw. It flopped off her boot and onto the deck. Inches away, the poisonous mane quivered and thrummed, then grew still as the life within faded to nothing. A saw protruded from its neck.

Hovering over her were the guards, lantern raised high. Blaise and Caleb, faces linen-pale. And Levi, standing by the tail, looking as the animal had only moments before. As if he wanted to kill her.

"'Oy, lion, look here'?" Levi said incredulously. "What were you thinking, Reyna?"

It was Levi who had killed the lion. Blaise would tell Reyna of it later. Realizing the futility of bow and arrow, he had swept up the saw Blaise had dropped: Master Noah's dreadful cranium incisor. Levi had used it, not as one would normally use such an instrument, but as a weapon, flinging it at the lion like an athlete's disk. The saw had caught the animal at the neck, severing something important. And that was how Reyna remained alive to sit by the mainmast with Levi. Who was nowhere near grateful.

His was an angry pacing. No one paid them any attention. The deck swarmed with men woken from their sleep by the excitement on deck. They surrounded the animal, close but not too close. Blaise was with them.

Reyna tried to reason with Levi. "Your arrows weren't working. What was I supposed to do? Watch while it ate you?"

Levi swung around to glare at her. "Yes! That exactly."

"I'm here to bring my friends home, Captain. I can't do that without you," she said, suddenly quite weary. Fear and relief—both were exhausting. She wrapped her arms around her knees and pulled them close, braced for more scolding.

The fight left him. He crouched before her, then said quietly, "You frightened me. I don't think my heart will ever beat normally again."

"The same." Her words were muffled, spoken into her knees.

Levi reached for her. His hand grazed her cheek. A second only. Hamish called Levi over. The captain's counsel was sorely needed. No one had any notion of how to remove a dead lion from the ship.

SIXTEEN

FIVE DAYS LATER, the *Truthsayer* entered the Strait of Cain. Reyna and Blaise watched from the deck, along with most of the crew. Within minutes they felt the first rumblings of the whirlpool, for to sail past the strait meant one had to first navigate around the maelstrom that spewed from its center. Maelstrom. Whirlpool. A bubbling pot of witch's brew. They were all one and the same.

The sun shone brilliantly in a cloudless blue sky. Despite its warmth, Reyna felt cold inside. She had not slept. She never did the night before this crossing. How could she? With one hand she clutched the railing. In her other arm was a clay jar, covered and sealed. She had packed it carefully on del Mar. It had a special purpose.

Blaise had kept her promise to Levi not to loaf. With Reyna's help she had gathered every spare pot, every empty bucket, and dragged them all onto the deck. They awaited the men who would be too weak to stand and aim their sickness over the rails. Blaise had heard the stories. Even these sailors, none of them new to the royal navy, could be leveled by the strait.

Levi spoke from outside the forecastle. The wind had picked up; he had to shout to be heard. "Well then, brothers! It's too late for us to join the army." Laughter greeted his words. "We will have to make the best of it. The Strait of Cain is a worthy adversary, but we have been here before, without a single man lost." This time there were cheers. "Today will be no different. Master Caleb!"

"Captain!" Directly opposite, by the helm, Caleb raised a hand, acknowledging the responsibility. The well-being of the *Truthsayer*, her passengers, her crew, was in his hands.

Caleb was a skilled pilot. While the men hurried about their tasks, he kept to the outer edges of the strait, a mere ten miles wide at its narrowest point, hugging the Coast of Ferdinand so closely that Reyna could see details in the houses built into the mountainside. Homes painted a cheerful red and yellow and pink, like a field of summer flowers. People gathered outside their homes to watch the *Truthsayer*. Some waved brightly colored cloth high above their heads. A festive atmosphere.

Blaise held on to the railing with both hands. "They seem friendly," she commented, watching the Ferdinese.

"Do you think so?"

Blaise gave her a quizzical look. "Don't you?"

"Not anymore." Reyna watched the figures gathered at the base of the mountain. They appeared to be readying their boats. "See those men?"

"Yes?"

"They're hoping the maelstrom swallows us up. By rights, any cargo that washes ashore belongs to them."

"I'm sure you're wrong," Blaise said, appalled.

"I wish I were." Reyna had once thought as Blaise did, the first time she had sailed these parts. She had even waved back.

Levi strode by, preoccupied. He stopped to ask, "What's wrong?"

Reyna was silent. Blaise answered for them. "Reyna says the Ferdinese are vultures."

"They're terrible people," Levi agreed, with a curious glance at Reyna's jar. "We stayed there once, to take on fresh water. They gather in the square, twice a day, for prayers. But they don't pray for normal things, like good health or . . . whatever."

"They pray for shipwrecks," Reyna said.

Levi nodded. "Even when they saw us standing there, listening. They prayed for our ship to wreck. The worst people."

Reyna and Levi were not the only ones who thought so. Behind Levi, she saw one of the men raise a hand to the Ferdinese; the rude gesture needed no interpretation.

"Do they bury the bodies, at least?" Blaise asked, subdued. "Maybe they consider the cargo payment."

"There are none." Reyna held the jar closer to her chest. "The maelstrom never releases them."

Levi said, "Look there."

A handful of men had paused in their tasks to peer over the sides. Blaise did the same. Her sharp intake of breath was instantaneous. Here, at the whirlpool's edge, the water was unnaturally clear: one could see directly to the sea floor, and the spirits roaming below. There were thousands of them. Men, women, children. Victims of the maelstrom since time immemorial. It was like looking down from a great height — the bell tower of a cathedral, perhaps — onto a square teeming with city dwellers. Too far away to make out individual features. Sometimes, though, they ventured closer to the surface. Where you could see clearly what they once were.

"You can't always see them," Levi said quietly. "But sometimes they're there, walking along the seabed, trying to find their way home."

"*Oh.*" Blaise slapped a hand over her mouth. "Oh, Reyna."

Levi's head came up sharply. It did not take long for him to understand. Shocked, he asked, "Reyna, who is down there?"

"My parents." She had been nine when she had first sailed through the Strait of Cain. Standing by the rails, saying a prayer for her drowned parents as the men were sick all around her. Her Uncle Ginés, his face tinged green, had stayed by her side long enough for her to pay her respects and throw a handful of del Marian sand into the sea before he too had emptied his stomach. Reyna had hoped the sand would help their spirits feel less lonely for home.

Now she removed the jar's seal and leaned as far over the railing as she could. She did not want the sand to blow back onto the ship. Levi's arm came around her waist. Strong and steady. An anchor. Holding her safe. She turned the jar over, like a sandglass, and del Marian sand drifted into the sea.

She spoke the words to herself and hoped that they could hear. *I miss you, Maman. Papa. Every hour of every day.*

Tears streamed down Blaise's cheeks. Reyna's eyes were dry. They had been dry for a long time. She stepped from Levi's hold and said, "Thank you."

"Reyna . . ."

There was a shout from Caleb as the ship lurched and men went flying across the deck. Ahead, a great churning mass of water could be seen.

"You'll be all right?" Levi said, and when Reyna nodded, he ordered, "Hold on." And he was gone.

There was no describing the Cain maelstrom to those who had not seen it with their own eyes. Words were simply not enough. It was a whirlpool, yes, but of monstrous proportions. To call it a whirlpool was to call a sea serpent, simply, a snake.

The maelstrom tossed the ship in every direction, first east, then south, before spinning full circle like a compass possessed. Waves crashed over the hull and left everyone aboard drenched. Reyna gripped the railing with one hand, a rope with the other. By some miracle only a faint queasiness had overtaken her. All around came the sounds of suffering as the men painted the deck with previously eaten meals. Some leaned over the rails and retched into open sea. A few clutched the pots and buckets that Blaise had managed to distribute before she too fell violently ill. Levi, pale but still standing upright, had taken over the steering oar. Neither Caleb nor the helmsman was capable of doing so.

They made it through. The *Truthsayer* continued to rock and sway, but the worst lay behind them. Along with some very disappointed Ferdinese. When Reyna found it safe to stand and looked behind her, she saw that the people watching them from land were no longer waving. The sight cheered her immensely.

She pushed sopping hair from her eyes and assessed the damage to the crew. Only a few men hung over the rails. The rest sprawled across the deck, dazed and exhausted. Blaise and Benjamin sat back-to-back near one of the masts. They held each other up. Blaise raised a feeble hand when Reyna came to check on them and bring water.

"I'm fine," Blaise croaked, adding that she was never going through the strait again.

"One more time." Reyna's smile was sympathetic. The Strait of Cain was the only way home.

"Never," Blaise vowed.

Reyna caught Levi's eye. He was a little green, but the smile he sent her was full of relief. *Not one man lost,* she thought, and smiled back.

It happened so quickly. The mast atop the sterncastle, weakened from the constant spinning and the relentless pressure of the sails, cracked. The sound was unmistakable. Levi looked up and, too late, tried to dodge the pole as it swung downward in an arc. It caught his midsection; Reyna heard his *oof* from where she knelt, paralyzed with shock. The pole swept him off the helmsman's deck, over the side of the ship, and into the sea.

"Levi!" Reyna's cry was lost among the shouts that rose as the men staggered to the rail. She made it to the side in time to see Levi, eyes closed, slip beneath the waves. The broken mast dipped and bobbed along the surface.

"Levi!" Caleb shouted. Clumsily, he tried to hoist himself over the rail to go after his friend. Reyna grabbed his collar and yanked, sending him toppling onto his back. She would not have been able to do it if he had been at full strength. None of them were at full strength.

Reyna did not think. She swung onto the railing and jumped, and just before she hit the water she heard Blaise, high above, screaming her name.

Reyna fought her way through waves that threatened to swallow her, gaining little ground, before discovering that she could make better headway by swimming underwater. The unnatural clarity and calmness made it a simple thing to spot Levi drifting toward the seabed. Even from this distance, Reyna could see that the spirits had grown still, no longer roaming, their faces turned upward in anticipation.

The thought galvanized her. They would not have him. Ignoring lungs that threatened to burst, she kicked and swam until — at last! — she was able to wrap her arms around Levi and head for the surface. He was unconscious, heavy in her arms. The progress was slow and excruciating.

The spirits would not be cheated of their prize. When Levi jolted, she thought he had woken . . . until she saw two ghosts holding fast to his legs.

They looked like real people. Men in shipman's garb. One young, one old. Though their mouths did not move, she heard the demands as clearly as if they had spoken aloud.

Let him go.

Their voices came from inside her head. Within her being. *His time has come. Let him go.*

Desperately, Reyna kicked at their faces. Her feet skimmed right through them. It was only then that she knew: They were not going to make it. Her arms loosened around Levi. He floated away just as her lungs gave out. And a third spirit appeared out of nowhere.

It was like standing before a looking glass. That was what Reyna would remember later. One where her hair streamed about and her dress, the color of the sun, rippled and flowed. Her *maman* pressed a kiss against her lips, and just like that, Reyna's lungs no longer hurt; she had all the strength in the world. In her heart she heard, *Go! Quickly!* And, fainter: *My sweet girl.* The spirits no longer held tight to Levi's boots. They were busy fighting off yet another spirit, who whirled around them like a dervish. Her father was holding them off. Alone, until her *maman* joined him.

Reyna did not go. Not quickly, not at all. How could she

leave them here? There was a powerful longing in her to remain close. She swam toward them. A hand clamped over her wrist. It was Levi, eyes wide as he looked from her to the spirits. He was solid, living. Even when she fought him, he didn't let go, but pulled her to the surface.

To safety.

SEVENTEEN

T HEY DID NOT SPEAK of it. Not until later, when the crew had fished them from the sea and Reyna had managed to convince a frantic Blaise that she was not hurt. Wonder filled the men's eyes. She and Levi had been underwater a long time. Yet neither looked close to drowned, or even out of breath. Thankfully, no one questioned them. It was not until the *Truthsayer* had left the strait behind and the sun had begun its descent that a knock sounded on Reyna's door. Blaise opened it.

Levi. Reyna, sitting cross-legged in her berth, was unsurprised. She had been waiting for him.

"I'll go find Benjamin," Blaise finally said when it appeared no one else would speak. Levi stepped aside to let her pass. He started to close the door, then thought better of it. Anyone who believed women terrible gossips had never spent time among bored shipmen. The door stayed open. Reyna remained in her berth. Levi took the chair opposite. And they just looked at each other.

Reyna broke the silence. "Your first ghosts?"

"No," he answered, surprising her. "I live in an old castle.

You see things." Leaning forward, he rested his forearms along his legs, and added quietly, "But these were the first to save my life. They were your parents."

"Yes." Gone but never, ever at peace. The weight of that knowledge threatened to smother her.

"This is not the first time you've seen them." The words were spoken with absolute certainty.

"It's the third." Her throat felt as if it would close up. "I was nine the first time, looking down from the rails, and they were just beneath the surface, looking back." Levi's only reaction was a muscle twitching along his jawline. "My *maman* is always in the same yellow dress. I remember it being made for her."

"*Reyna.*" This time his voice was unsteady. He came to his feet and would have gone to her. Something on her face stopped him. She didn't know what. All she knew was that if he touched her, held her, she would fall to pieces. Countless jagged, splintered parts, and she didn't know if she would be able to put herself back together afterward.

He stayed where he was. "You couldn't have known they would help when you jumped in after me."

"No."

"You did it anyway." When she did not answer, he asked very, very softly, "Would you have jumped, for just anyone?"

She sensed a different question behind the one he asked, and could not meet his eyes.

"I'm sorry. I don't mean to press you. I don't know why . . . I'll go." He turned away.

"Captain."

He looked back at her, the hand that gripped the door frame white-knuckled.

"I would not have jumped for just anyone."

She gave up trying not to cry. Levi swung the door shut, and as she wept hot, bitter, scalding tears, his arms came around her.

And stayed there, holding the pieces together.

The days passed as they usually did on a ship: slowly. The mast was replaced with another, kept aboard for a time such as this. Blaise found herself busy in the infirmary, a cabin that was large enough to hold her and one man lying prostrate on a table. The years with her Uncle Mori had served her well. She treated sprains and cooled burns, set broken bones and snapped dislocated joints back into place. One night, Levi and Caleb broke up a fight in the crew's quarters. A shipman had called another a drunken cow lover in a dispute over cards. The other had retaliated, saying his sister looked like an old she-goat. From there, violence had ensued. The stiches Blaise had sewn along cheekbones and foreheads had been much admired.

Reyna heard all this secondhand, for she spent most of her time in study, learning everything she could about Miramar and its people. Fascinating things. *No Miranese ship or boat whatever, nor any native of Miramar, shall presume to go out of the kingdom; who so acts contrary to this shall die, the ship with crew and goods be burned.* The solitude, relative on a ship, was something she desperately needed. It offered a balm, a bandage, if not a cure for grief. Eventually she emerged from the blackness that had threatened to suffocate her since leaving her parents behind.

Days after they sailed through the Strait of Cain, she found herself responsible for another task, one quite unexpected. It was midmorning. A fine, fair day. Seth, the cook, found her at her usual spot on a ledge below the sterncastle, a wooden tablet on her lap. She had set her book aside and was sketching Benjamin as she had seen him only minutes earlier, turning the sand clock that hung outside the forecastle. She was so intent on getting his cowlick just right that she did not hear Seth until he said her name.

"Master Seth," she said, surprised. He had never sought her out, not since the men had teased him for lending her his clothing on Lunes. Today it was on the flamboyant end, as usual. A rose-colored shirt, lacy at the cuff and collar. The outer seams of his trousers embroidered with intertwining vines and roses.

Seth scratched the back of his neck, distinctly ill at ease. "Master Reyna."

She waited, but it appeared he had nothing more to say. There were tattoos on his hands. Spiders, black as burnt twigs, inked onto each knuckle. That must have hurt. She prompted, "Is there something I can do for you?"

He scuffed a boot along the deck. "The captain says we're supposed to treat you like a scribe."

"Yes?"

"Scribes write death notes, don't they? Could you write one for me?"

Death notes? She clarified, "You want me to write your will?"

He nodded. "I never had time to take care of it back home. But after that maelstrom, and seeing as where we're going, I thought it would be a good idea."

He was not wrong. By going to sea, sailors put themselves three or four fingers away from death, the thickness of a ship's planking. And this was no ordinary voyage. In a perfect world, he would have secured a will before he left Selene and left a copy with their House of Trade. The *Truthsayer* could be sunk or burnt, with Seth's last will and testament suffering the same fate. But this was better than nothing.

"Of course. Hold this, please." Reyna thrust the wooden tablet at him. "I'll be right back." She hurried to her cabin, where she fetched more parchment, a quill, and a vial of ink. On deck she made herself a work chamber of sorts, sitting on her ledge and using the top of a barrel as a writing surface. Seth stood on the other side of the barrel and dictated his final wishes.

He had a mother and three younger sisters. Everything would go to them. His savings were hidden in a box inside his mother's home, beside the chimney and beneath the floorboards. Also hidden was a promissory note, proof he was owed a bushel of salt and a crate of nutmeg from a Master Allon, whom Seth occasionally worked for while on land. His mother would not know to look for the box. Seth had never told her it was there.

By now they had attracted a small crowd. Not Levi. He was halfway up the rigging lines in conversation with Benjamin. But one of the shipmen, Hamish, whistled. "A bushel of salt. That's a tidy sum. Where did you say you hid that box again? Ha-ha . . . It was a *joke*!" he added at Seth's baleful look.

"Like the earwax I put in your soup yesterday" was Seth's reply. "That was a joke too." Hamish's grin faded.

Smiling, Reyna finished the testament, then sprinkled sand on top of the ink to hurry along its drying. She said, "It's best if I leave this with the captain. He can keep it with the log."

When Seth offered her payment, she refused, saying her wages would come from the ship. She would not take his money, and when the other men heard that her services were free, a queue formed. This prompted Caleb to stomp over to see what was going on. Death notes? Exasperated, he ordered half the men away. They could return once they finished their tasks and not before.

The crew began to disperse, but Caleb, unexpectedly, turned back to her and said, "That was a brave thing you did back there, for the captain. Mad but brave."

Several of the men called out, "Hear, hear." Hamish said, "Brave, puh. Lady's got bollocks the size of Mount Samson. Maybe bigger."

More shouts from the men, louder this time, and Caleb winced. "I'd beg your pardon, but I think you've heard worse. And Hamish is right. Bollocks the size of Mount Samson."

Caleb pulled off his blue cap and bowed with a flourish. "Master Reyna, you have our thanks."

"Master Reyna." The rest of the sailors followed suit. Moved beyond measure, Reyna searched the rigging lines and found Levi's eyes on her already.

The remainder of her day was spent writing wills and, once or twice, letters to loved ones in case the men did not make it home. Sometimes she sketched their portraits to include with the letters.

Levi came by much later. They had not spoken privately since that day they had crossed the strait. She had taken great care to avoid being alone with him for the simple reason that she did not know what to say.

"I'm told I owe you money," Levi said.

The wills. So he did. She held out a hand. "Four double-shells, please."

He stared at her. "That's absurd."

She did not blink, and she kept her hand out. Her uncle had told her never to take less than what she was worth. "If you pay peanuts, you get monkeys. I did good work here."

Amused, he took a pouch from his belt. "I don't carry double-shells. Will you take Lunesian silver?"

"Yes. Thank you."

He dropped the coins in her hand. "You're feeling better."

He had noticed. She had thought she had put on a convincing public face since leaving the strait. Only Blaise had witnessed the cracks, in the privacy of Reyna's cabin. She had held Reyna while she wept. She had put herbs in her tea to help her sleep.

"I am." Reyna set the coins on the barrel top. "It's hard for me after. I'm sorry I've been loafing."

"You don't have to tell me about grief," he said quietly. A reminder of his own loss. "What do you mean, loafing? You just spent the day writing wills for my men."

Reyna gathered the parchment in a neat stack and rolled them together. "Hold this, please," and when he obliged, she used a bit of twine to tie them together. "I meant to help with the fishing."

Levi surveyed the deck. Four men with poles had tossed their lines overboard. Two by the prow, two by the stern. An odd look came over Levi's face.

"What is it?" she asked.

"I've never heard a lady say those words before," he confessed. "'I meant to help with the fishing.'"

Reyna's lips curved in response. She asked if he would keep the wills with the rest of his official papers, and when he agreed, she thought he would go. But he merely skirted the barrel to lean against the rail beside her. Arms folded, legs crossed at the ankle, rolled-up wills in hand. He was not going anywhere.

He said, "I'm glad your friend called in that favor."

Blaise was by the forecastle with Samuel, inspecting the hand he held out to her.

"I am too." Worried as Reyna was, she would have been lost without Blaise on this voyage.

Levi said, "Asher's university is in Caffa. There's a school for medicine nearby, and I seem to remember they admit women. From all over the Sea of Magdalen."

The medical school at Caffa. It was a sore subject. "I've heard of it."

She felt his sideways glance. "Has Blaise?"

A nod. No one knew more about the school than Blaise. "It's why she taught herself Caffeesh."

"Then why . . . ?"

"The students require noble patronage," Reyna explained. "Some lord or lady who will write a letter on their behalf, vouching for their potential."

"You're a lady," he pointed out. In case she had forgotten.

"Blaise will accept the letter from me, but she won't take the coin that must accompany it. The fees are dear."

Levi frowned. "Why won't she take it?"

Pride, Reyna thought. *Stubbornness.* She did not say these things. "She says you don't take money from friends. Not if you want them to remain your friend."

"That's understandable. You don't think so?" he asked when he saw her expression darkening.

"It's ridiculous," Reyna said. "What is the use of having all this money if I'm not able to use it to help her? Anyway, she's been saving for years now."

Levi looked thoughtful. "Why did you owe her a favor?"

Reyna angled her chin so that he could see the tiny scar, shaped like a crescent moon. "This would have been far worse if she had not helped me."

He studied the scar. "How did it get there?"

She should not tell him. He would not take it well, though many years had passed since that awful day. She found herself saying, "A man's boot."

"Holy hell, Reyna!" A shocked whisper. No one looked at them. To her, it had felt like a shout. "How old were you?"

"Nine."

The year was not lost on him, and she winced as the parchment — her day's work — crumpled in his fist. "Many things happened when you were nine."

She took the parchment from him, tugging at his fingers until his grip loosened. She had worked hard on these. "It was a long time ago, Captain. It doesn't hurt anymore."

"And you don't wish to speak of it," he said under his breath.

"Maybe someday." Or never. The memory of that time clawed at her like broken fingernails. She reshaped the rolled-up wills before offering them back to him. "What will you do after we're done here?"

His expression said he knew that she was trying to change the topic. Still, he answered her question. "Take my brother home. After that, I'll go where I'm needed. One of our territories, maybe."

Which Reyna knew were always vulnerable to invaders. "You're used to pirate attacks."

"Oh, all kinds."

Her curiosity was getting the better of her. "Did you always wish to be a captain?"

"Of the *Truthsayer*, yes. I was born on this ship."

"Really?"

He nodded. "My father was a second son, which meant he was expected to go to sea. My mother always sailed with him. When his elder sister died, he had to give up the ship."

"It went to you?"

"No," he said. "I was young still. My uncle took over as captain, and I was his page. I was four."

"Four!"

"Mm." Some of the tension left his shoulders as she questioned him. It had been her intent. "I have been a page, a deck swabber, a diver, a carpenter, a helmsman, and for about six months when I was fourteen, I was the cook. What?" he said when he saw her astonishment. "You thought I was a spoiled princeling?"

"No! Well, perhaps a little," she amended.

He smiled. "Spoiled princelings sink ships. My uncle made sure I could sail the *Truthsayer* alone, if I absolutely had to."

"Prince Asher is third born. Does that mean he'll become a priest?"

Levi burst into laughter. It happened so rarely all she could do was stare. "Never" was all he said. "What about you? What will you do?"

Reyna pushed the cork back into the vial of ink and tapped it down with a thumb. "I'll be eighteen in six months." She looked up. "How old are you?"

"Twenty," he answered. "What happens when you turn eighteen?"

"Lord Braga, our royal navigator, has said he'll consider my masterwork then and not a day earlier."

"A masterwork? So you'll what? Draw a map? Build a globe? *Can* you build a globe?" he asked curiously.

"Yes, but so can everyone else. Lord Elias's daughter, Sabine, can build a globe, and she's three," she added. Levi smiled. "It has to be something a three-year-old can't do."

"Why do you look worried?"

She busied herself gathering up her things — parchment, vial, quill. "I don't think Lord Braga wants to give it to me. A mastership."

"Because you're a girl."

"Yes. And girls should want babies and husbands and all the things they come with."

Levi was quiet. "You don't want those things?"

"Maybe I do. Later." She shrugged. "Babies and husbands. I can't even picture them. Sailing across the world I can picture. Discovering something new — to me, to del Mar — I can picture. I've dreamt about these things my whole life." She realized that she was rambling on. Self-conscious, she added, "This is a strange conversation we're having."

"Oh, we've had stranger," he commented.

It was true. From that first meeting on the dock until now, theirs had not been a conventional friendship. Reyna laughed then, as she had not laughed in a long time. And Blaise, wrapping a bandage around Samuel's hand, looked over at that rare, fleeting sound, her smile full of relief and wonder.

EIGHTEEN

THE FOLLOWING DAY, Reyna found Blaise in the infirmary examining a flask full of urine. Holding the glass up to the light, pulling the stopper and sniffing.

"That smells foul." Reyna would not ask whose it was. She did not want to know.

"It does, doesn't it?" Blaise dipped her small finger into the flask and placed its tip on her tongue, her expression thoughtful.

Reyna's stomach revolted. She went straight to the window and poked her head out, breathing deep. The air felt different here, heavier. She could have sworn she smelled nutmeg. The atolls and islets passed them by, along with the occasional sandbar.

Behind her came the sound of drawers opening and closing. "Where did I see it? I'm sure I — ah." Another drawer shut. "What are you looking at out there?"

Reyna shifted so that Blaise could see. The flask, thankfully, had been left on the table with the shears and lancets. "These are part of the Sandrigal Islands. Remember our bedtime stories?"

"I remember. The sirens used to live here. How did that rhyme go?"

"'A bird in the air,'" Reyna recited. "'A fish in the sea. A beautiful lady come screaming for me.'"

"*Singing.*" Blaise turned to look at her, askance. Their noses nearly touched. "Not *screaming.* What sort of nursery rhyme is that?"

"Jaime always said 'screaming.' It made him laugh." Her voice faltered on the last word. Would she ever hear Jaime laugh again? "Do you think they're still alive?"

"Yes," Blaise said. "All of them, and so do you. Otherwise you would not be here." Her arm came around Reyna's shoulders. "We'll see Jaime before you know it, and he'll be swearing his love for you, and for me, and likely even for your handsome, brooding captain. You know he's not particular."

The image coaxed a smile from her. They turned back to the window.

"Blaise," Reyna said.

"Mm?"

"I'm glad you're here."

A smile from her friend, without a trace of smugness. "I know."

The next day, they sailed through an estuary, home to barbets, cockatoos, and other colorful species of birds. Some were unfamiliar. Reyna drew what she could see. They would find Lord

Elias soon, and he would be able to tell her what birds they were. From the estuary, they turned in to a wide winding river, the Chrysanthemum River. Mangroves lined the banks in a tangle of exposed roots. The constant appearance of sandbars kept Caleb on his toes. Reyna and Levi consulted their maps. If they could avoid wrecking in the shallows, the river would lead them directly to the kingdom of Miramar.

"Is she a siren or a harpy? I can never remember the difference."

"A siren."

"But she has legs. And . . . you know. Lady parts. No fish tail."

"They're not always painted with tails. Sometimes they look like humans. Sometimes they have feathers . . . Quit ogling the rugs. We have work."

A knock on the door put an end to Reyna's dreams. It was early; the light of dawn filtered through the window. Half asleep still, she called out, "Jaime?"

The latch rose. Levi's head appeared around the door. "Nothing's wrong," he said when she sat up quickly, fearing the worst. "I thought you'd want to see this." He took in her bleary face and the white nightgown covering her toes. A smile from him, quickly hidden. "Will you come up?"

"Why? What's happened?" Embarrassment turned her voice surly. She looked like a banshee most mornings, hair tangled and wild around her.

"Come see" was all he said before closing the door.

A stubbed toe resulted from stumbling around, trying to put herself in order. Muttering her uncle's favorite curses, she threw on her clothes, braided her hair, washed her face, and hurried up to the deck. What would she see? Samuel and Hamish had been assigned the night's watch. They stood by Levi at the railing, pointing and exclaiming. She followed their gaze. Seconds passed before she realized that what she saw was real. Not part of any dream. She ran up to the rail beside Levi and gawked, provoking chuckles from the men.

There were three mountains, beyond the riverbank and across a rolling expanse of foliage. The center mountain stood taller than its sisters. And at the peak of that mountain was a ship. She did not need to squint or rub her eyes to be sure. The day was clear and the mountains were not so far away as that. It was a ship perched dead center on a mountaintop.

Levi was grinning, immensely pleased by her reaction. "I was in the ropes and I looked over and there it was! It came right out of nowhere!"

"Nearly fell off the ropes," Hamish commented, shaking his head. "Thought I was going to have to catch him."

From Samuel: "Not something you see every day, eh, Master Reyna?"

"A ship, Reyna!" Levi exclaimed. "Look at it!"

She found her voice at last. "I see it! How is it possible? It looks like it dropped right out of the sky!"

The four of them fell silent, considering the possibilities.

"The Great Floods?" Levi offered.

"Those were eight hundred years ago," Reyna said. The brothers looked dubious, but she thought about it. "It's the only thing that makes sense. But how could no one have seen . . . ?" She craned her neck this way and that, trying to get a better look. "It's so high up — perhaps the clouds have been hiding it . . . or the landscape has shifted. I've never heard of this ship. It's not on any map —" Her heart seized at the thought. She whirled around and grabbed Levi's shirtfront with both hands, startling a laugh from him. "Will you anchor?" she begged him. "Please? Or sail slower? I'll be quick, I promise —"

Levi covered her hands with both of his. He spoke over her babbling. "We can wait a little. Go."

Releasing his shirt, she raced back to her cabin and grabbed everything she would need as quickly as she could. Parchment and charcoal, quill and ink, a wooden tablet to write on. Her clattering woke Blaise and Benjamin, who slept in the cabins nearest hers. They stumbled to her doorway and watched.

"What are you drawing? What time is it?" Blaise's question ended on a yawn.

"A ship, Blaise! A ship on a mountain!" Reyna cried, and bowled past them.

She worked like a dervish. Drawing sketches of the ship and its mountains, noting markers of the surrounding area. Levi had ordered the anchor dropped, but she knew they could not remain here for long. They were not here to survey. That was not their mission. All her work was completed on deck with others crowding around to watch. Her notes piled up beside her, the parchment weighted by ballast stones Benjamin brought up from the hold. She did not have the time or equipment to climb the mountain herself, but with these maps, others could follow.

Or she could come back.

Much later, Levi ordered the anchor raised. It was time to go. Reyna took great care with her final sketch, done in ink with a simple ivy border. She drew the mountains in the background, the river in the foreground, and the *Truthsayer* in the river, which garnered approval from the men. The cartouche came last. Within its square borders she wrote: *Mapmaker: Lady Reyna, Tower of Winds, Kingdom of St. John del Mar.* Above that she wrote *Explorer.* She looked around for Levi and found him near. He and Caleb stood with their shoulders propped against the mainmast as they watched her work. She offered him the quill.

Levi crouched beside her. He didn't take the quill, only looked at her with his brows raised in question.

She said, "Captain. This is not my find."

All around them, silence fell.

"Are you sure?" Levi spoke under his breath.

Only then did she understand that he had meant for her to have it. This discovery, and the glory that went with it. Moments passed before she could trust her voice.

"Levi." It was all she could think to say.

He took the quill, signed *Prince Levi, Captain of the*

Truthsayer, *Kingdom of Lunes* in firm, bold strokes. And then he just looked at her.

Behind them, Caleb whistled. "I wonder what the queen will think about that."

No chance for Levi to respond. The arrow struck the mainmast an inch above Caleb's head. Levi shouted, "Down!" and, together, they hit wooden planking. Reyna pressed against the floorboards, Levi a shield on top of her, his heart beating hard and fast against her back. She went still and listened. To the arrows flying overhead and the men shouting. Not just Levi's men, but those on land, speaking a language she had heard once before on a dark, terrifying night in the Sea of Magdalen. Coarse and guttural. Coronad but not Coronad.

They had come looking for Miramar. Miramar had found them first.

"Stay down."

The order came from Levi. Loud enough to be heard by those on deck even as the Miranese shouted and threatened from the riverbank. Reyna assumed they were threats. She could not understand them.

"Are you all right?" Levi spoke near her ear.

No. She could not breathe. "Get off."

Levi rolled from her into a low crouch. Cautiously, Reyna lifted her head.

Blaise was safe, hunkered down by the railing with Samuel.

Not one person appeared hurt. A glance at the mainmast showed her this was deliberate. At least twenty arrows had lodged in the pole, a perfect, straight line that ended beneath the lookout. A warning, then, as well as proof the Miranese trained excellent archers.

Levi had moved to the railing. He called out in Caffeesh, "Listen here!" And, when the Miranese fell abruptly silent: "I am Prince Levi of Lunes. Captain of this ship. We're here by personal invitation of your prince, Jian-so."

Silence, followed by one word in heavily accented Caffeesh. "Stand."

A man's voice. All eyes turned to Levi, who shook his head. They were to stay as they were. But he was not. Reyna's heart stuck in her throat as he stood, arms extended to show he held no weapons. He posed no threat.

Another order. "All people. Stand."

This time Levi turned his head to the side and nodded. Everyone rose.

Three men on the riverbank. They might as well have numbered a thousand, for each pointed an arrow directly at the *Truthsayer*, the arrowhead alight with flame.

Reyna nearly forgot to breathe. A hull carved from oak and sealed with tar. Wooden barrels, canvas sails. There was no greater threat to a ship than fire.

Reyna inched her way to Levi's side. The archers' shared ancestry with the Coronads was unmistakable, though these men were rangier, not as large and hulking as their Coronad cousins. She noted other differences: the topknots, of course; also, they cared for their appearance in a way the Coronads did not. They wore leather tunics the color of freshly turned earth. A wide amber sash served as a belt. She could see the polished gleam of their boots from where she stood.

The Miranese on the right spoke. "Drop your anchor."

Levi had lowered his arms. His eyes never strayed from the arrows. His words were terse. "We're here by invit —"

An arrow twitched. Levi clamped his mouth shut. Reyna counted ten distinctive pops as he cracked the knuckles on one hand and then the other. He looked to the prow and saw Caleb nearest the anchor. "Drop it," he ordered. Caleb did his bidding.

Reyna said, "There's some sort of protectant on those arrowheads."

"I see it," Levi said. The flames remained on the tips, not extending along the shaft to burn flesh.

"Captain," Samuel said. "There's only three of them. I'll slip off the back, circle around, and *tzzzt* —" Here, he sliced a hand against his throat. "Simple."

Beside him, Blaise's eyes grew round.

Levi said, "We can't leave the ship, Sam. Look in the water."

A quick glance was all that was needed. Samuel groaned. Beyond the prow, a school of piranha churned up the water. Orange-and-gray scales, snapping teeth. Reyna had never seen a school so large.

A fourth man appeared beside the three, holding not a bow and arrow, but a horn nearly as tall as he was. It looked like a pipe: the mouthpiece at the man's lips, the bowl resting on the ground. The sound that emerged was reminiscent of a ship's horn, deep and melodic, rippling the water's surface. Before it died away completely, another horn sounded from afar, in the direction of Miramar. And another. And another. It was their version of beacon fire.

"Why are there only four of them?" Levi asked.

"Four's enough," Samuel said. "Only takes one of those arrows."

"True," Levi said. "Still, this is the main waterway to Miramar. You'd think there would be more men."

The grumbling began after an hour had passed and nothing had changed. Except the position of the sun, which lay directly above them, blazing hot. Levi called out once, "My men are thirsty. I'd like to bring fresh water from below."

The Miranese refused. "Wait."

Levi's lips tightened, the only sign of his growing anger.

At last, after three hours had passed, and Reyna thought she might die of thirst, she heard riders approach.

At least thirty men in full armor. One carried something Reyna recognized. She had seen a drawing in her book. The Miranese flag: a chrysanthemum in full bloom, orange petals blazing against a background of solid, ominous black.

NINETEEN

I

T'S HIM?" Levi murmured.

Reyna's chin dipped in the barest fraction of a nod. She had recognized the sea raider the moment she saw him. He rode ahead of the approaching riders dressed in bronze chain mail. Of similar age to Levi. The knot above his head as perfectly round as she remembered. Pits and scars covered his face. If there had been a sliver of doubt in her mind, it was gone now. Her raider and Prince Jian-so were one and the same. "It's him."

A young woman rode among them. She wore a white robe with an amber sash. Her hair, black as the animal she rode upon, was cut in a severe line below her ears. As far as Reyna could tell, she was the only female in the entourage, which fanned out behind Jian-so.

The prince led his horse dangerously close to the edge of the embankment. Raising a hand in greeting, he called over in Caffeesh, "Levi, my friend! My friend! Welcome to Miramar!"

But Levi had been left to simmer in the heat for hours. Sweat soaked his white shirt, and what looked to be the beginning of a vicious sunburn marred his neck and ears. His response was not so cordial. "Am I a friend, Jian-so? This was not the welcome I had expected."

"What is this?" Jian-so no longer smiled. "What has happened?"

"Your man there has aimed arrows at my ship since we arrived. Fire arrows. We've not been allowed to move about. We've not been allowed water."

"Is this true?" Jian-so demanded, his question aimed not at Levi, but at the Miranese who had kept them in the broiling, rolling heat. The man's expression, only moments before one of cold competence, shifted to unease. He answered in rapid Miranese. Jian-so held up a gloved hand, cutting him off.

"Prince Levi," Jian-so said formally. "Your treatment in my home dishonors me. I beg you to consider this a sincere reflection of my regret." Before Reyna could fully register his intent, Jian-so had removed the axe at his back and swung it through the air in a wide, graceful arc. The man toppled off the embankment and into the water, his head in one direction, his body in the other. A deathly silence fell.

The crew moved as one to the railing and looked into the river. An unlucky day for the Miranese who had lost his head. Not so for the piranha offered an unexpected treat. Like a marionette, the body thrashed as it was nipped and bitten to the bone.

Swallowing hard, Reyna grabbed for Levi's hand beneath the railing. Her nails dug trenches into his palm. He did not flinch, only shifted so that his fingers intertwined with hers.

Offering reassurance. All the while, he looked impassively into the water, then at Jian-so, who waited for a response.

Levi said, "I accept your apology. Jian-so. My friend."

"Good! Very good!" Jian-so's grin returned. All was well. Without bothering to clean his axe, he returned it to his back. "Follow that boat there." A galley had appeared at the river's bend. "It will show you the way. Welcome!"

Levi gave a small bow in response. Jian-so rode off with a final wave, and the rest followed on horseback and on foot. In the water, the body performed its macabre dance. Its severed head floated downstream, mouth gaping up at the heavens, pulled along by some unseen creature beneath the water.

Reyna could not bear to look any longer. Releasing Levi's hand, she spun around, fist pressed against her stomach.

Blaise had sidled over. She patted Reyna's shoulder absently and kept on watching, eyes wide in horrified fascination. "He just chopped off that man's head. Chopped it right off! What *is* this place?"

"We're about to find out," Levi said. Now that the Miranese had gone, his carefully controlled expression melted away. He looked flummoxed. Facing his equally burned and wilted crew, he said, "Listen here. Once we arrive, Benjamin, Samuel, Hamish, and Reyna will come with me. Benjamin will go back and forth with messages. Until I return, this is Master Caleb's ship. Understood?"

There was a round of nods and ayes.

Except from Caleb, who said, "Will you take more men,

Captain?" He pointed to the body in the river. "That prince is not right in the head."

There were murmurs of agreement all around. Levi refused. "More men and it will look like we're nervous —"

"We *are* nervous," Caleb pointed out.

"There's no reason to be. Remember, this is a trading visit, nothing more. That is how we will conduct ourselves." To Reyna Levi said, "I've changed my mind. Blaise is coming with us."

Blaise, still watching the piranha, looked around at that.

"What? Why?" Reyna demanded.

"Because I don't want you alone in the women's quarters."

"But —"

"She's coming." The look on Levi's face said this was not an argument she would win. "Blaise, you'll be her . . . her . . ."

Swallowing a defeated sigh, Reyna said, "We should stick as close to the truth as possible. Otherwise we'll get caught out. Blaise is a terrible liar."

"Thank you, Reyna," Blaise said. Several of the men snickered.

"So, what?" Levi looked dubious. "A lady scribe and a lady barber? You don't think they'd find that odd?"

"You're a foreign prince," Reyna answered. "You can be as odd as you want. They'll say you're eccentric."

Grim humor sliced across Levi's face. "Fine. Once we dock, neither of you will speak del Marian. We can't risk anyone over-hearing you." When Reyna and Blaise agreed, he continued. "Some of you might be asked to deliver the clay. Fine. Otherwise, if you must disembark, you don't go alone and you don't go far. We might have to leave here in a hurry." The Miranese galley they were to follow had begun to sail off. Levi looked into the water, said quietly, "I didn't mean for this; I am sorry," and turned away. "Caleb, Samuel, Hamish. With me."

Great iron chains blocked entry into the harbor. As the *Truthsayer* approached, escorted by the smaller, elegant galley, the chains fell away. This was a river port. Ships anchored here in a single row. Fewer than Reyna had imagined, but then, how many did one need in a kingdom kept so isolated? The sight of two carracks in particular sent a deep anger rolling over her. Both ships were painted black. Neither bore a flag or a name along the prow. These were the carracks that had attacked the *Simona*. She pressed fingers against one eye to stop the tic threatening to form there.

According to her book, this was Ota, the capital city of Miramar. It sprawled among dense foliage. White stone walls and black-tiled roofs, each roof swooping upward at the tips like a precisely twirled mustache. There were no grand cathedrals here, no pointed spires reaching for the heavens. Ota felt low and hidden and watchful. And everywhere, the flowers bloomed. One color only.

"What are those?" Blaise leaned forward, squinting. "Orange roses?"

"Chrysanthemums."

Reyna and Blaise wore crisp blue dresses. Simple, practical, and — thank every saint who'd ever lived — made of cotton, not wool. Before Reyna had locked her sea chest, she had been careful to remove anything suspicious. The book on Miranese history, written in del Marian. The drawings and charts of the magnificent ship on a mountain. All of it was now buried beneath a floorboard.

Levi stood atop the forecastle. Polished and shined in his captain's uniform. Anyone who did not know him would think him remote — cold, even. She knew better. He would be worrying greatly behind his captain's mask. Thinking through every possible obstacle. Weighed down by the lives — so many of them — that depended upon him.

Blaise might have read her thoughts. "Does the captain have any sort of plan?"

"We keep our eyes and ears open, I suppose. Try to find out what they might have done with the men."

A small silence. "That's it? That's our plan?"

"That's it. They might not even be here. There are a hundred slave markets between Miramar and Lunes." She would not think of it. Taking Blaise's hand in hers, she said urgently, "Do you remember how to make a compass?"

The abrupt switch took Blaise a moment. "Yes," she said, wary. Reyna had shown her how to build one years ago. "Why?"

Beyond the harbor, the river curved along a bend and disappeared. "That way is east," Reyna said. "Commander Aimon will be coming from there. Eventually. If something happens —"

Blaise snatched her hand away. "Like what?"

"Something. *Anything.* If you need to leave here, follow the river. If you come to a fork, keep to the east and watch for our ships."

Blaise was quiet. "I'm not leaving here without you, Reyna."

"I'd rather you didn't either," she confessed. "But you've seen what Jian-so can do. You need to know all the ways out. Will you remember?" She reached into her pouch and held out her hand. In her palm was a small black pebble. A leading stone, a magnet. Blaise would need it to make her compass.

The ship rocked slightly as the anchor dropped. On the docks, the Miranese gathered to watch their arrival.

"East," Blaise repeated, though she did not look happy about it. She took the stone. "I'll remember."

They were met at the waterfront by the steward of the imperial household, an efficient little man who saw to their chests, which were strapped onto the backs of stoop-shouldered porters and sent ahead. He spoke slow, careful Caffeesh. Even so, Reyna had to listen carefully. This version of the language was both familiar and unfamiliar and would take some getting used to. Royal guards kept the onlookers at bay. Men, women, and children.

Some wearing simple smocks and trousers. Most shielded from the sun by straw hats so their faces were not clearly visible. Levi nodded and waved. In response, some bowed at the waist. Others merely stared.

As they made their way to the horses, Levi asked Reyna, "Do you notice anything strange?"

"Yes," she said immediately. "This is the cleanest harbor I've ever seen."

Where were the stray dogs? The wandering chickens? The fishmongers and fruit sellers hawking their wares? This harbor had no market, which could account for some of its tidiness. But not all. There was not a single mound of horse dung to be found in the dirt, steaming or otherwise. To Reyna, who had visited more waterfronts than she could remember, the harbor was an anomaly. Sparkling and pristine. Perfectly improbable.

"You're right." Levi looked around in bemusement. "It's the exact opposite of Coronado."

Unflattering but true. Coronado's waterfront was heaped with filth and waste, from dogs, humans, horses, and bears. Bear-baiting was a favored pastime there. But Levi had not been speaking of the harbor's unusual cleanliness.

She asked, "What do you find strange?"

"Where is everyone?" Levi gave another regal wave, a smiling nod. "This isn't a small harbor. There should be more people here."

Reyna did not have a chance to answer. The steward came

forward to fuss over Levi and lead him to where the grand horses awaited. Majestic creatures, their saddles adorned with amber tassels, ribbons of a similar shade entwined in their manes.

They rode from the harbor surrounded by guards. The journey took them through the city, where a smattering of Miranese stepped from their homes and storefronts to watch them pass. Cold trailed up Reyna's spine. Unlike those gathered at the harbor, these onlookers were close enough that Reyna could see the scars riddling so many faces, young and old. Just like Jian-so.

Blaise noticed too. She brought her horse close to Reyna. "Something bad happened here."

"The pox?" Reyna remembered Levi's puzzlement. *Where is everyone?*

"I think so. It couldn't have been too long ago either." Blaise smiled at a pair of young girls peeking from behind their mother's skirts. They were only a few years past infancy. Both were scarred. "I wonder how the pox is treated here."

They rode deeper into the jungle. Chrysanthemums lined the roadside in such quantities that it looked as if their path were lit by fire. Only Hamish appeared unimpressed. He had taken one look at the flowers and erupted in a fit of sneezing.

After a time, they entered the gates of the palace, which was unlike any Reyna had seen before. White stone walls and elaborate, black-tiled roofs. Terraces too numerous to count. The greenery rioted here, growing along borders and in heavy pots, twining up the walls. Giant tortoises roamed the grounds, much to Reyna's and Blaise's delight. Reyna counted fifteen of them. If she were to stretch out beside one, there would be no great difference in length. She had never seen tortoises so large.

Jian-so met them in the courtyard. He had exchanged his armor for a brown leather tunic with a chrysanthemum embossed across the breast. Buttons gleamed orange and gold in the sunlight. He greeted Levi with clasped arms and genuine pleasure. Levi appeared to do the same. *They look like real friends*, Reyna thought. This was how she would greet Blaise. Or Jaime.

No one mentioned the dead man in the river.

The same woman accompanied Jian-so. Up close, she appeared even younger than Reyna had imagined. Her own age, perhaps. She did not look like a Miranese. Truly, she did not look like anyone Reyna had ever seen before: her face narrow, her chin pointed, a birdlike quality to her appearance.

"You travel with an interesting cortege, my friend." Jian-so's attention went from Reyna to Blaise. Blaise's grip on her physician's bag tightened ever so slightly. "Or are they gifts?"

Levi threw a disinterested glance in their direction. "This is my scribe and my healer. My queen sends gifts. But they're still on the ship."

It was only because Reyna was watching Jian-so's companion that she saw it. A flinch at the word *healer*; her expression showed a brief, bitter loathing.

"Too bad." Jian-so's eyes slithered back to Reyna. "A scribe, you say? Our scribes are all men, older than the mountains, who smell like cheese. I like yours much better."

Amused, Levi said, "We have plenty of those in Selene. Old men make poor sailors."

"And are harder on the eyes." Jian-so reached out, lifted Reyna's chin with a finger. Levi's smile slipped. "What is your name, scribe?"

"Reyna, Prince Jian-so." His was not the hand of a pampered prince. The callus on his finger scraped against her skin. Uneasiness coiled inside her. She reminded herself that he could not know who she was. He had not seen her that night on the *Simona*. His interest was of the regular, repulsive sort. Which posed another set of problems. Beside her, Blaise was as still as a rabbit sensing a trap.

"Reyna-si?" Jian-so's finger lingered against her skin. "As lovely as the goddess whose name you share."

Abruptly, Levi shifted the attention from Reyna to the woman beside Jian-so. He bowed. "Lady."

Jian-so dropped his hand and frowned at his companion, as though he'd forgotten she was there. "She's not a lady. Ana-si is my . . . scribe," he said, and laughed. Brushing the back of his hand across her neck, he ordered her to "show them to the women's quarters. Unless you prefer they be nearer?" The last was meant for Levi. Jian-so's smirk had returned.

Levi smiled. One man to another. "The women's quarters will do. For now."

Jian-so laughed.

Ana-si spoke for the first time. "Come with me."

As they followed, Reyna noticed two things. First, Ana-si's voice was deeper than Reyna had expected. It did not match her tiny, frail form. And second, she carried herself strangely. Her movements slow, as if trying not to limp. As if some injury, hidden beneath her clothing, was causing her pain.

TWENTY

ANA-SI LED THEM into the labyrinthine corridors of the palace, the silence broken by the occasional "Down here" and "We go there." As soon as they'd left the company of men, she began to scratch her arms. Forearms, elbows, wrists. Absently, as if she did not realize what she did. Reyna watched and wondered. A glance at Blaise showed her following Ana-si's every move. Noting the way she carried herself. Eyeing the endless scratching.

The quiet ended the moment they entered the women's quarters. Females everywhere. They spilled from chambers that opened directly onto a courtyard. Most wore robes like Ana-si's. One or two of them had a tiny red circle painted on her lower lip. For Reyna, a novelty. Conversation dropped off the moment the newcomers were spotted.

For herself and Blaise, Reyna felt only curiosity. The looks their guide received were less friendly. Ana-si was not liked by the women of the palace. She did not appear to care.

They stopped before a door. "You sleep here," Ana-si informed Blaise.

"Thank—"

Ana-si had already walked off, Reyna at her heels. She looked over her shoulder at Blaise, standing alone with her physician's bag, and mouthed, *I'll come back.*

Her chamber was down the passageway from Blaise's. It was small but lovely: dark and cool, with louvered windows. The bed consisted of a feather mattress placed not on a frame, but directly on the floor. Gauzy white coverings hung from the ceiling. Before she slept, she would pull them around her to keep the insects at bay.

Ana-si stood in the center of the chamber with folded arms, frowning at Reyna. "This will do?" she asked.

"It will. Nicely. Thank you."

Reyna's chest had already been delivered, left at the foot of the bed. Ana-si knelt by it. Without asking permission, she opened the lid and rummaged through Reyna's things. Ignoring the parchment and vials of ink, instead holding up one of Reyna's dresses for inspection. It was identical to the one she currently wore, in serviceable, sensible blue.

"This is all? No lace, no silk? Nothing more?"

The disdain in Ana-si's voice was evident, and Reyna smiled. "I'm a scribe, Lady. Lace just gets in the way."

"I am no lady," Ana-si reminded her, her tone stiff. "That is not who I am."

Strange and prickly. Reyna lowered herself onto the bed. A glance into the chest assured her Ana-si hadn't tipped over the tray full of ink. "What shall I call you then? Ana-si?"

She did not like that, either. "When we are with others, I am Ana-si. When we are here, I am Ana."

"I understand," Reyna said, though she did not. "My name is Reyna."

Ana-si's lip curled. She crumpled the dress on her lap. "Named for a Miranese goddess."

More scorn. With an inward sigh, Reyna decided not to take it to heart. Clearly, Ana-si was unhappy. It could not have anything to do with Reyna. She had just arrived. However, she was *not* named after a Miranese goddess. She said, "Reyna was my grandmother's name."

Silence. Reyna thought she saw something different in Ana-si's eyes, before she tossed the dress aside to look over Reyna's possessions. Cloak, underthings. Reyna pretended not to mind. Struggling to find some neutral topic, she said, "The red dot on the women's lips. What does it mean?"

A shrug. "The dot says, 'Look at my lips. I am prepared to marry. Maybe I will marry you.' After they marry, there is no more dot." She eyed Reyna's bare mouth. "I will find paint for you if you wish it."

"I don't." Reyna was certain she did not want strange men looking at her lips. "It's a mating ritual, then. Like the men who paint their teeth black?"

"Yes," Ana-si said, surprised. "How do you know this?"

The lie came easily. "Prince Levi mentioned it, I think. Are you from Miramar, Ana?" The girl only looked at her, and Reyna added hastily, "I don't mean to pry. Only I've traveled to many kingdoms with the prince, and you . . ."

"Yes? I do not look like everyone else. That is what you are trying to say? You think I am a changeling?"

Oh, for heaven's sake, Reyna almost said. This was exhausting. "I don't think you're a changeling. Forgive me. My curiosity runs away from me sometimes."

Ana-si was done with her. She dumped Reyna's nightgown on the bed, then walked to the door. Not limping, not quite. "The baths are just past the courtyard. Someone will fetch you for supper."

"Thank you."

"You will not see your prince until then. Jian-so will have much to say to him." Ana-si's hand rested on the door latch. She looked over her shoulder, and the silence stretched onward until she said quietly, "Ana was my grandmother's name."

With that admission, Reyna felt the first thawing of frost. Ana-si did not return her smile, but she did not scowl, either. "You are not like the others," she told Reyna. "The women. You are not unkind." A pause, as if she were coming to some decision. "I will keep your secret."

Reyna's smile faded. She made herself look puzzled, not a difficult thing to do. "What do you mean?"

"You are no Lunesian," Ana-si told her. "Neither is your

curly-haired friend. I have traveled to many kingdoms too." The door opened and shut.

Reyna was alone.

Reyna and Blaise wandered in what they hoped was the direction of the baths. *Just past the courtyard*, Ana-si had said. But where was it? Reyna had begun to wonder if she'd misheard until, finally, they came across an old woman scrubbing the floors. Reyna asked for directions. Unfortunately, the woman did not speak Caffeesh. After much gesturing — Reyna lifted an arm and mimicked scrubbing beneath it — the old woman pointed them this way.

Reyna could not get her mind off Ana-si. Not only her final words to Reyna, or the very real danger they were in. She said, "I think I've seen her before."

Blaise's head whipped toward her. "Where?" she demanded.

"I don't know. At a harbor, maybe. Just a glimpse. There's something about her that's familiar."

"Did she tell you where she's from?" When Reyna shook her head, Blaise mused, "That's strange, isn't it? As many places as you've been, you should be able to tell."

It was not the only thing that was troubling. "What is the matter with her? You saw the way she walked. Something isn't right."

"It might not be anything sinister," Blaise said. "Perhaps she's never sat a horse until today, and is sore. Or perhaps . . ."

"She was beaten," Reyna said flatly. She knew what it was to be kicked, hit. She had carried herself as Ana-si did, once.

"Possibly," Blaise acknowledged quietly. "It doesn't explain the scratching. Did you see her face when the captain said I was a healer?"

"Yes." They turned left, down a passageway Reyna was certain they had already walked through. Some geographer she was. "She doesn't like doctors."

"I wonder . . ." Blaise lowered her voice. "I wonder if she needed help from a doctor once, and whoever it was made it worse."

On that wretched note, Reyna spotted a separate structure beyond a courtyard. A courtyard, but not *their* courtyard. Ana-si had left out that detail. Three women disappeared inside, each with a bathing sheet draped over an arm. "I think we're here."

"Good." Blaise marched that way. "I need a bath after meeting that creepy prince. Which reminds me: Do you have your dagger?"

Reyna could still feel Jian-so's callused finger against her skin. She shuddered. "Yes. Do you?"

Blaise opened the door to the bathhouse, where a wall of steam enveloped them. "Oh yes."

The same could be said in any kingdom — nowhere was gossip more freely exchanged than at the public baths. And it occurred to Reyna that if any of the palace women knew about the missing men, this was where she might hear about it. The bathhouse was a pleasant chamber with two separate pools and vaulted ceilings. Water droplets clung to walls tiled a soft green. The floors were cream-colored stone, the surface rough to prevent slips and falls.

Every stitch of clothing had to be left behind in the antechamber. They were new, and they were foreign, and that meant the pool they'd chosen to bathe in quickly became a crowded one. At least two dozen women shared the waters. Others gathered along the edge and pulled combs through damp hair. Pretty combs made of wood and tortoiseshell. The ladies of the court were not present. They bathed in the privacy of their chambers. Reyna's companions were the palace's middle and upper servants. Most of them spoke Caffeesh. And what they most wanted to discuss was Levi.

"He is very handsome, your prince," one said.

From another, her tone wistful: "His eyes are like lapis lazuli."

"Are all the men on Lunes so handsome?"

The water came up to Reyna's neck. She would have to tell Levi about the lapis lazuli. "Prince Levi is more handsome than most," she said, ignoring the smile on Blaise's face before her friend ducked beneath the water to soak her head.

The questions continued, with Reyna's answers translated for those who did not understand. Did the prince have a princess? No, he did not. Was the prince here in search of a princess? Prince Levi's private affairs were not for her to share. The thought of Levi with his own princess struck an unpleasant chord inside her. Of course he must marry, someday. It would be foolish to think otherwise. The next question had to be repeated, for she had not heard it. Why did the Lunesian crown go to a woman and not to Prince Levi?

"Every kingdom is different," Reyna explained. "On Lunes, the king's eldest child inherits the crown, no matter the sex. Though Queen Vashti's husband isn't a king, merely a consort. Other kingdoms require a male heir always. Like your Prince Jian-so, for instance."

An unexpected silence fell, thick as the steam that filled the chamber. What had she said? She looked to Blaise, who shrugged.

Just then, Ana-si walked into the baths carrying a bucket. She did not speak, or even look in their direction, but knelt to fill it at a nearby pump. She rose with some difficulty, gripping the bucket with both hands. Water sloshed over the brim.

Reyna started to rise, ready to grab her robe and offer help. Blaise beat her to it. "I'll walk with you, Ana-si," she called out. "I'm finished here."

"No." Ana-si did not glance Blaise's way. She left the baths as the women watched in silence. Blaise sank lower into the water, her expression troubled.

"Don't think anything of it," an older woman advised. Her eyebrows had been plucked bare. She must draw them in with a pencil. "She's a strange one."

"Strange how?" Reyna asked.

It was all the prompting the woman needed. "In every way.

The girl arrived a year ago. Prince Jian-so brought her on his ship."

"She did not look like a lady then," a second woman with a large mole by her nose said. "Not even the beggars would have worn her rags."

"And that voice!" another exclaimed.

"Like a man's!"

The women tittered; their breath turned to vapor. Reyna had not been wrong. Ana-si was not welcome here.

The first woman said, "We see nothing of her for days, and then one evening she comes to supper. The prince introduces her as Ana-si and says she is to be his guest. Nothing else."

"But where did she come from?" Reyna asked. "Does no one know?" Who was this Ana-si who insisted on being called Ana in private? How had she recognized Reyna as not being from Lunes?

"The slave markets on Caffa," another woman said. "So they say. We've asked her, but she doesn't waste her breath speaking to us."

"Did she come here alone?" Blaise asked.

"We didn't see anyone else," the woman said. They promptly lost interest in the topic. Reyna did not mind. She learned other things. The women had been born here and raised here and never left. It was the same with their husbands. Except one woman. Her husband, a carpenter, sailed frequently on a ship captained by Jian-so. He never spoke of where he went or what he did.

"That sounds mysterious," Reyna commented with a smile,

even as her heartbeat quickened. Blaise had moved farther down the pool to speak with others.

"He tells me only that it is the prince's business and no one else's." The woman was quite put out. "There should not be secrets between a man and his wife."

"Your husband sounds loyal," Reyna offered.

"For all the good it does him," the woman said with a snort. "He's always in a temper when he comes home. He doesn't eat. He barely sleeps."

"Oh?" Reyna said, but the moment was lost. A younger woman had sidled up to Reyna, eyes bright with curiosity. "You have seen Caffa?" she asked shyly.

Reyna managed a smile and said yes, and spoke of it. The women were hungry for any news of the outside world. The younger women in particular. They pried from Reyna the history she had invented for herself. How her parents had died when she was a young girl. How she had been raised by her grandfather, a royal scribe, who had trained her to become one herself. How he was gone too. And so on, and so forth. Reyna told her story easily. Lies were best remembered when they bore some semblance of truth.

That evening Prince Jian-so threw a splendid welcoming feast for his friend Prince Levi.

Reyna saw this: a great, sunken courtyard out in the open, the sky turned gold from dusk. Two rows of artfully sculpted trees. The tree behind Reyna was shaped like an open-mouthed carp. Another had been trimmed to resemble a hawk. Otters were represented, as were tigers, tortoises, pigs, and horses. She could see Blaise beneath the otter, Benjamin near the pig. They would dine among the Miranese tonight and try to learn what they could of the missing men.

Low tables had been arranged on the grass, weighed down with platters of carp, pig, and other dishes Reyna could not readily identify. There were no chairs, only large tasseled pillows. The Miranese knelt upon them while they dined. Though no one was kneeling at this moment. Jian-so's father, His Imperial Majesty Botan-so, had yet to arrive.

Reyna stood within earshot of the royal table. Beside her was a much smaller table covered with parchment and ink. A meal would come later for her. She was Levi's scribe; this was an official function. Her duty was to record all that transpired. At least she would not have to worry about the gathering darkness making it difficult to see. Ample light came from torches blazing on the walls and from the tortoises that roamed among the guests and harpists, slow and amiable, lanterns strapped to their shells. Reyna had come to Miramar on some dark journey, it was true. But there was beauty here as well. Everywhere she turned.

A chirping distracted her. She looked up, searching the branches overhead, smiling when she saw a nest tucked away just out of reach.

Levi arrived with Jian-so. His eyes searched the crowd,

found hers. She spread her arms slightly to show that she was in one piece, no disasters here, which made him smile. Jian-so appeared distracted. Constantly looking to the main archway, where, presumably, his father would make an appearance.

Only it was not Miramar's imperial majesty who arrived, but a younger man dressed, not for dinner, but in a traveling cloak and gloves. She judged him to be four or five years older than Jian-so and Levi. He bore a striking similarity to the Miranese prince, without the scarring, without the twist to the lips that hinted at some deep anger or unhappiness. When the steward introduced the stranger to Levi, he could not keep the shock from his voice.

"*Crown* Prince Ken-so?" Levi said. The sweet notes from the harpists trailed away. The courtyard was silent. Levi recovered quickly and returned the short bow offered. Beside him, Jian-so's face had flushed a deep, sullen red.

Reyna did not understand. Jian-so was the king's only child. How could he not be his heir? And why had he kept it from Levi?

"You look surprised, Prince Levi," Ken-so observed with a sardonic glance in Jian-so's direction. And he tugged his glove from each finger with brisk efficiency. "No. Astonished. Has my dear cousin been telling tales again?"

"I'm no liar, *Cousin*." Jian-so's words sounded bitten off at the ends. "Your kingship is not a certainty."

"But it is," Ken-so replied evenly, "when your own father, His Imperial Majesty, decrees it so." A servant stepped forward to remove his cloak and gloves.

"Much can happen before my father leaves us."

"So you keep telling me," Ken-so said, tight-lipped. He shrugged off the cloak, which a different servant whisked away. "I will offer a reminder that you, also, are not invulnerable."

Levi's eyeballs were the only parts of him that moved, cautious eyeballs, flicking from cousin to cousin. On the steps behind the royal table, Samuel and Hamish watched, alert.

"Come." Ken-so visibly reined in his irritation. "We are making our guest uncomfortable. Take your place here, Prince Levi. Eat. Drink. Welcome to Miramar."

The steward clapped his hands sharply, making Reyna jump. The harpists started up again and everyone else knelt by their tables. Conversation resumed, but it was muted. More than one ear strained in the direction of the royal table.

Reyna dipped her quill in ink and wrote feverishly. Her king's words came back to her. *Why would the heir to the Miranese kingdom be conducting sea raids? He could be killed. It seems a foolish move to me.* The answer was simple: Jian-so was not the heir. Why not? What horrible deed did one commit to be disinherited from the throne?

Ana-si dined closest to Reyna at the end of the royal table. Alone, for the woman beside her had turned her back, speaking to others. Reyna watched Ana-si for a moment, knowing she had not shared her suspicions with Jian-so. If she had, Reyna would not be here. And neither, she suspected, would Levi.

Ken-so said to Levi, "You'll forgive my late arrival. I've only just arrived in the city."

"No apologies are necessary." Levi accepted a glass of wine from a servant. He knelt on one side of the croown prince. Jian-so knelt on the other. "I should have sent word ahead. Prince Jian-so has been very welcoming."

"Has he? Now it is I who am astonished." Ken-so's smile was meant to soften his words.

The look Jian-so sent him could have curdled bathwater.

Ken-so sighed. "I'm told you've brought clay for us, Prince Levi."

Levi said that he had. "Bricks of them."

"Forgive me, but . . ." Ken-so turned to his cousin with a puzzled frown. "For what purpose?"

"It's a gift for Father," Jian-so muttered. He stabbed a thick slab of pork with a knife, with enough force that the tip broke off. Instantly, a servant stepped forward to offer a new, unbroken knife. A girl, about twelve. Was it so common, then, for Jian-so to destroy knives at the supper table?

Ken-so waited for further explanation. None came. He eyed his cousin with displeasure and weariness.

Levi cleared his throat. He went from honored guest to peacekeeper. "Will His Imperial Majesty be joining us?"

"Regrettably, no," Ken-so said. "You may have noticed that our numbers" — he gestured toward those dining around them — "are somewhat less than what is usual for a palace this size."

Reyna brushed excess ink from her quill. It was impossible to miss. The palace was mammoth, yet it did not have the servants to support its upkeep. On the way to supper, Reyna and

Blaise had passed several wings that had been roped off. You could see the dust thick on the ground. No one went there. And the guards . . . there should have been more of them.

"I have, yes," Levi said. "Was it the pox?"

"Two years ago," Ken-so said. "There were many losses. My uncle survived but was sorely weakened. To our great sorrow, he is not expected to be with us much longer."

Levi looked past him to where Jian-so had abandoned his meat. Both fists were on the table, on opposite sides of his plate.

Levi said to him, quietly, "My friend, I am sorry to hear it."

Jian-so dipped his head in acknowledgment.

Ken-so said, "Is there pox on Lunes, Prince Levi?"

"Not for many years," Levi said. "Not since I was a boy."

"And were there many deaths?"

"Not as many as here, I think. Our doctors know ways to treat the pox so that fewer suffer. Fewer die."

Levi had the attention of both cousins.

Ken-so waved away a servant offering more food. "I would be interested in learning more about these ways. It is not something I wish to see ever again."

"My kingdom is open to you," Levi said. "Our hospitals as well. If you wish to send physicians to Lunes, I will see they have all they need."

When Ken-so did not answer straight away, Jian-so smirked. "My cousin is trying to find a polite way to reject your offer, Levi. We do not send our physicians abroad, ever. We prefer death and ignorance."

"You're an ass, Jian-so. You always have been," Ken-so said mildly, without bothering to look at him. Instead, he eyed Levi with a thoughtful expression. "We are isolationists, it's true. I believe isolation has done much to preserve our way of life. Our language. Our culture. All that makes us who we are. Do you find that strange?"

A tortoise padded by Reyna's table. She paused in her writing long enough to reach out and touch its shell, hard and smooth beneath her fingertips.

Levi said, "It's a different custom from my own. I won't deny it. But my father told me, long ago, that there are no foreign lands. It is the traveler only who is foreign." He held up a hand, refusing more wine. "I've been treated well by your countrymen. I will not come here, to your home, and criticize how you rule it."

Reyna was unaccustomed to this side of Levi, less like a captain and more like . . . what was it Mercedes had once said? A diplomat is someone who will tell you to go to the devil in such a way that you actually look forward to the journey. Levi had a way with words, and people. Just like Mercedes.

Ken-so smiled. "You are a credit to your kingdom, Prince Levi. Miramar could use more like you." He shot a glance at his cousin, who snorted. Turning back to Levi, he said, "I lost three sisters to the pox. Nieces and nephews, all gone. I accept your offer with gratitude and . . . who is that girl over there?"

Reyna, parchment raised to her lips as she blew the ink dry, did not immediately realize the crown prince was speaking of her. When she looked over at the royal table, she found everyone else looking back.

"Master Reyna is my scribe," Levi said with a neutral expression.

Heart racing, Reyna set aside the parchment and jumped to her feet. She curtsied low and held it.

"A scribe? But she's female," Ken-so said, utterly perplexed.

"I've already told him it's odd," Jian-so said. For once the cousins were in agreement.

Levi was unruffled. "There are men and women in our writers' guild," he explained. "Master Reyna was chosen by my queen. She can read and write the languages of our neighbors. It's a useful skill."

"Is that so?" Ken-so beckoned to her. "Come here."

Reyna did as she was told. Her palms were damp. She clasped them together as she stood before Ken-so. Behind her, the rest of the palace continued to dine and laugh and enjoy music and conversation. Before her, the royal table had fallen silent to hear what the crown prince had to say to her.

"Master Reyna, you said?" Ken-so inquired of Levi, who nodded.

Ken-so addressed her. "Tell me, scribe, what do your parents think of your position at court? Your father allows this?"

"I'm sorry to say my parents died many years ago, Prince Ken-so."

Jian-so chewed his pork, bored.

"Ah. Then you're an orphan, taken in by the royal family.

Commendable of you," Ken-so said to Levi, who inclined his head and looked gracious. "How old are you?"

"Seventeen, Prince Ken-so."

"A good age to marry. Are royal scribes allowed marriage?" Ken-so asked Levi.

At that, Levi appeared to have swallowed something unpleasant. "If she wishes it."

"Then you'll lose her," Ken-so predicted. Levi glanced at Reyna, and glanced away. "The pretty ones don't stay unmarried for long. Is it not a waste to educate a female so thoroughly only to see her married and gone?"

Mercedes would not like this man, Reyna thought. *Not even a little bit.*

"Lunes is ruled by a queen," Levi reminded him. "A wise one. A married one. My sister is a great believer in free will for her women."

Jian-so swished the wine around in his cup. "There is free will for women, and then there is too much free will. Where is the line drawn?" Laughter rippled down the table. Levi merely smiled.

Ken-so said to Reyna, "Prince Levi says you speak the languages of your neighbors."

"I do, Prince Ken-so."

"Do you know Coronad?"

Reyna lifted her eyes to his. She answered in Coronad. "Very well."

Ken-so was quiet. She braced herself for more questions, but he waved her away.

Reyna smiled at Ana-si as she walked back to her place. As usual, the smile was not returned. Reyna retrieved her quill in time to hear Ken-so say to Levi, "Don't take offense, but Jian-so has never mentioned you. He's been very secretive about his adventures."

"It's no secret. It's not your business," Jian-so said.

To Reyna, it seemed as if the entire table held its breath. Jian-so's rudeness was breathtaking. Ken-so merely drank from his cup, his eyes never leaving his cousin's. He set the cup down. "It will be," he said softly, in a tone that had Reyna wondering which cousin was scarier.

"You speak as if you're king already," Jian-so spat.

"Enough. Your temper is an embarrassment. We'll discuss this later."

"We'll discuss nothing —"

A squawk had Reyna look up in time to see a small bird tumble from its nest. It landed on the thick grass. Ana-si's head came up sharply, and she and Reyna rose in unison. A number of guests had finished their meals and left their tables, strolling about the courtyard or clustering beneath the trees in conversation. Before Reyna could reach the bird — she had meant to scoop it up and return it to the nest — a nobleman walked by and, not seeing the creature, stepped directly on it.

Ana-si's cry turned heads. As the nobleman looked down in puzzlement, lifting his boot to see what lay beneath, Ana-si flew at him, wailing, her small fists pummeling his chest.

"Ho! Hey! What!" The man raised his arms to ward her off, then tried to grasp her wrists. "Get off me, woman!"

Everyone stared. Jian-so appeared, pulling Ana-si from the man. His grip was gentler than Reyna had thought him capable of. He whispered something in her ear, and the fight left Ana-si. Her shoulders slumped.

Jian-so turned a cold gaze on the hapless nobleman. "Idiot."

The man blanched. "My prince, I did not see it. Forgive me." He backed away, turned, and fled the courtyard.

Ana-si's tears were silent ones. Reyna had never seen anyone look so despondent over the loss of a nameless, solitary bird. Reyna scooped it up. A cardinal, clearly dead. It fit in the palm of her hand, crushed and bloody, perfectly horrible. "I'll bury it for you," she offered quietly.

An irritated Ken-so called out, "Jian-so, for pity's sake. Control your woman."

Jian-so looked down at Reyna. He said, gruffly, "There's a grove by the women's quarters. That will be a good place."

"Yes, Prince Jian-so." Reyna curtsied and belatedly glanced at Levi, remembering that she needed his permission to leave. He dipped his head once — *Permission granted* — his expression asking, *What in the name of all strange things is happening here?* Reyna had no answers. Without having to be asked, Hamish came down the steps to take her place at the writing table.

Reyna swiped a spoon from the royal table and tucked it

into her belt. A moment's hesitation only before she took Ana-si's hand in hers. To her surprise, the girl did not protest.

"Scribe." Jian-so's words stopped her. "My thanks."

Reyna curtsied again. She left the courtyard, dead bird in one hand, and Ana-si weeping beside her.

Reyna dug a small grave using the spoon, which took no time at all. Twilight had come, and there were no tortoises to shine a light on her sad task. Ana-si sat with her back against a tree, watching as Reyna placed the cardinal in the hole, covered it with dirt, and patted the mound.

Reyna offered the only words that came to mind. "It was a pretty bird." Lame, useless words.

Ana-si's face was half lost in shadow. "Do you have family?"

Reyna sat beside her. "An uncle. And I have friends who are like family." Blaise and Jaime. Lord Elias and Mercedes.

"No one else?"

"No." Reyna brought her nails close. They were encrusted with dirt. She did not like to talk about the rest of her family. "Do you?"

"Yes," Ana-si said, but her voice had turned to prickles. Reyna did not press for more. They sat for a time in silence. The grove was situated on a small rise behind the women's quarters. All but one of the windows below were dark. Most people would be at supper still.

Ana-si pressed a hand to her ribs as though they pained her.

Reyna could stay quiet no longer. She had to try, prickles or not. "You're hurt," she said.

Ana-si dropped her hand.

"Prince Levi's healer —"

"No."

"Blaise is gentle and kind," Reyna persisted. "She might not be able to fix what is hurting you, but perhaps she can. And she would never cause you more pain than you're already —"

"No one can help me, Reyna-si. I am beyond healers." Ana-si rose, dusted herself off. She turned away, then turned back. "Thank you for the bird," she said, and made her way down the hill.

TWENTY-ONE

WELL, THAT WAS the strangest supper I've ever attended," Levi commented.

It felt wrong to smile. Reyna could not help it. They were in yet another courtyard, this one outside Levi's chambers. The moon was high, and the torches spiked into the ground helped keep the darkness at bay. Reyna sat across from Levi, her supper plate pushed aside, replaced by parchment and inks. Anyone passing through the covered archways would only see the foreign prince dictating letters to his scribe in the late hours of the night. But Levi had brought her outdoors because it was the one place they could be certain no one would overhear their conversation. They had both grown up in castles. A castle without a peephole or a hollow wall was simply not a proper castle. Samuel and Hamish stood guard by a pillar.

Reyna reached for a quill before deciding on a stick of charcoal instead. "It was horrible."

"Oh, it gets worse. I found out why Jian-so was disinherited." Reyna glanced up. "Why?"

Levi's answer was to crook two fingers at Benjamin, who

was playing chess with Blaise at a nearby table. The boy made his move on the board — Blaise groaned — and then came running. "Tell her what you heard," Levi said. "About Jian-so."

"It's because of the scars, miss." Benjamin reached over and righted a torch that had begun to tilt. "One of the other pages told me that after the pox, the king took one look at the prince's face and fell right over."

"Seizure," Levi clarified.

"He hasn't left his bed since," Benjamin said.

"Ken-so was next in line for the throne," Levi said. "They summoned him from the provinces and named him crown prince in Jian-so's place. Being so far away from the city, he and his wife and son had escaped the pox."

"But . . ." Reyna could not take it all in. "You're saying Jian-so was disinherited because his father thinks he's *ugly?*"

Levi looked just as flabbergasted. "Samuel heard the same," he said. "There are others in the palace with scars. Noblemen and servants. But they're not allowed in the king's presence. He refuses to look upon them."

"Even his son?"

There was laughter at the other table. Hamish was keeping Blaise company. At Benjamin's wistful look, Levi sent him back to the game. "Jian-so is the exception," Levi said. "Samuel heard he's been trying to find a way back into his father's good graces ever since."

It's a gift for Father, Jian-so had said of the clay. Reyna felt an unexpected sympathy welling up inside her and clamped down on it, hard. Jian-so was a kidnapper, a murderer, a brute. Still. "Is the king crazy?"

"I'm starting to wonder if the entire family is. It's nothing new, is it? The old woman you spoke to on del Mar. Didn't she say something similar?"

The royal family of Miramar values beauty and strength above all else. My father made it so I was no longer valuable. The memory of Niemi-si's words sent a shiver down Reyna's spine. "I'd forgotten."

"Whatever anyone's appearance, it's moot. I don't think Jian-so intends for his cousin to live long enough to sit on any throne."

"Ken-so doesn't seem like an easy person to kill."

"No," Levi agreed. "What a family! And I thought mine was troublesome." He slouched in his chair, dropped his chin on his hand, and said morosely, "That's not all. There are no slaves in Miramar, Reyna. There never have been."

Reyna was quiet. The news did not come as a complete surprise. There had been no mention of slavery in her book. She had hoped it had simply been something the author had chosen not to record. "Then . . ."

"Then why did Jian-so take our men in the first place? What purpose could they serve here? If they're here at all."

"They're here, Levi," she insisted, because she could not bear the thought that they were not. "It only means we don't understand *why* they are."

"Mm," he said again, which could have meant anything. Eyeing her unfinished supper, he said, "Are you done there?"

Her appetite had vanished since burying the cardinal. She nudged the plate toward him.

Levi said, "What about Ana-si? That was an awful business with the bird." He speared a piece of meat with her knife, then stopped and took a closer look. "What is this?" he asked suspiciously.

"Quail."

More bird. Grimacing, Levi set the knife aside.

Reyna told him all that she had learned, beginning with Ana-si arriving in Miramar in rags.

Levi interrupted once, incredulous. "You learned all this at the baths?"

"It's the best place to hear things."

Levi opened his mouth, closed it. "I won't ask why," he decided.

Reyna's smile faded when she spoke of Ana-si's suspicion: that Reyna was lying about being from Lunes. "What are we going to do? If she tells that wretched Jian-so, we won't be safe here."

"We're not safe here either way." Levi picked up the knife again and twirled it absent-mindedly between his fingers. "She seems to like you. We'll have to hope she keeps her promise. I've been invited to tour the royal tombs tomorrow."

Reyna picked up her charcoal. "That's a strange thing to show a guest."

"I thought so too. Jian-so said he wanted me to see how they're using our clay. What are you doing?"

Between them was a bowl filled with water. Three chrysanthemums drifted within, freshly plucked and fully in bloom. The bowl was high enough and large enough that he could not see what Reyna was scribbling across the parchment.

"Pretending to be your scribe," she answered without looking up.

"Let me see."

She refused. "It's not finished."

He held out a hand.

This time she looked up, cross. "I'm not really your servant, you remember."

"Give it over."

The instant the parchment left her hand, she wanted to snatch it back. Too much of her heart lay exposed there. What had she been thinking?

It was a sketch of Levi in the *Truthsayer's* forecastle, palms flat on the table as he studied the chart before him. She had drawn him in a three-quarter profile, showing the curve of his lips, a straight nose, eyebrows lowered in concentration. Reyna watched him study the sketch for a long time. Red slashed his cheekbones.

He lifted his eyes to meet hers, and he spoke quietly so the others could not hear. "This is how you see me?"

She nodded.

His gaze returned to the sketch. "This isn't me. He looks like he knows what he's doing."

"Levi." She waited until he looked up again. "We've made it this far because of you."

"Not only me."

"You're the captain," she reminded him. "You take the glory and the blame."

He smiled briefly at that. After a long moment, in a different voice, he said, "You came all this way to find him. This Jaime."

"And Lord Elias." And so many others.

But Levi was not interested in Lord Elias. "Do you love him?"

"Lord Elias?"

Levi gave her a look.

Reyna was quiet. "Do you have friends who are ladies?"

"No." There was no hesitation on Levi's part.

"What? Not even one?" she asked, nonplussed.

"If I even speak to a female in Selene, her mother becomes . . . hopeful. My sister becomes hopeful. It's not worth the aggravation. What does this have to do with Lord Jaime?"

"Everything," she said. "After I was hurt, I was in bed for weeks. I couldn't even sit up at first. I couldn't feed myself." Reyna touched the scar on her chin. It was not a time she cared to think about in detail. Plenty of terrible things had happened then. But this was one sweet thing. "Jaime was there. He is always there.

He read to me and he fed me. He knew I was not sleeping—I had nightmares, you see—and he would sneak back into my chamber and keep me company. And he paid the price for it the next day, because he could not stay awake for his lessons. You ask if I love him. I do," she said, and saw Levi flinch. "The same way I love Blaise. He is my friend."

Levi would not look at her. "I don't dream of my friends, Reyna."

She stared at him. "What?"

"You said his name in your sleep. The morning I knocked on your door." When he had discovered the ship on the mountain. His gaze hovered somewhere around her right shoulder.

"Levi . . ."

He stood abruptly. "It's late. Samuel will see you and Blaise back to your quarters. Get some rest."

Was he really going to walk away? "Levi."

But he did not listen, only walked off, stopping briefly to speak with Samuel.

Reyna gathered up the parchment and ink vials and returned them to the box. She studied the sketch she had drawn. It was not an appropriate picture for a scribe to have of her prince. Or even one Reyna should have of a Lunesian captain. By the time Blaise reached her, Reyna had torn the page into dozens of pieces and tossed them into the box.

Blaise waited until they had returned to Reyna's chamber before she brought up Levi.

"You both looked upset. What happened?"

Reyna flopped onto the bed and stared up at the netting. A single candle lit the room. "Do you ever wish you were normal?"

Blaise came over and flopped down beside her. Now there were two sets of eyes staring at the netting. "Am I being insulted?"

Reyna's smile was halfhearted. She told her all of it. When she was finished, Blaise rolled onto her side, propping herself up on an elbow. "He cares for you. Anyone with eyes can see it. Can you blame him for being jealous? I would be *seething* with it, if I were him."

"I told him about Jaime."

"Words," Blaise dismissed, and Reyna looked over, bemused. "You said the captain met him."

"At Vashti's coronation," Reyna confirmed.

"That explains it, then," Blaise said. "Jaime is handsome, Reyna. Unnaturally so. We both know this. We don't even think about it anymore. He's like one of those statues we used to ogle at the ruins. In Alfonse. Remember?"

"*You* used to ogle."

"And he's so charming that everyone wants to be his friend," Blaise continued, as if Reyna had not spoken. "The captain . . . everything about him is quieter. Not less, just different. Why wouldn't he look at Jaime and think your interest lay with him?"

"Because I told him so." Reyna sat up. "It doesn't matter, anyway."

"Why not?"

"When this is over, he'll go home. I'll go . . . wherever. He'll find a proper lady."

"A normal one, you mean." Blaise sat up too, her mouth turned down in annoyance. "You're right: there's nothing proper about you. You jump into the Strait of Cain to save someone you love. You sail across the Sea of Magdalen to rescue people you love. You distract lions . . . well, you understand what I'm trying to say. I can't imagine what the captain sees in you. Idiot," she added fondly.

The tears were falling now, silent down Reyna's cheeks. "He makes my heart hurt, Blaise."

"I know, dearest." Blaise wrapped an arm around her shoulders and pulled her close. "If it makes you feel better, I think you make his heart hurt too."

TWENTY-TWO

HE ROYAL CHAMBER reeked of death and dying. It was a dim room, no candles. A weak morning light filtered in through louvered windows. His Imperial Majesty Botan-so reclined on a bed similar to Reyna's. Low to the floor, with gauzy curtains. His bed, however, was ten times the size of hers. His robes were white, as were his bed linens, and from where Reyna sat, off to one side in the scribe's corner, all that was visible was a bald, shrunken head surrounded by a sea of white.

". . . a great honor to meet you at last," Levi said from his position at the foot of the bed. Jian-so stood beside him, somber as he looked upon his father. Crown Prince Ken-so was alone by a window, set apart from a trio of councilors clustered near the door. All relatively young, especially for such an old king. Not one of them visibly scarred by the pox. Levi was also studying the councilors. He glanced from them to Reyna. She looked away.

"Come . . . closer." Botan-so's order came in wheezes and gasps. Levi moved to the side of the bed.

Botan-so studied Levi in silence, for so long Reyna thought he had fallen asleep. Her quill hovered over the parchment.

Beside her was a Miranese scribe. An older man, bony and disapproving. Every time he looked at her, his lips pressed thinner than before and his pointy nose twitched and quivered, as if she were the cause of the chamber's bad smells.

Botan-so said, "I have only seen a Lunesian . . . in the histories. Drawings in the . . . margins. When I was a boy."

"It is the same for me, Your Grace," Levi said with a small smile. "I had never seen a Miranese until your son visited my home."

Eyes like raisins glared down the length of the bed to Jian-so. Disgust rippled over the old man's face. "You look strong," he said to Levi. "Healthy. Like . . . my nephew there. Your father would have been pleased with such a son."

Jian-so did not react. Only stood stone-faced as his father showed his contempt for him in front of visitors. What sort of father thought such things?

Levi kept his voice neutral. "I hope he was pleased, Your Grace."

Botan-so erupted in a fit of coughing that shook his frame and went on forever. He hacked and spat into a handkerchief. It came away thick and bloody. Reyna's stomach churned; she could smell the sharp, coppery tang of it. Crown Prince Ken-so had spoken true: Jian-so's father would not live to see another spring. A robed physician crawled across the wide expanse of bed coverings. Rump in the air, sandals flapping against ancient, flaking heels. He exchanged the soiled handkerchief for a fresh one. The king waved him off in irritation. The physician scuttled backward off the bed. Reyna wrote down all that she saw and heard, in Lunesian.

Once he'd caught his breath, Botan-so said to Levi, "You have . . . family."

"An older sister and a younger brother. My sister, Queen Vashti, sends her greetings to you, along with her best wishes for your health and happiness."

"Kind . . . of her." Botan-so closed his eyes briefly. "Ken-so will write a letter . . . on my behalf."

Ken-so bowed. "Yes, Your Grace." This time, a little of what he felt showed as he glanced at his cousin, compassion in his eyes.

Jian-so stiffened perceptibly. Rage flashed before he schooled his features. For some, there was no greater insult than pity. The meeting ended shortly thereafter. Reyna returned her writing materials to her chamber and changed into clothing more appropriate for riding outdoors. Then she went to fetch Blaise. They were to visit the royal tombs this morning. First the king, now the tombs. It was to be a day filled with the dying and the dead.

When Reyna knocked on Blaise's door, it opened a crack. A single eyeball peered back at her.

Instantly suspicious, Reyna lowered her voice. "What are you doing? Let me in."

The door opened wider. Blaise stuck her head out, curls

bouncing as she looked one way down the hall, then the other. Finally, she stepped back, pulling Reyna inside with her.

Blaise's first words were "I couldn't leave her like this."

A young woman knelt at the foot of the bed. She wore her hair in a braid over one shoulder. Protruding from her bare, elegant neck was a hideous boil the size of a plum. The woman eyed Reyna apprehensively.

"This is Tori-si," Blaise said in Caffeesh. "She brews tea in the kitchens. You saw her in the baths yesterday, remember? This is Reyna, Prince Levi's scribe."

Reyna did not remember. "Hello."

Tori-si nodded and would not meet her eyes.

"I need to lance it." Blaise indicated the bowl and cloth placed by the bed. A needle the length of Reyna's hand lay on the cloth. "It's a simple thing, really."

Knowing it was rude but not caring right now, Reyna switched back to Lunesian. "Why do you both look so shifty about it?"

Blaise answered in Lunesian. "It's strange here, Reyna. The Miranese believe that any sort of disease or disfigurement" — she glanced at Tori-si's neck — "is caused by bad behavior committed in a past life."

Reyna's gaze snapped back to the boil. "This is a karmic society?"

"There's a word for it?" Blaise said. "Whatever it is, it's peculiar. No one likes to admit they've sinned in any lifetime, which means they don't seek out treatment. They hide their illnesses."

Karmic societies no longer existed in the Sea of Magdalen. Or anywhere else, Reyna had thought until this moment. There was no mention of it in her book. She must remember to write this down.

Blaise said, "I only saw her boil for a second yesterday. She covered it with her hair. I couldn't stop thinking about it, so I went to look for her this morning. I had to convince her to let me help."

"And she told you about karmic societies?" Reyna asked.

"Eventually." Blaise smiled at Tori-si. "Anyway, I wasn't being shifty, just discreet. That boil needs to go. It's hurting her."

Reyna thought fleetingly of Jian-so, who could not hide his disfigurement. Not unless he wore a mask. "We're supposed to ride to the tombs."

"No one will miss me. And if I stay here, I might be able to learn something useful. Someone must know *something*." Blaise knelt beside her patient and picked up the needle. A whimper came from Tori-si. She covered her eyes with one hand.

Reyna stepped back involuntarily. There would be plenty of blood in a boil that large. And other oozing fluids. "I would offer to help, but . . ."

Blaise looked over and smiled. Reyna was fooling no one, least of all Blaise. "I'll see you later. Be careful."

To Reyna's surprise, they were joined at the palace gates by fifty noblemen and noblewomen, along with their cortege. Crown Prince Ken-so and his cousin kept their distance from each other.

On the palace steps, Jian-so spoke with a serving girl. Reyna recognized her from the night before. She was the efficient one who had handed Jian-so a new, unbroken knife. As Reyna watched, the girl, smiling, reached for his hand and kissed it, then hurried off.

Reyna had swung onto her horse when Levi came by.

"Where's Blaise?" he asked, frowning up at her. There were shadows beneath his eyes. Seeing them made her feel a little better. Benjamin trailed behind, leading both their horses.

"Tending someone." She explained briefly.

"I don't like her staying here alone."

"I'm not her keeper. Tell her so." Reyna wished he would go away. She took up her reins. Levi caught them. When she looked down at him, stony-eyed, he said, "Forgive me."

Her horse's tail swished back and forth. A carriage rolled past them through the gates. The others were departing.

"For what?" she said.

His hand tightened on the reins. Exasperation tinged his words. "You know what. Yesterday. Lord Jaime is not my business."

Reyna wanted to reach down and shake him. "That is a coward's apology." She had not meant to speak of it, ever again. But she was tired, and sad, and the words came pouring out. "You were upset last night for a reason. Why not say it? Why pretend?"

"I —" Levi's hand fell away from her reins. "I have no right to say it."

"Who says you don't?"

"Your king," he snapped. "My queen. You're better off with that worthless Jaime —"

"Worthless! You don't even know him!"

"What's this? Troubles with the scribe?"

Several feet away, Jian-so and Ana-si watched from their horse. Jian-so was grinning. Ana-si sat behind him with her arms wrapped around his middle. The sight of them together made Reyna's skin creep. That was not all. She cursed her carelessness. Hers and Levi's. What were they doing, going on about different kings and queens? Even though they had spoken Lunesian, it had been reckless. She saw her thoughts reflected in Levi's eyes before he smoothed his features and shrugged. He switched to Caffeesh.

"Sometimes she's difficult," Levi said to Jian-so, who laughed. Ana-si, her cheek resting against Jian-so's back, looked off in the distance and said nothing.

"Have you brought your ink, scribe?" Jian-so said. "You'll see much worth writing about today."

Heart thudding, Reyna lifted the flap on her satchel so that he could see the writing box tucked within. "I have, Prince Jian-so."

"Excellent. Come, Levi. My wretched cousin has already left. We can't let him take the lead here."

The road followed an ancient aqueduct that wound past the city to the river. Levi and Jian-so rode together at the front. Jian-so's mood had improved greatly once leaving his father's company. He joked and laughed, pointing out sights along the way: the aqueduct; the amphitheater; the spice market, six hundred years old. He was knowledgeable and well-spoken, a man who clearly loved his kingdom and knew its history. Reyna could almost see why Levi had taken to him back on Lunes.

Reyna and Benjamin rode in the middle of the cortege, largely ignored by the Miranese. The conversation around them was subdued and occasionally punctuated by odd stretches of silence. Jian-so seemed to be the only one in good spirits. Crown Prince Ken-so did not look bothered at having his cousin in the lead. He rode near Reyna, content with his young son in front of him. A boy, about five years old. Reyna had learned his name was Ippen-so.

Despite her best efforts, her eyes strayed frequently to Levi. To the curve of his ear; to the way he sat on his horse, self-assured, easy.

Benjamin nudged his horse close to Reyna's and whispered, "Why does everyone look so sad?"

Even though they spoke Lunesian, Reyna kept her voice low. "Do you remember how the Miranese kings are buried with their councilors and soldiers?"

Benjamin nodded.

"I think these are the councilors and soldiers."

Benjamin's eyes widened. A carriage rolled by, filled with women. He said, "But those are ladies!"

"They go too, sometimes."

Another voice broke in, speaking Caffeesh. "Is something the matter?"

Crown Prince Ken-so had ridden up on her left. His son looked over at her and smiled. The boy was a miniature of his father, with tidy, knotted hair and a dagger hanging from his belt.

Reyna returned the smile, then said, "Nothing is the matter, Prince Ken-so."

Clearly, he did not believe her, eyes resting on Benjamin before turning back to her. "What were you speaking of?"

There was only curiosity in his words. He did not give her the same bad feelings as Jian-so. She decided to tell him. "Benjamin was asking about the tombs. About *tutto mortise.*"

"I see. This is not the custom on Lunes?"

Reyna shook her head. "Or anywhere else that I know of."

An eyebrow rose. "Not even Coronado?"

"Not for centuries." Uneasy, she wondered why he bothered to speak with her. She was just the scribe.

Ippen-so was peeking over at Benjamin, twice his age, with unabashed interest.

"You must think it an archaic custom," Ken-so said to Reyna. "Cruel."

"It's not my place to think these things."

"No? Who better than someone who has lived beyond here? Seen how others live?"

Levi looked over his shoulder at them. His brow creased before he turned back, responding to something Jian-so said.

Reyna answered Ken-so's question with another. "Do *you* think it's archaic and cruel?"

The answer was yes. She saw it in his eyes. Ken-so looked around, realized that others had begun to take an interest in them. Including his cousin. She did not miss the cold look Jian-so threw in their direction, or the way Ken-so set his shoulders and met his cousin's gaze unflinchingly.

"What a question, scribe," Ken-so answered lightly. "Certainly I don't. In life and death we serve." He nudged his horse forward and left her.

At Benjamin's questioning look, Reyna lifted a shoulder. She could not begin to guess what that exchange had been about.

They rode past the harbor, clean and tidy. Reyna saw the *Truthsayer* bobbing peacefully in the water and wondered how the men were doing, stuck aboard the ship. Benjamin had not had a moment to spare for messenger duty.

They followed the river. Mountains sprang up to the left, and on the right. The royal tombs had been built into these mountains, their facades carved into the stone. Each tomb the size of a cathedral. One tomb for every ruling family. Centuries of evolving architecture. Even knowing the urgency of their mission, Reyna was tempted to grab her parchment and charcoal and spend the day by the river, sketching away.

They dismounted in front of the last tomb. Hundreds of wide, shallow steps led up to the entrance.

Ana-si came up to her. She inclined her head toward the

steps and spoke to Reyna for the first time that day. "We walk?" she asked.

Reyna watched Levi climb the stairs with a royal cousin on each side. She nodded grimly. "We walk."

Once they climbed the endless steps and walked past massive, iron-spoked doors, Reyna found they immediately had to descend another staircase. This one steeper than before, leading them into a dark abyss broken only by the torchlight carried by servants. The doors closed behind them with a thud, and a muffled scream emerged from the rear. The air turned chilly. Reyna sniffed; she smelled not dirt exactly, but something similar.

Something cold and damp.

Clay.

She smelled clay.

Ana-si remained by Reyna's side. As they neared the bottom — Reyna could see a brighter light — Jian-so spoke from the front of the crowd, loud enough to be heard by all.

"For centuries," he began. "The rulers of Miramar have been buried beneath these mountains. Accompanied by those they loved best, men and women who chose to follow their sovereigns into the afterlife. In life and death they served."

Only the smallest hesitation before the Miranese said, in unison, "In life and death we serve."

The words echoed around them. Reyna rubbed her chilled arms.

"But these are different times, my lords and ladies," Jian-so said. "Illness has decimated our numbers. Isolation has left us friendless." Reyna saw him look toward Levi. "Nearly. I believe there is a way to honor our past and protect our future. Therefore, when my father takes his final journey, he will be guarded by the most powerful army ever created." They reached the bottom and walked into the main part of the tomb. A great cavernous space. Over the gasps, Jian-so finished: "Carved by our most gifted sculptors."

Reyna stood at the edge of an immense sunken pit and looked down. Rising from the pit was a replica of the palace, the steepest roof only twenty feet high. At the entrance to the palace, where elaborate doors had been left open, she could see the pedestal that would hold King Botan-so's coffin. A reflective pool surrounded the replica; beyond it were the most lifelike statues Reyna had ever seen.

Clay soldiers filled the pit. Hundreds of them. They stood in orderly rows, dressed in full battle gear: some with visors and helmets, others bareheaded. The men were armed with shields on their backs and lances in their grips. There were swords, axes, and clubs; every possible weapon was represented here. And not only men. A boy, no more than eight, held a strawlike object to his lips, preparing to shoot a poisoned dart directly up into the crowd. The craftsmanship was an extraordinary thing.

A nobleman stepped forward and looked into the pit. A woman clutched his arm, her expression both frightened and full of hope. The man asked Jian-so, "There will be no living sacrifices?" His voice shook.

"None," Jian-so confirmed. "This is my gift to you. To your wives, your children. Do not forget my generosity when the time comes." Jian-so looked over at his cousin, smiling faintly.

Ken-so, his son by his side, wore an unreadable expression. "Your father knows of this?"

"I told him before we left. I've never seen him so pleased."

The look on Ken-so's face shifted; it went beyond skepticism. "Where did these statues come from?"

Jian-so extended a hand toward Levi, who was also looking upon the soldiers with astonishment. "The clay came to us from our dear friends on Lunes," Jian-so said. "Their first shipment. The craftsmanship you see is from Miramar's finest sculptors."

"What sculptors?" Ken-so demanded. "Most of them are dead. How were these carved so quickly?"

Jian-so's expression hardened. "You think too little of our craftsmen, Ken-so. And bore our guests with your questions." He raised his voice, smiled once again. "You will want to look closer. Come!"

They followed him down the steps into the pit and spread about exploring. The mood was lively now that the Miranese realized they would not be suffocating and starving in the upcoming days. There were tears, and many crowded around

Jian-so, kissing his hand and looking eternally grateful. A few dropped to their knees and kissed his feet. Jian-so was gracious. He played the part of the beloved prince well.

Only Ken-so looked displeased. And mystified.

Reyna wandered off on her own, intrigued despite herself. Studying the detail, as fine as the statue she and Jaime had discovered in the storage vaults back home. The Miranese sculptors had been open-minded with their art, for the statues bore the stamp of other kingdoms and races. The men without helmets looked like Caffeesh and Bushidos and more than a few Pyrenees. No two were alike. The artists must have studied paintings in great detail. Unless, of course, they had been given special permission to leave the kingdom. These were the thoughts running through her mind as she turned down one aisle. And that was when she saw, among the clay soldiers, a familiar, beloved face. In the eighth row, four soldiers in, wearing no helmet.

Lord Elias.

His hand on the hilt of a sword and his expression trapped in a ferocious scowl.

TWENTY-THREE

WHO WAS TO SAY what Reyna would have done, with every drop of blood rushing to her head and her entire body trembling? Cried out? Or flung herself at the statue, trying desperately to understand what she was seeing? She might have done both these things, had not a hand clamped hard around her wrist and Ana-si hissed in her ear, "Do not look so, Reyna-si! He will see you. And you will join your friend here."

There were others nearby. Ana-si took her arm and forced her to move on. Somehow, Reyna pretended to be calm. She marveled with the rest of the cortege. She oohed and aahed and pointed, even as they passed men from the *Simona*, the *Amaris*, sprinkled among strangers. They walked by Ken-so, who stood with his arms folded, studying a Coronad warrior.

The others gradually drifted off. When they were far enough away, Reyna rounded on Ana-si. "What *is* this?"

"Do not stop." Ana-si drifted down another row, forcing Reyna to follow. "They are alive," Ana-si told her. "All of them."

"How is that possible?"

"They are stunned only," Ana-si explained. "Their hearts

still beat. The clay preserves them. It makes them look like statues. What Jian-so said is not true. He says it only to gain favor with his people. He knows his father requires living sacrifices. Anything less will not do."

Horror seeped through the shock. "Stunned only." Reyna wondered how she could have been so stupid. She had never set eyes upon Ana-si before coming to Miramar. But she had heard her. That voice. That strange, beautiful voice aboard the *Simona.* "*You* are the one who stunned them."

Ana-si looked at her, wary. "Yes."

"With your voice." It had turned men to mindless sheep. But not Reyna, not Gunnel. Ana-si had no power over women.

"Yes."

Reyna stayed where she was, though every part of her wanted to run away. "What are you?"

"Don't you know, Reyna-si?" she said softly.

The stories from her childhood came back to her. Sirens who lured sailors to their death with music. Or the other. *When a man vanishes so completely, it's said he's been carried off by the harpies.*

Reyna said, "A siren?"

A shoulder lifted. The answer could have been a yes or a no.

"A harpy?"

"These are the names you give us," Ana-si dismissed. "Foolish names. We are the same as you."

"We're nothing alike."

"No?" Delicate brows rose in a pale, tired face. "I am

someone far from home, who wishes only to return. What are you?"

Reyna no longer heard her. Because she had found Jaime. He too wore Miranese armor and clutched a plumed helmet beneath one arm. He stared directly ahead, his expression somber. Reyna stood on her tiptoes and looked into his eyes. Searching for some sign that what Ana-si said was true. That somewhere, deep inside, these men still lived. These men still breathed. She saw nothing. Only a statue, with the face of her friend.

"Jaime," she whispered.

"Do not look so!" This time the warning came with a vicious pinch on Reyna's arm.

Reyna flinched; she came back to herself in time to see Jian-so and Levi looking down at them from above. Immediately Reyna smiled, turned to Ana-si, and exclaimed, "Truly?" She pointed at Jaime's muscled arm and tittered behind her hand. Jian-so turned away, disinterested, but Levi watched her for a moment longer. His eyes skimmed over Jaime without recognition, before he followed his host.

"I will help-you, Reyna-si," her strange companion said. "But you must help me first."

Outside the tombs, Reyna readied her horse for the ride back to the palace. Levi stopped beside her.

"What's wrong?" His voice was pitched low. Unnecessary,

for no one would have heard him even if he had spoken in a normal tone. The conversation around them was loud and lively. The Miranese might have just come from visiting the spring carnival rather than a sacred tomb. Their lives had been spared. Their prayers answered. Reyna could not help thinking what an unflattering display this was for the king. "Besides me, I mean," Levi added. "Did something happen?"

"Levi." Reyna was staggered by the immensity of the task before her. The clay soldiers far outnumbered the men she knew to be missing. Not the officers and crew of four missing ships, but ten ships, or more. Where had these other men come from? How were she and Levi supposed to save them all? "Will you come to my chamber tonight? When everyone is asleep?"

Levi stared, and as Reyna watched, his ears turned the color of rubies. "Yes," he said.

Her face had to be as red as his. She saw where his imagination had led him. It was not as he thought. This was what Ana-si had told her to do. Ensure Levi was in her chamber with her, alone, before the witching hour. Everything would be explained then. But there was no time to tell him this. Jian-so headed their way.

Levi saw him too. "I'll be there," he said, and went to meet the prince.

Ana-si rode behind Jian-so. Reyna kept her eyes on her the entire way back to the palace. A siren? A harpy? Villains from her childhood tales. Reyna had stumbled into someone else's story. One that would not end well, not for anyone.

Once there was a cardinal, crushed beneath a boot.

The wait was excruciating, the sun's descent impossibly slow when one checked its progress as frequently as Reyna had. By dusk, she had developed a crick in her neck. At supper, she missed half of what was said at the royal table. Part of her record that evening was pure invention.

Ana-si had said the men were alive. Stunned only. Reyna did not see how that could be true. She had looked into Lord Elias's face, into Jaime's. There had been no signs of life. Lunesian clay had filmed their eyes, coated their nostrils. In Jaime's case, it had sealed his lips together. How did they see? How did they breathe?

When Reyna had told Blaise what had happened, her reaction had been a peculiar one. She had lowered herself onto a chair, slowly, and said nothing.

"What is it?" Reyna said. Blaise was rarely speechless.

"I've seen one of them before. A harpy."

"When?" Reyna, sitting cross-legged on Blaise's bed, was astounded. "*Where?*"

"Back home, a few days before I met you. Uncle Mori and I were walking on the beach. By the cove near your tower, and she was lying on the sand. It looked like a large bird had washed up."

"Was she alive?"

"Dead." Blaise grabbed a water goblet from her table and drank deeply. "Her face was human. And her hands and feet the same. But everything else was covered in black feathers. Most of them torn from her."

"Torn? How?"

"Some animal had found her before we did. You're saying Ana-si is like her?"

"She won't say what she is," Reyna told her. "What happened to the harpy? Did Master Mori bury her?"

"He wouldn't touch her." Blaise set the goblet on the table. "He fetched a torch and threw it on her. And he made sure every bit was turned to ash before we left."

Blaise painted a hideous image.

"You've never told me this before."

"I don't like to think about it," Blaise admitted. "It scared me. The captain is coming here tonight?"

"Yes." Reyna told her of her conversation with Levi, and his misunderstanding. Blaise smiled briefly.

"He's in for a shock. Reyna, promise me you'll be careful. Uncle Mori isn't easily frightened. I've never seen him so afraid of something, not before or since."

Reyna had promised. In her chamber, she paced the length of the room too many times to count. The moon rose in the night sky. She could see it through the slits in her louvered windows.

At last, there came a knock at the door. One knock only. Very soft.

Reyna opened the door. Torchlight on the walls showed Levi dressed informally in a loose white shirt and trousers. Samuel, Hamish, and Benjamin were with him. All three appeared scandalized. Not one could look her in the eye. Farther down the hall, a door opened. A woman poked her head out, and then back in just as quickly. Levi slipped into the chamber and shut the door behind him, leaving his companions outside.

"I couldn't get rid of them," he said, apology in his voice.

Reyna would have been mortified if she had not already been frantic. "It doesn't matter."

"No? Listen to me, Reyna, about yesterday —"

"It doesn't matt —"

"It does to me." He came closer, rested his forehead against hers, looked into her eyes as he spoke. "I don't mean to be this way. Turning into some kind of bear every time his name comes up. Jaime's. I feel like a lump. There are a thousand other things I should be thinking about. Asher, for one. No, let me finish," he said when she tried to interrupt. "All I can think of is that when this is over, you'll go back to del Mar, with him. And I'm not sure I can —"

His words were like the rapids of a river. Fast. Impossible to slow down. Partly to silence him, partly because she needed to, Reyna leaned closer and pressed her lips against his. Shock coursed through Levi; she felt it in the arms that pulled her close. Then shock became something else.

She was the first to speak, later. She stayed close in his arms because she needed him to *hear* her. "Listen to me, Levi. And remember, someone might be listening."

She told him all of it. From the moment she had come face-to-face with Lord Elias. Every word Ana-si had uttered, Reyna repeated. His arms around her had gone rigid. He said, "Asher?"

She cupped a hand to his cheek, shook her head. "I don't know what your brother looks like. I'm sorry."

A screen covered the wall behind Reyna's bed. Mountains and cherry blossoms had been painted onto the rice paper. It shifted, the sound causing Reyna and Levi to spring apart. Both reached for their daggers. Behind the screen was a hole, a tunnel, no more than three feet high. Ana-si's head emerged. She held up a lantern, and saw them standing in the middle of the chamber, gaping at her. She gestured impatiently. *Come!*

Reyna had frozen. The tunnel had been there all along. Right by her head! Levi said under his breath, "She's Jian-so's girl, Reyna. Are you sure this is a good idea?"

"I trust her." Instinct told her Ana-si meant her no harm. She scrambled across the bed, then paused when she reached Ana-si, who pointed to the passageway behind her. Reyna crawled past and found, after ten or so feet, that she was able to stand. She dusted the grit from her knees and palms. Levi and then Ana-si appeared. The light from the lantern showed them to be at a juncture that led in eight directions, like the wind points on a compass.

Levi would have spoken, but Ana-si shook her head. Cupping a hand to her ear, she mouthed one word: *Listen.*

Somewhere down a tunnel came the sound of a man snoring. These secret passageways led to a great number of bedchambers. Reyna and Levi followed Ana-si through dark, twisting passages. Up a set of stairs and down others. A route so confusing Reyna knew they would not be able to find their way back without Ana-si's help.

As for Levi, he did not miss the way Ana-si carried herself. Carefully, slowing once or twice to press a hand to her chest and breathe deeply. He turned to Reyna, a question in his eyes, but she could not tell him what she did not know. Finally, he stopped.

Ana-si glanced back, annoyed. "Come."

"You're hurt," Levi spoke quietly. "We should rest. Or I can carry you."

Ana-si turned around fully. Her entire frame had stiffened. "No."

Reyna said, "It's getting worse. I can see it. Let him help you."

"Take my dagger." Levi invited. "If I do anything you don't like, you can stick me with it. I won't hurt you, Ana-si."

Reyna thought Ana-si would accept — there was a moment when she wavered. But she merely turned and continued on without answering. Levi's expression remained troubled.

They descended another set of stairs. The air grew warmer, constricting. And once, when Reyna braced a hand against the rough stone wall, her palm came away wet. Not long after, she discovered why.

When they finally emerged from the tunnel, slipping around a jagged crack in the wall, they found themselves by an underground river. A narrow waterway with closed-in walls that glinted and sparkled from some unrecognizable stone. A small boat had been tied to a stake.

By now, Levi's patience had worn thin. He was not accustomed to following blindly. "Where are you taking us?"

Ana-si pointed down the river. "Back to the tombs. Don't speak."

Reyna could almost hear his teeth grind. After they climbed into the boat, he untied the rope from its mooring post, took up the only oar, and pushed off.

Reyna was not fond of caves. Caves usually meant bats. Fortunately, the lantern did not reveal any nocturnal creatures hanging above their heads. At one point, the ceiling dropped so low they were forced to hunch over, hugging their knees tight to their chests, or risk impalement by jagged rocks. Ana-si extinguished the lantern as they emerged from the cave. The royal tombs were ahead. Reyna could see a pair of guards at the top of the steps. Behind them on the wall, two torches blazed.

Reyna and Levi dragged the boat onto the bank and hid it behind a large shrub. They crept toward the steps, Ana-si leading the way. One of the soldiers yawned widely, which provoked the other into yawning as well.

Ana-si's smile was strange and unsettling. She whispered to Levi, "Do not listen."

Levi's eyes grew round. He clapped his hands over his ears just as Ana-si turned around and began to sing. Her voice drifted up the many steps. A strangled noise from Levi. Horrified, Reyna saw that covering his ears was not enough. His eyes had glazed over. He sank to his knees. She dropped in front of him and clamped her own hands over his, pressing inward to further hinder the sound. Blue eyes focused on hers; his pupils returned to normal. They were so close her nose brushed his and their breath became one in the darkness.

The Miranese soldiers did not have a chance. They pitched forward. Two thuds followed.

The singing stopped. Ana-si cast a disinterested glance at Levi. She no longer whispered. "We go."

"Are you all right?" Reyna asked Levi.

"I don't know." Levi stared after Ana-si. But he did not protest when Reyna grabbed his hand and dragged him up the steps.

"What will happen to them?" Reyna asked as they passed the guards sprawled face-down on the stone.

Ana-si pulled one of the torches off the wall. "They will wake later. Hopefully after we have gone."

They went through the doors and down more steps. The sunken pit was as Reyna remembered. Here the torches had not been snuffed. They burned as bright as before.

Levi said, "Where is my brother?"

"I do not know your brother," Ana-si said, frowning. "What are you saying? Jian-so admires you. He leaves your ships alone."

Levi glared at her. "Asher was on a Caffeesh messenger, not a Lunesian ship. It disappeared a month ago."

Ana-si's expression cleared. "I remember." She looked over the men, shrugged. "He is here. Somewhere. There is no order to it."

Aggravated, Levi spun around and went in search of Asher. Reyna could not help him. Feeling useless, she left Ana-si and made her way to Lord Elias's statue. She sat by his boots, arms around her knees, and thought of Mercedes, home on del Mar.

Much later, Levi's muffled cry had her leaping to her feet and running through the maze of stone men. She found him gripping a statue by its shoulders.

The resemblance was there, though Prince Asher looked much more like his sister, Queen Vashti. He wore full battle armor, his visor raised; otherwise Levi would not have been able to see his face.

Ana-si drifted over. "I can help you," she said to Levi. "I can help both of you."

"But we must help you first," Levi said coldly. "That is what you told Reyna."

"Yes," Ana-si said.

"How?" Reyna asked.

Ana-si sat cross-legged on the dirt floor, and after a moment Reyna joined her. Ana-si said to Levi, "I will tell you. But do not hold him so. They are fragile."

Levi snatched his hands from his brother. He crouched beside Reyna, his body turned so that Asher remained in his sight.

Ana-si folded her hands. "I have a sister named Mei. She is only eight. We lived on an island that is no longer our home. It is just the two of us now. Everyone else has gone."

"You're the last of your people?" Reyna asked.

"There are others, we believe. We hope it is so. We have heard whispers of them, far away. Mei and I went to search for them, but we were captured by Jian-so. He took my sister and hid her from me. He said that as long as I helped him, he would not hurt her. He would give her food. He would make sure she is not cold. She is small, you see. But he would only do these things if I listened."

Ana-si spoke softly, without inflection, her eyes on her folded hands. "I sing to the ships and the men come. Jian-so makes them wear the Miranese armor. He leaves them in vats full of clay so they look like statues, not real men."

"*Why?*" Levi asked.

"So many died during the last sickness. They do not have enough to sacrifice. The Miranese do not want to anymore. There has been unhappiness. There have been threats."

"Against the royal family?" Reyna asked.

"Yes. That is why Jian-so promises no more sacrifices. He will use statues instead. It will be good symbolism. The people are happy. They will stand by him when he kills his cousin and takes back the throne."

Reyna exchanged a look with Levi. She said, "But his father wants living sacrifices."

"The king *needs* them," Ana-si said. "If the sacrifices are not real men, there will be no one to protect him in his second life."

"Is that true?" Reyna asked.

Ana-si lifted a shoulder. "It is what he believes."

"Do the Miranese believe it?" This from Levi.

Another shrug. "I do not speak to the people. They are like every living thing, I think. They want to live. But they will not be pleased to know others are kidnapped in their place. It would cause difficulty."

"How did Jian-so even imagine this could be done?" Levi asked. "Why clay? Why *my* clay?"

Ana-si hesitated. "I do not know this for certain. Jian-so keeps a book. A history. It has been done before, I think. There is something in the Lunesian clay that preserves them, makes it so they do not need to eat or drink. It is the thinnest layer of clay, but it is powerful. Their hearts still beat; there is no need for breath. When they wake, it is a simple, delicate shell to break free from. But if left too long, the clay will become part of the man. They will become real statues."

Reyna turned to Levi. "Have you ever heard of this before?"

Levi had gone pale. "It's just a story."

For the first time, Ana-si smiled. "Am I a story too, Prince Levi?"

Reyna looked at him, and waited.

Levi said, "Our clay comes from the quarries outside Selene.

Sometimes, during the worst storms, the quarries flood over. They become rivers of mud, torrents. Villagers disappeared, and it was thought they had drowned, been carried away by the floodwaters." He stopped, looked around at the silent, staring men. "But sometimes, the villagers came back."

Reyna rubbed at her chilled arms. "From where?"

"They all told the same story. They had woken up by the river, picked themselves up, and walked home. Once, a man went home and found that fifty years had passed. His wife was dead and gone. But some of the older villagers recognized him."

"What happened to him?" Reyna said.

"The villagers were afraid of him," Levi said. "His grand-daughter lived in his home, but she would not take him in. I think he went mad. Ended up being cared for by the nuns."

Suddenly Reyna clapped a hand over her mouth. She pictured Jaime strolling from the storage vaults, a clay head tucked under his arm.

Levi said, "What is it?"

Reyna had to take several breaths to keep the nausea at bay. "Jaime and I found a statue back home. A clay statue, like these. It fell over and broke. The inside was full of ash."

Levi winced. "That was an old statue," Ana-si said.

Reyna shied away from the memory. There was something else she needed to know. "Where are the women?" At Ana-si's blank look, she added, "The ones you capture. They're not here. Where do you put them?"

"Jian-so captures no women."

"There was one, Ana!" Reyna came to her knees. "Her name is Gunnel. On the *Simona*. A del Marian ship."

Ana-si stared at her. Comprehension dawned. "That was you."

It was not a question, and Reyna did not answer.

Ana-si said, "Jian-so was angry when you escaped. And he did not like the tall woman. She spat in his face."

Dread swept over Reyna. She could picture Gunnel doing such a thing. "What happened to her?"

Ana-si was quiet.

"Please," Reyna said.

"He made her go into the water."

Reyna dropped her head in her hands. Gunnel had never learned how to swim. Reyna could not even grieve properly for Gunnel. Not yet. There would be a time for mourning later, when other lives did not hang in the balance. A hand came to rest on the back of her neck, warm and comforting. Levi.

Ana-si said, "We must leave soon."

Reyna lifted her head as Levi asked, "You can wake all of them?"

Ana-si nodded. "It is just another song. Simple."

Levi gestured to his brother. "Then do it. Please."

But Ana-si shook her head, resolute. "You will find Mei first."

"No, you'll —"

Reyna touched Levi's arm in warning. They must tread carefully here. She did not want him turned into a statue too. "Of course we'll help you find your sister," she said.

Ana-si had been holding her breath. She exhaled now, long and shaky. She was as much a prisoner as these clay soldiers. All alone in a hostile kingdom, separated from her only family. Threatened, scared. At least Reyna had Levi and Blaise and the crew. Ana-si had no one.

"Do you know anything that could help us?" Reyna asked.

"Where they might be keeping her?" Levi added, more subdued. Perhaps realizing how similar their troubles were. Her sister. His brother.

"Jian-so brings her to my chamber every month," Ana-si said. "If I do not make him angry. She is somewhere in the palace, but I do not know for sure. We are never left alone and cannot speak freely. Her guards, they are all women. Old and young. They are different every time."

Silence fell as Reyna and Levi absorbed this.

Ana-si said, "We must go."

"She's right." Levi stood. "We need to think how to do this first. Find the girl, wake the men. Escape. What will they be like afterward?" he asked Ana-si. "Can they fight?"

Ana-si said, "It will be as if they woke from a normal sleep. But the clay . . . they will be clumsy."

The pool surrounding the burial chamber lay undisturbed. The water had come from the mountains. "They'll need to wash," Reyna said. "Their weapons, too."

Levi went to his brother, then looked back at Ana-si. "Just another song, you said. Simple."

"Yes."

"Show me," Levi said.

Ana-si rose. She shook her head.

"One man only," Levi insisted. "As a show of good faith. And I promise you I will find your sister."

Ana-si's fists were clenched. She spoke, not to Levi, but to Reyna. "One man. Your Jaime."

Levi looked furious and . . . stung. Reyna could not risk Ana-si changing her mind. She ran, and was the first to reach Jaime.

"Stand there," Ana-si said.

Reyna moved aside. Levi hung back. Using a fingernail, Ana-si tapped around Jaime's eye sockets until the clay cracked and crumbled away. She did the same with his ears, then stood on her tiptoes and brought her face close to his. Her voice was soft, the song for him only.

Jaime blinked. One moment his eyes were blank and the next they were his own, staring down at Ana-si with a bemused expression.

"Hello there," he said, and smiled. Or tried to. "What . . ." He looked past her, to Levi rooted in place, to Reyna with both hands clamped over her mouth. A puzzled frown. "Reyna, love. What —"

A whisper from Ana-si, and Jaime was gone, locked inside his clay prison once again.

Ana-si turned to them, her expression apologetic but determined.

"My sister first."

TWENTY-FOUR

WHY WOULD SHE HELP US?" Levi said.

They were back in Reyna's chamber. Once Ana-si had led them through the tunnels, she had not lingered. They sat on the floor in the middle of the room, as far away from the walls as they could get.

"What do you mean?" Reyna said. They spoke in whispers, heads close together.

"We find Mei, reunite her with her sister, and then what? Why would Ana-si help us? If I were her, I would disappear. I would just go."

"She gave us her word."

"She's not human, Reyna." Her hair was loose about her shoulders. He reached for a strand, twined it absently between his fingers. "Or not entirely. I still don't understand what she is. But Jian-so, who *is* like us, has done her nothing but harm. Why would she keep that promise?"

A fair question. But. "She loves her sister."

"Yes."

"As much as you love Asher. She understands family."

Reyna pressed her fingers to his lips when he would have spoken. His lips were warm against her skin. It was an effort to remember what they were discussing. "How can we say she doesn't understand other things, like keeping her word? We're more alike than we're different. I believe her." She dropped her hand. "Besides, what choice do we have?"

Levi's expression was troubled. "I hope that's true. Because one pretty song from her and we're helpless. Everyone except you and Blaise."

At that, Reyna looked around the chamber. The candles here were not made of tallow, a stinking, smoking substance that filled the lungs with smoke and the eyes with tears. These candles were the color of honeyed cream. Their light burned bright, accompanied by the pleasing aroma of pure beeswax.

"What are you doing?" Levi asked when she rose and went to stand in front of two lit tapers. She beckoned him over.

With Levi watching, Reyna blew a candle out and broke it into many little pieces. She held one near the remaining flame, far enough away not to burn her fingers. The wax softened; once it did, she rolled it between her palms to form a ball. Not too big, not too little. Roughly the size of a marble. She set it on the table and did the same with the second piece, then blew on them until they cooled. "Here. Come closer."

Levi lowered his head toward hers. Reyna pressed a ball into each of his ears. "Can you hear what I'm saying?" She spoke in a normal tone, neither whispering nor shouting. Levi's gaze dropped to her lips, saw them move. His brows drew together in a small frown before his eyes met hers, his question clear: *What are you saying?*

Good. Carefully she removed the plugs. They had molded to the unique shape of his ears. These were more efficient than the wax plugs one could buy at the markets. Because they had been made to fit his ears specifically, they would be better able to keep out sound. Any sound. From anyone. She hoped. She offered them to him.

"You're brilliant." Levi took her hand, kissed her knuckles, and she smiled.

"They're still a little soft," she warned. "Keep them with you always, Levi, and the *instant* you hear —"

"I'll be careful." Levi glanced at the door. "Can you make more?"

"Yes."

He let Samuel, Hamish, and Benjamin into the chamber. They shuffled in, red-faced and avoided looking at the bed at all costs. Then they saw Reyna standing by a candle, fully dressed and rolling balls of wax between her palms. Their embarrassment turned to confusion. Levi explained all that had occurred while they had stood guard outside.

"What did you think we were doing?" Reyna could not help asking Samuel.

"Ah . . . uh . . ."

"Hmm." Reyna pressed the wax into his ears.

The three newcomers looked sheepish, Levi amused. They left soon after. Reyna eyed the screen behind her bed. Five seconds later, she crept down the hall to Blaise's room. If she was to be murdered in her sleep, at least she would not be alone.

Reyna could not say what woke her. Not Blaise, who slept quietly beside her, one arm flung over her eyes. Reyna only saw the faintest outline of her friend. There were no candles, just moonbeams through the windows. She held herself still beneath the blanket and listened to the sounds of the night.

Crickets chirped beyond the walls. Sleepy footsteps padded by outside the door. Across the chamber, a voice spoke softly.

"Please help me."

"Ana?" Reyna bolted upright. She shook Blaise's shoulder hard enough she nearly fell off the mattress.

Blaise mumbled, "What? *What?*"

Reyna batted aside the netting. She fumbled around until she felt the candle on the table. Within moments the chamber was bathed in a soft light. Ana-si crouched by the door, her arms wrapped around her knees. Her face bathed in sweat.

Blaise, beyond vexed, had started to drag a pillow over her face before catching sight of their visitor. She froze. An instant later, she was by Ana-si's side. "Help me move her. Careful, Reyna."

They lifted Ana-si beneath each arm and walked her to the bed. They sat her down and knelt before her. Unlike Ana-si, still in the dress she had worn to the tombs, they wore long white nightgowns, ruffled at cuff and collar.

"Where does it hurt?" Blaise asked.

Ana-si's head had drooped. She lifted it long enough to say, "Where does it not?"

Blaise was quiet. "We need to remove your dress. All right?"

Ana-si nodded.

"Good. Reyna, another candle."

Reyna lit a second taper, then helped Blaise undress Ana-si. She thought she had braced herself for what she was about to see. Nothing could have prepared her.

Ana-si had a woman's body. On it, innumerable red bumps covered her skin from shoulder to hip. As if every pore were inflamed. Reyna knelt with the candle and wondered that her hand could remain so steady.

"What happened?" Blaise said quietly.

"When I first arrived here," Ana-si said, "after they took my sister, there was a man. A doctor. Jian-so told him he wanted my feathers pulled and my wings . . . cut. He said the same would happen to Mei if I did not do as he asked."

Reyna looked around to Ana-si's back, where, in addition to the red holes, she saw a long, hideous scar in the shape of a V. The candleholder shook in her grasp.

Feathers plucked. Wings cut. "Will they grow back?" Reyna said.

"No." Ana-si closed her eyes briefly. "Never."

Blaise, paler than she had been a minute ago, took Ana-si's hands, spreading her arms to better see the damage Jian-so and his doctor had caused. "Do you scratch these?"

"Yes."

"Do they appear to heal somewhat before you scratch?"

"Yes."

Blaise looked at Reyna. "Sound familiar?"

Reyna touched the scar on her own chin. "She needs aloe."

"Plenty of it, among other things. I don't have close to enough."

"There are aloe plants in the courtyard," Ana-si said.

"Are there?" Blaise turned to Reyna, who was already on her feet.

"How much do I need?" Reyna asked.

Blaise said, "As much as you can carry. Don't get caught."

Reyna left the candle by the bedside and grabbed Blaise's cloak before slipping from the chamber. A single torch on a wall lit the corridor. Reyna would not have to stumble blindly in the dark. She did not rush. Hurried footsteps would provoke curiosity if someone happened to be awake in their bed. In the courtyard, beneath a full moon, she searched for the aloe, eventually discovering two large pots in a corner. She spread Blaise's cloak on the grass and, using the dagger Mercedes had given her, began slicing off the leaves above the root. She tossed the leaves onto the cloak.

"What are you doing?"

Reyna bit back a scream and spun, dagger in hand. It was Tori-si. Blaise's patient. A bandage lay flat against her neck where her boil had once grown unchecked. Seeing Reyna's dagger, she stepped back, eyes fearful.

Reyna lowered her dagger. She stammered, "It's for Blaise."

Tori-si looked down at the small mountain of aloe leaves. "Only her?"

Reyna could not think of a lie that would help her. "And the prince's companion. Ana-si."

Tori-si was quiet. She pointed to the opposite end of the courtyard. "There's more over there. Come on."

One found help in the most unexpected places. They dragged the cloak across the courtyard.

"What are you doing out here?" Reyna asked.

"I was returning from the privy when I saw you. We must be quiet. There could be others."

While Reyna cut the leaves from one pot, Tori-si sped the task by snapping off the leaves from another. After they had decimated every aloe plant in sight, Tori-si gathered the edges of the cloak together and handed the sizable bundle to Reyna.

Reyna thanked her, and Tori-si said, "She must not be in Blaise's chamber after dawn. Otherwise, it will not be good for your prince. There are eyes everywhere."

"I understand."

Tori-si's chamber was down a different corridor. They went their separate ways.

Blaise made quick work of mixing the aloe with additional medicines from her box. Reyna held Ana-si's hand as Blaise applied a thick coating of salve across the girl's torso, back, and arms. Ana-si could not lie down; she had to remain upright so as not to smear the ointment. When Blaise was done, she wrapped Ana-si in winding strips of linen.

Reyna went to the window and peered out. Dawn was not far off. "I'll walk her back to her chamber. Others will be waking soon."

Blaise protested, but Ana-si said, "She is not wrong. I will go myself. I am better."

Reyna and Blaise helped her dress. It did look as if the salve had worked wonders. Ana-si's movements remained slow, but the pain in her eyes had lessened. She said, simply, "Thank you," and was startled when Blaise kissed her, once on each cheek, and said, "I am very sorry you were hurt."

When Reyna told the men what had happened to Ana-si, she was met with a full ten seconds of silence. They were in Levi's courtyard, where a table had been set up for their breakfast. Four Miranese servants stood patiently at one end of the courtyard, waiting to be summoned.

Samuel was the first to speak. "We used to pluck the chickens back home when we were boys. It was our job. We lived on a farm." He looked spooked.

"They weren't still living when we plucked them," Hamish said, a touch defensive. "We wrung their necks first. And they were just *chickens*, Brother."

"How do you know they were just chickens?" Samuel demanded.

Blaise pushed her food around her plate without appetite.

"They won't grow back?" Levi was dressed all in brown with

a short green cloak. He would be leaving soon to spend the day hunting with Jian-so. Benjamin had spread Levi's arrows along the far end of the table, inspecting each one before the hunt. The arrows lay forgotten as he listened to Ana-si's story.

"She says not." Reyna's own plate lay before her, untouched. "If you could have seen her face. She spoke of finding another group like theirs. I'm not sure they'll accept her the way she is. I have never ever in my life seen anything so cruel."

Levi took one of the arrows and inspected its point. "We have to find her sister. The question is how?"

"All we know is that she might be in the palace and that she's guarded by females, though we don't know whom."

"That's not much," Samuel said.

"No," Reyna agreed. "But Blaise and I can start there, in the women's quarters."

Levi was thoughtful. "Then you'll stay behind today. Two women aren't going to be missed on a hunting trip."

Blaise finally spoke. "Reyna will be missed," she said. "She's your scribe. Even if she weren't, you've seen the way he looks at her. He'll wonder."

"Let him." Levi's expression turned flat. "Let him wonder. Let him ask." He tossed the arrow back onto the table. "I'll think of something. You two stay here. Find Mei. I'll keep his attention off the both of you."

TWENTY-FIVE

FIND MEI. Words easier said than done. Over the next few days, Reyna scurried about the grounds with her notebook, befriending the women of the palace by drawing their portraits, writing down their songs, and playing with their babies. Her efforts to learn Miranese made them laugh. Not only the females in her living quarters, but noblewomen as well, who found her foreignness intriguing. They grew used to seeing her; they spoke comfortably in her presence. To no avail. If there was a child named Mei anywhere in the palace, no one mentioned her to Reyna.

But what she noticed was this: There was a girl who dined in the great hall who had peculiar habits. Around twelve years old, the same servant who had replaced Jian-so's broken knife at supper that first night. She always dined alone; she spoke to no one and, as far as Reyna could tell, no one spoke to her. The girl ate her meal quickly, one arm curved around her plate in a way that had Reyna wondering if she was part of a large family. Whenever Reyna visited Blaise in Montserrat, she noticed her friend eating the same way. Fast, arm guarding her food from grasping, grabbing siblings. Before the girl left the hall, she always filled a second plate and took it with her.

"Who is the girl?" Reyna asked her dining companion.

Poma-si looked around. She had a red dot painted on her lip. "Hama-si? She is no one. A maid. An orphan."

Blaise, kneeling across from Reyna, paused in her chewing, expression carefully blank. Reyna bristled at Poma-si's words and tried not to show it. Was the girl a no one because she was a lowly maid or because she was an orphan? Or both? Indignation filled her on behalf of all orphans everywhere.

Tori-si was kneeling beside Blaise. The bandage on her neck was smaller today. She eyed Reyna curiously. "Why do you ask?"

"I only wondered. No one talks to her."

"They're not being unkind," Tori-si said. "The girl does not speak."

That interested Blaise, who turned to look. "Never?"

"Only a few years," Tori-si said. "Since the sickness took her family. Her parents and eight brothers and sisters. Hama-si was the youngest."

Poma-si said, "Her father was the head gardener, but now . . . Prince Jian-so has been kind to her. He kept her in the palace and did not leave her to the streets. He is generous, our prince."

"Very," Reyna agreed absently. She watched Hama-si fill the second plate and paid attention to what she put on it. Chicken but no boar's head. Strawberries but no eggplant. No vegetables whatsoever from what she could see. Three puffs full of cream. The sort of meal that would have delighted Reyna as a child.

When Hama-si left the hall, Reyna and Blaise followed her.

They stayed well behind, not wanting to scare the girl but not wanting to lose her either. It was a good thing they wore their soft slippers. Boots would have given them away. Hama-si had not looked back once.

Around corners they went, past giant, roaming tortoises, through courtyards that grew smaller and less busy the farther they withdrew from the central confines of the palace. Here the air was not so sweet. Reyna raised an arm, pressed her nose into the crook of her elbow. Blaise wrinkled her own nose and whispered, "*Blech*. There must be a cesspit nearby. Or a bog."

Reyna found she had to breathe through her mouth. "Why would she bring food here?"

Blaise had no answers. Hami-si turned a corner and disappeared. Reyna sped up, leaving her friend a few paces behind. She swung right . . . and stepped ankle deep into a cloying, congealing pool, its contents unspeakable.

"Oh, that is *foul*," Blaise said from behind her. Reyna groaned.

The cesspit spread out before them in a large, lumpy pool that guttered downward into a tunnel. The dying sun aimed its rays on the flies that hovered above the pit in a great teeming mass. Reyna had been too hasty, rounding the corner and plowing past the gate that would normally have been closed, keeping all but the gong farmer, the sewage master, at a safe distance.

Reyna glanced over her shoulder. Blaise looked away quickly, lips trembling. Yes, very funny. *Her* slippers were safe. As for Hama-si, she was nowhere in sight. But on the opposite side of a wall came the sound of footsteps in rapid retreat, and the high, tinkling sound of laughter.

"You're smiling," Reyna said.

"No," Levi said, smiling. "I'm sorry about your shoes."

It was the following morning. They walked along a tiered garden, shallow steps ripe with staked tomatoes and bushy herbs. The gardens had been extensive once. Now, only half the plots were used. Benjamin and Samuel waited at the top, along with two burly Miranese guards.

"It's a good thing I packed an extra pair." She kicked at some pebbles. "Smart girl. I could have sworn she hadn't seen us."

Levi walked with his hands clasped behind his back. "I've seen her with Jian-so, many times. You think she knows where Mei is?"

"I'm not sure of anything. But I've noticed . . ." Feeling foolish, she told him about the second plate Hama-si always made up before leaving the hall. "Yesterday, she didn't bother with the vegetables or the boar's head." She glanced at him. "Did you like boar's head when you were a boy?"

"I still don't like it."

"Neither do I," she admitted. "And the other day, she left out the peas and onions. It was just ham and cake. So much cake."

Levi turned her words over in his mind. "She's guarding Mei, but she feels sorry for her. The sweets are a kindness."

"It's thin, isn't it? It sounds ridiculous." And it was all she had. They were doomed.

"Oh I don't know. I think it sounds like a hunch," Levi said with a smile. "I know someone who swears by them." Whatever else he would have said was interrupted by a sharp whistle piercing the air. Jian-so stood at the top of the terrace, hand raised in greeting. He beckoned. Ana-si was with him.

Reyna said, "Did he just whistle at you?"

"He can whistle all he wants." Levi waved to say he understood, smiled. "He's a means to an end, that's all. Still, I'm going to be glad to leave this place."

They retraced their steps.

"Where are you going today?" Reyna asked.

"Back to the ship. The clay still needs to be unloaded and sent to the tomb. I said I'd see to it, but Jian-so wanted to join me. You'll have to come with us after today. Otherwise, it will start to look odd." The men had gone on hunts these last two days. Levi had merely explained that Lunesian women were not allowed to attend them. Samuel had taken over her duties on these outings.

Blaise would be on the *Truthsayer*. Seth had burned his

hand at the cookstove, and she had left early this morning, not trusting anyone else to treat him. Hamish and Benjamin had accompanied her.

Frustration seeped into Levi's voice. "I'd rather stay here, Reyna. Help you search. Botan-so won't last much longer. Days maybe."

If that. But what did Botan-so have to do with them? "What is it?"

Jian-so, impatient with the wait, descended the steps toward them.

Levi said, "The Miranese don't hold wakes. Not like we do. Their dead must be buried the same day."

Reyna stopped. "But if they seal the tomb . . ."

"It can't be opened again," he finished. Their eyes met, Reyna's stomach churned with renewed panic. "I'll see what else I can learn," Levi added. "You'll be careful?" He reached up to touch her face, then dropped his hand, remembering who was watching.

"I will."

Reyna was determined not to lose Hama-si today. She needed to find out who the girl was feeding.

Reyna went about it differently this time. Instead of following Hama-si after the midday meal, she skipped the meal altogether. She retraced her steps from the day before until she came to a smaller hall with a staircase tucked into a corner. No one was about. Reyna climbed halfway up, then sat in the shadows and waited.

It felt like forever. Several people passed through. An old woman carrying a basket full of clothing. A bald man with a falcon on his shoulder. Reyna glanced over the banister each time before sinking back in disappointment.

Just when she had started to nod off, she heard footsteps. Light and quick and lively. Hama-si. Reyna followed; she kept farther back than she had the day before. At an open gate, the girl did not turn right, toward the cesspit. She kept straight on a path that led to the palace's outer walls. Stone covered in trailing ivy. Hama-si nudged aside the vines with a shoulder and disappeared from view.

Moments later, Reyna peeked through the vines to see Hama-si entering a house at the edge of the woods. It stood at least a hundred feet away. White stone and a black slanting roof, strawberry plants wilting in boxes at the windows. From its remote location, she thought it might have been built for a palace woodcutter or gamekeeper.

No conveniently planted trees offered cover. Anyone who glanced out the window would see her approach. And then where would she be? Best not to think about it. Holding her breath, she dashed to the side of the house. No one yelled, no one charged. She tiptoed back and peered around. The first thing she saw was Hama-si scowling at her; the second, a spiked club swinging toward her face. Reyna ducked, heard the lethal whisper of wood and metal above her head. A loud crack sounded . . . but it was Hama-si who slumped to the ground, her eyes closed.

Standing behind Hama-si was an even younger girl. No more than eight or nine. She wore a shift that reached to her knees. Her feet were bare. Dark hair lay tangled around her shoulders, and her eyes were big and frightened. Clutched in both hands was the stone pitcher she had used on Hama-si's head.

Slowly, Reyna rose. The girl's hands tightened on the pitcher.

"Mei?" Reyna said, her voice a little strained. Small wings peeked above Mei's shift. Three inches above her shoulders, feathered in red.

The only answer was a flicker of awareness in the girl's eyes.

"Mei, my name is Reyna. Ana sent me."

The pitcher lowered. "Ana?"

Reyna managed a smile. "Your sister will be so pleased to see you. She's been very worried."

"Where is she?" The pitcher tumbled to the ground. Tears fell from Mei's eyes. "She said she would come. I thought you were her."

"I'm here to bring you to her." Hama-si remained unconscious, but Reyna could see the rise and fall of her chest. Relief filled her. Still alive, then. "Ana said you had guards. Women. Is that true?"

"They are different some days," Mei said. "Today is

Hama-si and the other. She went to the well to fetch water." Mei pointed toward the deeper woods. "She'll be back soon."

That galvanized Reyna. She grabbed Hama-si's arms. "Then we must hurry. Take her legs."

Together, they carried Hama-si inside. The house had one chamber, separated into different areas: a bed, a kitchen with a table and two chairs. A tall ladder led up to a sleeping loft. Reyna took care when lowering Hama-si's arms and head. Mei dropped the girl's legs, and they hit the floor with a thump. Reyna ran outside and fetched the club and the pitcher. Leaving them inside the door, she said, "Where are your clothes . . . ?" She trailed off in dismay.

Mei was at the table, devouring the food Hama-si had left there. She ate like she had not eaten in days, shoveling food into her mouth with her hands, barely taking the time to chew.

Quietly, Reyna approached. Beside Mei was a cup half full of water. "Mei."

When Mei looked up, Reyna offered the cup. "Not too fast or you'll be ill. Drink this."

"You said hurry." But Mei took the cup.

"We have a little time." A horrible suspicion filled Reyna. She looked at the girl's arms. Painfully thin, like twigs. "Don't they feed you?"

"Sometimes." The girl set the empty cup on the table and eyed the plate with longing. "Hama-si brings food and eats while I watch. It makes them laugh when I ask for a little bit."

Careful to keep the anger from her voice, Reyna pulled out a chair. "Sit. We won't leave until you're done."

Mei first, Ana had said.

When the girl began to eat, more slowly this time, Reyna freed her dagger from its ankle strap and went to stand by the door.

Eventually, the guard returned from the well. She was whistling. Reyna listened to her, rigid with wrath. What sort of person starved a child, kept her prisoner, and still felt like whistling?

Mei heard it too. She jumped to her feet, terror in her eyes. Reyna held up a hand. *It will be fine. Stay there.* Mei nodded, trusting in a stranger even after all she had been through. When the door opened and a woman — older, stern-faced — stepped in, Reyna was not gentle. She smashed the hilt of her dagger directly between the guard's eyes. Just as Mercedes had taught her. The guard collapsed onto Hama-si with a grunt. The bucket she had been carrying overturned, spilling water everywhere.

Reyna returned the dagger to its sheath. "Where are your clothes?"

Mei had one dress, one cloak, and one pair of shoes. She was only allowed to wear them once a month, on the day she saw her sister. The rest of the time she wore her shift and went hungry. The cloak was not for cold, but to disguise her wings. They appeared undamaged, though they were, like the rest of Mei, in need of a wash.

Reyna helped her into her clothes and braided her hair quickly.

"We're going to see Ana?"

"We are," Reyna promised. "First I need to find a safe place for you."

"Which safe place?"

"My ship."

This was not the original plan. She and Levi had discussed this. Reyna was only supposed to learn where Mei was being kept and *then* they would decide how best to rescue her. The plan must change. Mei needed help now. Reyna would hide her on the *Truthsayer*, find Ana and Levi, wake the men, and escape. Somehow. The details of how all this was to be accomplished were a little hazy. Levi would help.

They stepped over the unconscious guard and Hama-si. When Mei stepped on Hama-si's hand, Reyna ignored it. But when the girl picked up the spiked club, Reyna took it from her.

"You're not like them." Reyna tossed the club aside. She took Mei's hand in hers and they ran.

TWENTY-SIX

THEIR LUCK FALTERED at the main gates. By some miracle they had managed to skirt the palace grounds without being stopped. A light rain, warm and pleasant, fell from the sky. Mei and Reyna were able to conceal their faces with hoods without looking suspicious.

Reyna had thought the gates the best possible route for escape. Enough people coming and going that they could simply sidle up to a group departing and pretend they were traveling with them. They kept their hoods up and their gazes straight. They walked with a purpose, Mei's hand in Reyna's.

"Stop."

The guard clearly recognized Reyna as a member of the Lunesian cortege, because he relayed the order in Caffeesh. She tightened her grip on Mei, whispered, "Keep walking," and pretended not to hear.

"You there! Stop!" This time there was the unmistakable sound of swords sliding from their scabbards. Reyna looked at the guards: two large men scowling their way. Everyone else had frozen in place. A bearded man on a cart. Three older men on foot, wearing straw hats.

"Where are you going?" the guard demanded.

"To the harbor," Reyna answered. "I have a message for my prince."

The guard turned to Mei, still hooded, pressed against Reyna's side. "Who is this?"

"My apprentice." An answer she instantly wished back. One did not hold an apprentice's hand, as she did. She should have said sister. No, that would not have done either. She should have said —

"Take off her hood," the guard ordered.

"My message is urgent. My prince will be angry —"

His sword twitched. "Now."

Mei's hand slipped from hers. From beneath her hood came a song, light and sweet and sad-sounding. A different melody from Ana's. Though Reyna could not understand the words, their effect was immediate. The guard had started toward them. He stopped in his tracks, eyes rounding, sword falling to the ground. He burst into tears. The first one to do so but not the last. As Reyna stood rooted in place, the second guard, the man on the cart, the three travelers wept, their expressions filled with sorrow and grief. One man dropped to his knees and pulled at his hair. Reyna and Mei had been lucky after all. No other female was present.

Reyna's hand trembled only slightly as Mei's hand slipped

back into hers. "Good girl," she said. They walked on and did not look back.

They stayed on the main road, the one that led directly to the harbor. She had considered using a side road, but Miramar was unfamiliar to her, and she did not want to risk becoming lost. Three women on mules rode ahead, too huddled against the damp to notice the foreigners in their midst. Reyna pulled her hood lower and did her best to look uninteresting.

"Almost there, Mei."

"We'll see Ana soon?"

"Soon," Reyna promised. She glanced behind them to make sure they were not being followed. A flash of white in the dirt caught her eye. "This is yours, isn't it?" She picked up a necklace. The pendant was not made of stone or metal. It was a seashell, an inch around, with a tiny hole at the top to fit a leather string. The edge of the string had frayed, which was likely why it had fallen. Mei saw the necklace and gasped. Her hand flew to her throat.

"Here, I'll keep it for you until we can get it fixed. Come on." Reyna tucked the necklace away and took Mei's hand. They were nearing the harbor when they heard the horses. Quite a number of them, approaching from behind.

"*Hama-si,*" Mei breathed.

"Don't be afraid," Reyna said quietly. Their hands were clammy from fear and rain. There was nowhere to go. A few inches to the right, the road dropped into a ditch, a sharp, twelve-foot fall.

The riders were not for them. The horses galloped by. Reyna counted ten men wearing the chrysanthemum tunics. Every one of them carried a black banner high above his head. Solid black, no crest. As the riders disappeared around the bend, the women on their mules began to wail.

Mei pressed close to Reyna's side. "What's wrong? Why are they crying?"

Reyna listened to the Miranese weeping — on horses, on carts, standing desolate in the road — and felt the hairs rise along her neck. "The king is dead, dearest. We must hurry."

The sounds of mourning followed them the rest of the way to the river. Reyna wiped the mist from her face and scanned the ships anchored at the docks. Quickly at first, and when she did not immediately see the *Truthsayer*, she made a slower, more thorough perusal.

"Which ship?" Mei asked.

It could not be. The harbor was small enough, and the *Truthsayer* large enough, that Reyna should have been able to see it right away among the other carracks, caravels, and junks. It should have been here.

It was not.

"Where is Ana?" Mei tugged on Reyna's hand. Her eyes were large and trusting beneath her hood. A reminder that Reyna could not let her panic show.

"Soon, Mei," Reyna assured her absently, and patted her

hand. Her mind worked fast. Where could the *Truthsayer* have gone? Peering through the drizzle and mist, she saw the great iron chain looped across the river. The chain could have been removed long enough for the ship to sail through. But Levi would not have left without her. Not if he'd had a choice.

Another possibility: the *Truthsayer* could have sailed east, to the tombs. Levi had come here to unload the barrels of clay. He could have decided, or Jian-so might have informed him, that it would be easier to sail the ship down the river as near to the royal tombs as possible. A simple explanation. Why did she always imagine the worst?

A hand came down on her shoulder. Reyna whirled, shoving Mei behind her. She saw a hooded figure and a dear, familiar face.

"Blaise!" Reyna flung her arms around her friend.

Blaise held on tight. When she stepped back, still gripping Reyna's shoulders, she said, "I am so glad to see you!" Tori-si was with her, the bandage on her neck concealed by a high collar.

"What's happened?" Reyna asked. "Where's the ship?"

"I'll tell you later." Blaise's tone was urgent. "We have to get away from the docks. I don't think we're welcome here any longer." Even so, she managed a smile for Reyna's companion. "Hello. You must be Mei."

"Come with me," Tori-si said. "I know where you can speak."

Tori-si led them away from the harbor to a beautiful spice market, an indoor bazaar with vaulted ceilings made of sparkling jewel-toned glass. On a prettier afternoon, sun rays would have drawn prisms and rainbows across the marble floor. Today the colors were muted, softer, as rain fell onto the roof.

Merchants packed the bazaar in untidy rows. Many wore flowing robes of white. Reyna walked past spices of every sort. Mounds of cardamom and sumac in clay pots. Burlap sacks full of cinnamon. Baskets of turmeric and star anise. Some spices were ground finer than sand and sculpted into miniature pyramids, bushels of gnarled ginger looked like the fingers of a crone. Reyna inhaled the scent of cloves and the sharp, bitter tang of newly crushed peppers. In other markets, the persistent cries of the spice sellers were a constant, each determined to be heard above the rest. Here the cries were of a different sort. The news of the king's death had traveled fast.

"Over here," Tori-si said. "This is my grandfather's booth."

They approached a man with a gray beard that tapered off at his navel. In addition to spices, he sold sweets and tea. He was the only merchant who did not look distraught by news of Botan-so's passing. While others gathered in the aisles, united in their grief, he remained behind his bushels and baskets, a faint smile on his face, polishing a glass with a cloth. His smile widened when he spotted Tori-si, who kissed his hand and introduced him as Sen-so.

Sen-so was most interested in Blaise, whom he thanked for helping his granddaughter. He spoke in halting Caffeesh and offered them crumbly, raisin-filled delicacies, along with tea that smelled strongly of mint. Reyna saw Mei lick her lips. The coins they offered were refused. Sen-so merely pointed across the aisle, where brightly colored floor cushions were strewn about a table, and said, "Sit there. Bring back cups." Tori-si remained with him, allowing them privacy.

No one noticed them. As soon as they settled, Blaise switched to Lunesian so as not to alarm Mei.

"I'd just left the ship," Blaise said. "Hamish wanted to go back with me, but I told him I was supposed to meet Tori-si at the spice market. She wanted to introduce me to her grand-father. It wasn't far. I was on my way here when I saw them."

Reyna's pastry remained untouched. "Levi?"

Blaise nodded. "With Samuel and Benjamin, all on horse-back with their hands bound. Surrounded by soldiers."

Reyna's heart dropped to the floor. "Were they hurt?"

"It didn't look like it. They were angry, though."

Reyna cast a look at Mei, who had eaten every bite of her pastry and was now licking her fingers with delight. "What hap-pened? Did you hear anything?"

"A little. I wasn't close enough. Jian-so said something like, 'I'm sorry, my friend. This was not my wish.'"

"Not his — What does that mean? Whose wish was it?"

"I don't know! He *did* look unhappy, but that could just be his face. After that, the captain said something very rude in Caffeesh, and then Jian-so just looked mad. I couldn't hear the rest."

Reyna said, "What about the *Truthsayer?*"

"Master Caleb could do nothing. The soldiers aimed fire arrows at the ship. A favorite trick of theirs," Blaise added bitterly. "After, everyone boarded the *Truthsayer* and those two black ships and they sailed off."

"Did Jian-so go with them?"

"No," Blaise answered. "But Ana-si did."

Mei looked up. "Ana?"

"Yes." Reyna smiled and offered Mei her pastry. The distraction worked. "Which way did they go?"

"East. Toward the tombs."

Reyna downed the contents of her tea cup. "Then that's where we're going."

"On foot?" Blaise said, askance. "It will take forever."

"We'll have to. Now. Before the funeral procession gets —"

Reyna looked past Blaise and down the long market aisle. Soldiers. Stopping at each seller. Looking for something. She pushed her cup aside. "We have to go."

Her companions followed her gaze, saw the soldiers. They scrambled off the cushions to their feet.

"Wait," Reyna said, for there were also soldiers in the opposite direction, blocking the market entrance.

"Where do we go?" Blaise whispered.

"There," Reyna said.

Across the aisle, Tori-si gestured — *Come!* Her grandfather held back a curtain that separated his booth from the room behind it. They did not hurry, only gathered their teacups and plates, crossed the aisle without looking right or left, and walked straight through to Sen-so's back room.

"Thank you," Reyna whispered as she passed them.

"No noise," Tori-si said.

The curtain snapped shut behind them.

It was a confining space, large enough for them to sit on the floor with their knees drawn up to their chests. They rested their backs against crates and listened as the soldiers came and went. Mei passed the time by watching the rain fall onto the glass ceiling. After a long while, Tori-si and her grandfather reappeared. They squeezed together even more to make room.

Tori-si spoke. "The soldiers are looking for the girl scribe from Lunes. They say she stole something." Her gaze rested briefly on Mei.

"She was stolen already." Reyna put an arm around Mei. "I'm taking her back to her family."

Tori-si and her grandfather exchanged a glance. Sen-so said, "The market is closing early. It will be safe to leave when everyone has gone."

"You're going to the tombs?" Reyna asked.

"Everyone, yes." Sen-so flicked the curtain aside, looked out, then shut the curtain again. "How may we help you? Do you need money?"

"We don't want to put you in danger," Blaise said.

"You helped my Tori-si when she was hurting," Sen-so told

her. "No one else would. You made her smile again. We are not all like the king's son. These soldiers are many. You" — he looked at each of them in turn — "are three children. So. You need money?"

"No, sir." Reyna blinked back tears. After Jian-so and even Hama-si, she had forgotten that such a thing existed — the simple kindness of a stranger. "We need to get to the tombs. As quickly as possible."

Another look shared between the tea seller and his granddaughter. Neither asked why they needed to go to the tombs, and for that Reyna was grateful. How could any of this possibly be explained?

Sen-so looked thoughtful. "Wait here. No noise."

And they left.

Mei said, "They're nice."

"Yes," Reyna whispered, and held a finger to her lips. Wide-eyed, Mei clapped a hand over her mouth and nodded.

The market grew quieter as the spice sellers departed. Reyna taught Mei to play the game stone-parchment-shears. While the girl was distracted, Blaise managed a quick inspection. Looking in her ears and her mouth, checking her skin for bruises and sores. She tried not to gawk too much at the feathers and wings. Blaise mouthed to Reyna, *Fine — just needs food*, and rubbed her stomach for emphasis. Relieved, Reyna mouthed in turn, *Thank you*. Before long, they heard only faint voices, and eventually those too faded.

The tea seller appeared. "I have a cart."

TWENTY-SEVEN

REYNA PEEKED THROUGH a gap in their covered cart. The rain had stopped. Above, the sun settled alongside an early moon, neither willing to cede its place in the sky. The road leading to the canal was slow-moving, full of mourners making the trek to Botan-so's tomb. She was dismayed at the sight. At this pace, who knew when they would arrive?

She scooted closer to the front of the cart and peppered their Miranese companions with questions. "Where is His Imperial Majesty now? Still at the palace? When will he be interred? After everyone arrives? Where I'm from, everyone may see the king before he is buried. To pay our respects. There's a long queue. Is this your custom as well?"

Better if Botan-so was on some conveyance behind them. She would have time to find Levi, find Ana-si, and put everything to rights before he even arrived.

Tori-si dashed her hopes. "The king does not travel this road. He goes by river. He is already there."

Reyna stared in consternation at the people — so many people — who stood in their way.

"The people do not see His Imperial Majesty." Sen-so spoke in that calm, quiet way he had. "We pray outside until the sun rises again. Then we go home."

"You don't enter the tombs at all?" Blaise asked.

Sen-so flicked the reins lightly. "The nobles only. The guards make sure." He glanced at Reyna. "They look for your face."

Reyna had not realized she was drumming her fingers along the cart floor until Blaise covered her hand with her own and squeezed.

"I can hear the wheels turning inside that head of yours," Blaise said.

"There are wheels in her head?" Mei whispered, full of wonder, which made everyone smile.

Blaise said, "It means she's thinking very hard."

Reyna looked through the gap again. "What about the road there? It's clear."

Their cart was at a standstill, along with everyone else's. But on the far side of the road, a path remained open, wide enough for carriages and horses to ride through unimpeded.

"It is for lords and ladies only," Sen-so said. "Anyone else who tries . . ."

"What happens to them?" Blaise asked.

Sen-so waggled the fingers on one hand. "They lose a finger. Sometimes two. But only the tips."

Mei shrank back against Blaise. Reyna instinctively curled her hands at the image his words had conjured. A carriage drawn by six horses came to a stop in the lords-and-ladies-only lane. It was well guarded. Soldiers came around to one side, where the driver knelt by a horse's front hoof. The curtain was whisked aside and a familiar face appeared. Prince Ken-so ... no, no longer a prince: His Imperial Majesty Ken-so. Impatient as he exchanged words with a soldier. Though most of the words were lost to her, she guessed that the horse had a stone in its shoe. The carriage would be going nowhere until it was removed.

Painful for the horse, but a chance for her.

Reyna shot to her feet. "I'm going ahead."

"What!" Blaise said. "Why?"

"I have an idea. Sort of," she amended. "I'll meet you outside the tombs at the foot of the steps. I don't know when. As soon as I can."

Mei said, "With —"

"Ana." Reyna had to hurry. There wasn't much time. She turned to Sen-so. "Sir —"

"Go," Sen-so said. "Do not worry. Your friends will be there, at the foot of the steps."

Blaise grabbed Reyna's arm. "Be careful."

"I will." Reyna pulled her hood low and hopped off the back of the cart.

Weaving her way through the mourners took some time. With every passing second, she was afraid Ken-so's carriage would simply roll away before her plan — her dangerous, uncertain plan — could even begin. But when she reached the carriage, the driver was still crouched by the horse, muttering under his breath. The soldiers, distracted, irritable, were pushing him to work faster. Reyna went around to the opposite side, opened the door, and slipped inside.

Ken-so and his wife wore black, the lady's veil lifted off her face and spread about her hair and shoulders. They had expected to see one of their soldiers. Reyna saw it on their faces: their impatience turned to surprise and then to complete bafflement when recognition settled. It gave Reyna enough time to sit beside the new queen, fold her hands in her lap, and say, "Your Grace. Your Grace. Greetings."

The queen reached for the curtain, exclaimed, "How dare—"

Her husband stayed her hand. He regarded Reyna with a frown. "There are many people looking for you, scribe."

"So I understand. I'm told I stole something. What exactly?"

"You would know better than I," Ken-so said.

"Would I? Surely Prince Levi has spoken in my defense?"

The queen's eyes flicked back and forth during the exchange, a silent observer.

Ken-so sat back, folded his arms. "Prince Levi left Miramar this afternoon," he said. "His business was done. Or so I'm told."

"Without saying his farewells? Didn't you find that strange?"

"I don't pretend to know what he will or will not do."

"But you wondered," Reyna said. "At his discourtesy. And then there's me. Does he strike you as someone who would leave behind a member of his cortege?"

Ken-so's eyes narrowed. "What are you trying to tell me?"

He would either believe her, or he would not. Reyna said, "The clay soldiers in the tombs are real, living men."

In the silence that followed, husband and wife looked at each other. They looked at her.

"She's mad," the queen announced, and reached for the curtain once again. This time her husband stopped her by leaning forward and placing a hand on her knee.

He watched Reyna with an odd light in his eyes. "She doesn't look mad, my love, though I don't know many Lunesians. Explain yourself. Now."

"You knew something was wrong the moment you saw them," Reyna said. "Miramar doesn't have the sculptors needed to create so many so quickly. And they would have to be master sculptors, Your Grace. Not apprentices, not journeymen, to create such . . . lifelike images."

Lord Ken-so straightened, his hand falling from his wife's knee.

Reyna said, "You're isolationists. Curious, then, that there's not a single Miranese statue in that tomb. Those men look like Lunesians and del Marians and Bushidos. Why would your sculptors, whoever they are, not make statues in their own likeness?"

Ken-so said, "There are a few —"

"They're Coronads," Reyna said, her tone flat. "Coronad shipmen who disappeared from the Sea of Magdalen three months ago."

Another silence fell.

"You're not a scribe," the queen said at last.

Reyna's smile was faint. "No, Your Grace. I'm not even a Lunesian." The carriage dipped as the driver climbed back onto his perch. They were on their way. Reyna said, "Please, this is important. I would like to tell you a story."

The queen's veil was difficult to see through. The black lace made navigating the steps to the tomb a tricky business. Holding on to Ken-so's arm helped. At least the dress fit Reyna reasonably well and the shoes did not pinch. The queen had remained behind in the carriage, wearing Reyna's dress and cloak. Reyna had wondered how she was going to get past the guards. Switching clothing had been the queen's idea.

They shared the steps with other members of the nobility. Murmured greetings were exchanged, but the grave occasion, thankfully, discouraged any more than that. Reyna kept her mouth closed and let Ken-so speak for them both. The veil hid her completely.

Behind them, the mourners spread out in all directions, along the riverbank and the roads. Torches and candles chased the dusk. There was no sign of the *Truthsayer.* Only Miranese ships, which Reyna assumed had escorted the king to his final resting place.

"It's the most preposterous story I've ever heard," the queen had said when Reyna finished telling her tale in the carriage. She turned to her husband. "I'm sorry to say I believe her."

"I do too," Ken-so said, his expression grim. "I wish I did not."

Reyna said, "We didn't come here alone. Others are near. If there is no word, they will come looking for us."

"Why didn't they come to begin with?" Ken-so challenged.

"Because no one wants a war," Reyna said. "My king least of all. He demanded proof before he would sail here and burn your kingdom to the ground. Now there is proof." She saw Ken-so's nostril's flare. "You'll need someone to speak for you."

A silent exchange between husband and wife.

Ken-so asked, "You can do this?"

"I give you my word," Reyna said.

Ken-so flicked aside the curtain, deep in thought. "Very well, I am listening. What do you propose?"

Reyna told him, and now they were here, passing through iron-spoked doors and descending into the heart of the tomb. They were among the last to arrive. The floor surrounding the pit was crowded, noblemen and noblewomen looking down at the statues in wonderment. Botan-so's coffin had been placed inside the palace replica on the pedestal. Jian-so stood at the edge of the pit beside a priest. Ana-si, as pale as Reyna had ever seen her, stood beside him. She was going to allow these men to die in order to remain in Jian-so's good graces. To keep Mei safe. She thought Reyna had failed her.

Reyna and Ken-so made their way to the front of the gathering, where they could better see into the pit, then maneuvered closer to Jian-so. Just before they reached him, Ken-so stopped. He said, quietly, "I am placing my family in your hands. My wife, my son. If you are wrong—"

She tightened her hand on his arm and said, her voice trembling, "Look."

The clay soldiers directly below Jian-so were different from the others, the red-brown clay darker. Not quite dry. One soldier stood with his legs braced wide. Both hands gripped a sword that pointed to the ground. He wore no helmet, and his head was lowered, following the line of his sword and making it difficult to see his face. Reyna did not need to see it. What she saw was enough.

Levi.

And surrounding him were Samuel and Caleb and the rest of the crew. Even Benjamin, with a bow and arrow notched and pointed straight at the mourners. A startled oath from Ken-so. He had looked closer, recognized Levi.

Jian-so turned to look at him. His lips pressed thin in displeasure. "You are the last one here, Cousin. I was beginning to worry."

Ken-so said, evenly, "I regret the hour. Your men attacked us in our chambers. It caused considerable delay."

Murmurs rose from those close enough to hear. Reyna had been practicing her Miranese with the women of the palace.

Every chance she could find. Still, she had to concentrate to understand the words spoken here.

"*My men?*" Jian-so said lightly. "You're mistaken. My men are all here." He turned to Reyna and bowed. "My dear, you must have been very frightened."

Ken-so had had enough. He raised his voice. "My lords, my ladies. Your Holiness. Prince Jian-so has placed our kingdom in grave danger."

"Silence him," Jian-so ordered. There was the clank of metal, the whisper of steel, as the soldiers loyal to Jian-so prepared to do his bidding. But Ken-so was not without protection of his own. Behind him, more soldiers stepped forward.

"Stop!" The priest jumped in front of Jian-so and threw his arms out to shield him. "This is a holy site. You cannot shed blood here!"

Reyna was close enough to Ana-si to touch. She lifted her veil, and when the girl's eyes widened, held out her hand. "I've kept my promise. Mei first."

Ana-si snatched the shell necklace from Reyna. Her expression was full of a desperate hope. "Where?"

"Outside, waiting for you at the bottom of the steps — Ana!"

Ana-si twisted around just as Jian-so's dagger arced downward. His blade missed, slicing through air, but Ana-si lost her balance and tumbled into the pit. The screams from the onlookers started when Samuel, covered in layers of clay, reached up and caught her. At the same time, Levi lifted his head. His eyes met Reyna's shocked ones. Blue eyes untainted by mud or magic. Because of his wax plugs. His sword came up, tempered by clay but still sharp enough to slice through the back of Jian-so's boots, severing the tendons at his ankles. The shriek that emerged was a hideous thing.

But the sound that followed was not.

Somewhere, deep within the pit, shielded by sleeping men, guarded by Samuel, Ana-si began to sing.

TWENTY-EIGHT

REYNA DID NOT BEGRUDGE the Miranese their screams. Had she not known the truth behind the clay soldiers, now slowly coming to life in the king's funeral pit like something from a nightmare, she would have screamed too. Though she liked to think she would have shown a little more dignity than these noble mourners, who were shoving others aside as they raced for the stairs, arms flailing above their heads in complete and utter panic.

The soldiers were an eerie sight. Unmoving at first, then looking around in confusion, their movements disjointed, like so many oversize marionettes. Clay shells cracked, giving them the appearance of broken pottery. Kneeling, Reyna reached into the pit for Levi. When he grasped her hand, she pulled with all her might, and he landed beside her, hard on one knee. He turned to look at her. Just looked at her and said, "You're safe."

"I was scared to death." Reyna placed her palms on his cheeks. Felt the tackiness of the clay. "The ship was gone and I thought —"

"Jian-so said it was his father's decision." Levi rested his forehead against hers. "He took one look at me and thought I'd make a nice addition to his army here. I will not lie to you. Being thrown into a vat of clay is an unnerving experience."

"How long were you going to stay in that pit? You could have been trapped here forever!"

"I was waiting for you to come," Levi said. "Preferably with Mei, or news of her. Something to tell Ana. I didn't have enough men to fight him off."

Reyna gaped at him. "*I* was your plan?" There were a thousand things that could have gone wrong. What if she had not arrived in time? It had not been a certain thing. She had nearly been too late.

He said, simply, "I knew you would come."

A voice behind them interrupted.

"This is all very touching," Ken-so said, testy. "However, these men are starting to look upset. They're also armed."

Ken-so raised his voice in order to be heard above Jian-so, who keened on the ground several feet away. The lone priest had stayed behind to tend him. His soldiers had fled. Ken-so was right. The baffled murmurs from the pit had changed to ominous mutterings. The clay soldiers had begun to move about. Who knew what they would do, left in the dark, carrying all manner of weapons?

Levi said to her, "I need your help." He scrambled to his feet, clumsy, and waved his arms high above his head. He shouted, in Lunesian, "Friends!" and had to repeat himself — "Friends! Friends!" — before the volume dropped noticeably.

All eyes turned his way. This time, when he shouted, it was in Caffeesh.

"Friends!"

And then, in Oslawn, "Friends!"

Levi looked at Reyna, expectant. Understanding what he needed her to do, she stepped to his side and said, in del Marian, "Friends!"

"Reyna!"

She could not see the man who shouted back at her, his voice full of shock. He was lost among so many others. But she recognized Lord Elias's voice. He was alive. He was safe. She would keep her promise to Mercedes after all.

Smiling now, she pressed a hand to her heart, where Lord Elias and Jaime and all the rest could see, and continued on — in Bushido, in Pyrenean, in Mondragan — so that the men might understand that however bizarre and inexplicable the circumstances, they were not in danger. "Friends!"

Ken-so came to stand with them. His face was the color of freshly scraped parchment, made even more stark against the black of his funereal robes. There was no point in him speaking Miranese. The pit was free of them, save the dead king. And so he called out once, in the language of his long-banished countrymen. In Coronad: "Friends!"

So began the painstaking process of explaining how the men had come to be here. Levi's tale was as brief as he could make it, for it was a story that had to be repeated over and over in a variety of languages. Interruptions were frequent. How long had they been here? It was midsummer, Levi had answered. Anger turned to fury. She knew it would only worsen once the men came to realize that not all their shipmates were there. Many, the ones deemed flawed by Prince Jian-so, had long since lost their lives.

Levi broke off only once, early on, spotting a face below. A young man was lifted high by the *Truthsayer's* crew, who clearly knew who he was. Here, at least, there was laughter and relief. Levi reached down and grabbed his brother, Asher, pulling him into his arms.

Reyna had to turn away. And that was when she saw Blaise kneeling by an unconscious Jian-so and his loyal priest. Jian-so's boots had been removed. His feet were bare. Blaise was tying strips of cloth above his ankles, slowing the bleeding inflicted by Levi's sword. The cloth must have come from the priest's robe. His hem was torn, speckled with blood.

Reyna knelt beside Blaise. "Where's Mei? Ana?"

"Gone." Blaise tied another strip tight. After one glance, Reyna kept her gaze carefully averted. There was an awful lot of blood here, seeping into the dirt. "Happy. Ana found us by the steps and they ran off." Blaise looked down at Jian-so. "I can't believe what he was going to do here. To everyone."

"Leave him." Ken-so had come to look down upon his cousin. "Let him rot."

The priest looked overwhelmed, close to fainting.

"Your Grace, listen to them," Reyna said of the men in the pit. "They'll need someone to blame. If he's gone, who is left?"

Ken-so was. His little boy, Ippen-so, was. The truth of her words sank in. He said, "Will he live?"

"He might," Blaise said. "I don't think I can save his feet."

There was no time to dwell on Jian-so's grisly injury. Lord Elias hoisted himself onto the ledge. He barely got to his feet before Reyna flung her arms around him.

"You're not hurt?" Lord Elias said, his arms coming around her. The embrace threatened to crush her bones. Bits of clay crumbled from him and fell to the ground. He stepped back, inspecting her from head to toe. "You're in one piece?"

Levi was nearby, still speaking to the men, urging them to leave the tombs. They would be able to breathe more easily in the fresh air, and bathe in the river. Some had already gone into the pool to wash off the clay. The water, once as clear as glass, had turned to mud. A mass exodus ensued. Asher sat at Levi's feet, elbows on knees, still a bit dazed. Levi kept a hand on his brother's head, as if afraid he would vanish once again.

"Yes," Reyna said. "What about you?" Ana-si had said the men would suffer no ill effects. Reyna needed to be sure.

"I'm fine," Lord Elias dismissed. "Midsummer, Reyna. Mercedes —"

"Was perfectly well when we left." Levi glanced over at that. But she would not frighten Lord Elias by telling him of his wife's true condition. Not when he was so far away from home and could do nothing about it. "The king wanted me to tell you he's watching over your ladies. You're not to worry about anything except returning home. Quick as you can."

Her lie cleared away some of his anxiety, enough that he noticed his surroundings for the first time. His mouth fell open. "*Blaise?*"

Blaise looked over and smiled. Her dress was splattered with blood. "Sir. I am very glad to see you."

"Who is that?" Lord Elias looked down at her patient, his expression hardening. His hand moved to the sword at his belt.

Levi stepped in front of him, deliberately pulling his attention away from Jian-so. "Lord Elias. We should speak. Outside."

Lord Elias did not move. "This is Jian-so?"

"Yes," Levi said. "I need him to live. For now, at least. Will you hear why first, before you put that sword through him?"

Reluctantly, Lord Elias agreed. Levi instructed some of his men to stay behind with Blaise. Jian-so would have to be guarded and moved. Reyna decided to stay too. Levi turned to speak to her; before he could, someone grabbed her hand. "This clay itches!" Jaime announced, and swung her around in circles, while she laughed and cried and held on tight. When Jaime finally set her on her feet, she saw that Levi was still there, watching.

"Lord Jaime." Levi's tone was civil. "I'm pleased to see you're well."

Jaime's smile was amiable even through the clay. He kept an arm around Reyna's shoulders. "Prince Levi. The same."

Levi paused, waiting for something. Lord Elias looked at

him, then at Jaime, then at Jaime's arm. Finally, Levi said to Jaime, "You'll join us? There's much to discuss."

"Oh, you don't need me, if Lord Elias is here," Jaime said. "I'll stay with Reyna —"

"Jaime." Lord Elias shook his head in exasperation. "Let her go before you get your head knocked off. Come on."

"What?" Jaime's arm slipped away. Before he could say more, Lord Elias marched him off. Levi went as well, but only after brushing Reyna's cheek with the back of his hand and saying, "I'll find you later."

TWENTY-NINE

ORROR AND PANIC. This was how the Miranese reacted to news of Prince Jian-so's crimes. Many fled the city, fearing retribution. The newly crowned Ken-so tried to reassure his countrymen. Miramar was under the protection of Lunes, he said. There would be no violence against them, he said. Who knew what concessions Levi had demanded in exchange? It meant that the kingdom of Miramar might not be burned to the ground, but it would never be as it once was, so isolated and remote.

Ken-so's first attempts at diplomacy were rebuffed. Sneers met his offer to house the captains of the pirated ships at the palace. They chose instead to camp with their men by the river, near the tombs. Undeterred, Ken-so sent carts full of food and clothing and tents. They were distributed by servants, their faces full of trepidation, which eased as the days passed and they found themselves returning to their homes each night, unmolested. Ken-so himself came by every day, with his son, to meet with Levi and others. Trying to find some way to keep his kingdom intact.

Messenger ships were dispatched to meet the fleet awaiting word near Aux-en-villes. The *Truthsayer* had been located downriver, undamaged.

Jian-so was kept under guard at the palace. His day of reckoning would come; privately, Reyna thought it had come already. Blaise had been allowed to visit once. She had found him near catatonic with pain, the stumps at his ankles wrapped in bloodied bandages.

Botan-so's tomb had been sealed, leaving him without a soul to guard him on his journey to the afterlife. The order had come from Ken-so. If there were any Miranese who protested his decision, who believed in the tradition of *tutto mortise*, Reyna did not hear of it. Not one person came forward to speak for their dead ruler.

As for Prince Asher, he kept to himself. Polite in mixed company, but quiet, and prone to taking long, solitary walks along the riverbank.

"Everyone else has had time to grieve," Reyna said when Levi brought it up. He was worried. This was unlike his brother, who had always been the livelier of the two. A thousand friends and no enemies. "Your father's death is still new to him."

"Asher was my father's favorite," Levi said. "I worry this will sink him."

"It might." Reyna remembered her own losses. Her parents, her grandfather. "But not forever. We both know this, I think."

She stumbled across Asher the next day while walking along the river. She came this way sometimes, keeping an eye out for ships bearing the royal flag of del Mar. Asher sat on a rock jutting out over the water. He looked over his shoulder, and when he saw it was her, rose and offered a bow. He wore Levi's clothing. A billowy shirt and rough linen trousers, both a little big on him.

"Lady Reyna."

"Prince Asher." Reyna smiled and would have continued along the path. She had no wish to intrude on his privacy.

His next words stopped her. "You don't have to go." He stepped to one side, offering her space on the rock. Surprised, she joined him. They sat side by side, legs dangling over rushing water.

"I wanted to thank you," he said. "Levi says we would still be in that tomb if it wasn't for you."

"You're very welcome," she said, though it was far from the truth. "I'm sorry about your father."

Asher looked at her with the same brilliant blue eyes as his siblings. "Your own parents must be worried. You've been gone a long time."

"No. They died years ago."

"Then you understand." Asher turned back to the water. "Being an orphan sounds better in the fairy tales, doesn't it?"

"I . . . hmm?"

"It's not as fun when *you're* the orphan," he explained.

Reyna found herself smiling. "I suppose that's true."

They shared a brief silence, before Asher said, "I was very

young when my mother died. I don't remember her well, like Vashti and Levi do. But my father . . ."

Asher was my father's favorite, Levi had said. *The youngest child.*

"When my parents died," Reyna offered quietly, "I remember thinking that there was no one else on this earth who would love me, as they had."

"Yes." Asher's head bowed; he breathed deep. "That's how I feel too."

"Except you're wrong." She touched his arm, just for a moment. "We're here because your brother sailed through the Strait of Cain looking for you. Because your sister bullied my king for reinforcements." Asher's lips curved at that. "I wish I could be there to see her face when you go home."

Asher's shoulders hunched even more, drawn up around his ears. He closed his eyes, and Reyna was reminded once again of Levi, alone with his grief at the docks.

When Asher lifted his head and looked at her, his eyes were blurred with unshed tears. "You're wrong too, Lady. About who loves you. I've seen how my brother looks at you when he thinks no one else is watching."

And Reyna decided that she liked this brother of Levi's, very much. They did not speak for a time, only sat there companionably, the silence broken by the river beneath them and the men back at the campsite, calling out to one another.

Late that evening, a light disturbed her sleep. Reyna rolled over in her tent and opened her eyes. Ana and Mei were there by her feet, sitting beside a lantern. They wore white Miranese robes with amber sashes.

"I thought you'd gone." Reyna kept her voice low. She sat up on the mat. Hers was one of a dozen tents erected in the makeshift camp. Blaise slept in one beside hers. They were surrounded by men who made their beds beneath the stars.

"We were far away," Ana said. "Mei found something in the river and wanted to come back to give it to you." The look she gave her sister was indulgent. "So that you will not forget her. And . . . there is something I need to do as well."

Reyna gathered Mei close, careful not to crush her wings. She was so frail. They would be journeying far. How would they manage?

"You don't have to give me anything, Mei. I won't forget you," she said, then stared when the child opened her palm and showed her what was in her grasp.

A pearl the size of a mandarin. Flawless and translucent. In a year spent at Aux-en-villes, its riverbeds blanketed with oyster shells, she had never seen one this large.

Mei asked, "It's pretty?"

Reyna smiled and kissed her temple. "Very pretty, thank you. I'll keep it with me always." To Ana, she said, "Won't you wait a bit? The ships will be here soon. We can take you wherever you need to go."

The smile faded from Ana's face. "No more ships," she said. "No more men. Come, Mei." She took her sister's hand in hers, then went still, ear cocked, listening. Her expression cleared. "It's only your captain. Goodbye."

"Goodbye," Reyna echoed.

Ana lifted the flap on the tent, and, with a final smile from Mei, the sisters were gone.

Reyna found Levi by the water, sitting with his back against a tree.

"I saw Ana go by," he said when she had settled by him. He hooked an arm around her neck, pulled her close. "Do you think they'll be safe?"

"I think so. I hope. You didn't speak to her?"

"I hid behind a tree until they left," he admitted, making her smile. "She terrifies me."

She did not tell him that Ana had known he was there. The night was warm, breezy, and the moon beamed silver in the sky. A crescent moon. It reminded her of Lunes. Of Levi. She wondered if she would ever look at a moon again and not think of him. Before she could think better of it, she said so.

He did not answer right away. "Looking at the moon and thinking of me sounds sad, Reyna. It sounds like I'm nowhere near." His fingers played absently with the end of her braid. "Lord Elias says he'll leave on the first del Marian ship he sees."

Levi's eyes were troubled. Why would that bother him? "He's worried about Mercedes."

"He says you'll go with him."

"Oh. Does he?"

"What 'oh'?" His fingers in her hair grew still. "Was he wrong?"

"He assumed. I've never told him otherwise."

A gentle tug on her braid. "Was he wrong?"

"Yes," she said. "I won't go home just yet. I don't think I'll stay here, either. I should. It's an obvious place for a masterwork. It could write itself, practically, and I've already made good progress."

Now Levi just looked confused. "But?"

"There's something I'd like to do more." An idea had formed in her mind, a seedling only, one she could not stop thinking about. She told him of it.

When she was finished, he grew thoughtful. "You can't go alone. It's too dangerous."

"Maybe," she said, carefully noncommittal. "I thought I could take Benjamin —"

"He's your first choice?" He flipped her braid away. "Benjamin? He's ten."

"He's helpful." She smiled in the darkness. "No? What about Samuel? Hamish?"

Silence. A poke in the side had her giggling. She tipped her head to look at him. Levi's kiss was sweet, though cut short, for a voice in the night — Lord Elias, of all people — barked, "Who's out there?" Sending them both scrambling to their feet, laughter muffled, darting off in opposite directions.

When Ken-so next visited, he brought disquieting news. Early in the morning, the soldiers guarding Jian-so had been found unconscious at their post. Unhurt, but asleep. Jian-so was dead, floating face-down in a courtyard fountain. A trail of blood led from his bed to the fountain, and some wondered if he had crawled there on his hands and knees, pulled himself over the fountain rim, and drowned himself. The royal physician who had been tending Jian-so floated alongside him.

There is something I need to do as well. Reyna thought of Ana, feathers plucked, wings severed.

And said nothing.

A meal was served by the riverbank at midday. Pigs and rabbits roasted on spits while trout, freshly caught, sizzled in pans by the campfire. The men mingled freely with one another. Reyna and Blaise shared their meal alongside the Lunesian and del Marian crews. They sat on a fallen log, talking among themselves, until a voice called out, "Master Blaise."

It was Levi who approached, a wooden box tucked under one arm. Asher was with him.

"What is he doing?" Blaise asked in an undertone. All eyes had turned her way, making her even more self-conscious.

"Go and see." Smiling, Reyna took Blaise's plate from her. She had been waiting days for this, ever since Levi had brought up the idea.

Ill at ease, Blaise stood. "Captain."

Levi waited until those nearest had fallen silent. Smiling slightly, he said, "Someone once told me that if you pay peanuts, you get monkeys." His smile touched on Reyna. "You get what you pay for. And it occurred to me that every crew member on the *Truthsayer*, including Lady Reyna, has been compensated for their work. Except you."

Levi handed the box to Asher, who held it as his brother opened the lid.

Blaise stepped forward for a closer look. Levi reached in and produced five scrolls tied off with black ribbons. He said, "I'm told that the medical school in Caffa requires a letter of noble patronage before you may be considered for admission. Here are five. These were written by myself, Lady Reyna, Lord Elias, Lord Jaime, and Prince Asher. Each attesting to your skills, and to your good common sense under harrowing conditions. And this" — he indicated the box, tipped slightly by Prince Asher so that the silver coins could be more easily seen; the look on Blaise's face had those nearby chuckling — "is for your room and board. I hope it will suffice. No?" he asked, because Blaise was shaking her head.

"It's too much." Blaise reached for the box, then stopped, as if afraid Asher would close the lid on her fingers. On her hopes and dreams.

"On the contrary." Levi was no longer smiling. He understood what this meant to her. "You have kept my men in excellent health. And your kindness gave us friends when we sorely needed them." Reyna had told him of Tori-si's boil, and of her grandfather's assistance. "Lord Elias will be sailing home; he's offered to escort you to Caffa and vouch for these letters in person if need be. Once he returns to university, my brother will also be at your service."

It was hard enough trying to blink back the tears. Reyna refused to blubber. What had Blaise said to her, in a time that now felt so long ago? *There's so much else I don't know, and I want to know it.* Now she had a chance.

Smiling, Asher closed the lid and offered the box to Blaise. "Take this, please. It's getting heavy."

"To Master Blaise," Samuel called out. Words echoed again and again by those who had sailed with her.

Overwhelmed, Blaise took the box. Levi reached for the cup Reyna held out to him. He raised it up and said, "To Master Blaise."

When the rescue fleet arrived, too late for an actual rescue, many of the ships departed almost immediately. They would transport the stranded men back to the nearest large port, where they would then find one of their own ships to take them the rest of the way home. A few carried letters from Levi and Lord Kenso. Several had refused Ken-so's letter. An Oslawn captain who had lost half his men to Jian-so was one of them. He had spat at Ken-so's feet, vowing retribution.

Lord Elias would leave tomorrow, as would Blaise. Jaime had decided not to go with them.

"I think I'll stay," Jaime said to Reyna as they strolled around the campsite at dusk.

"What?" Reyna said, surprised. "Why?"

Jaime shrugged. "Why not? I need to start thinking about my masterwork, and this one fell into my lap. You're sure you don't want it?"

"I'm sure. How long will you stay?"

"At least a year, I think. Stay away from Lady Beatrice's husband a while longer. And I want to survey the city before too many people get here. Start painting the buildings Lunesian blue or something horrible like that. You know it won't look the same in a few years."

"No," Reyna acknowledged.

They walked for a time, each lost in thought as the camp fires were lit around them.

"Reyna?"

"Hmm?"

"Those notes you've written already. I was thinking, if you're not going to use them . . ."

She stopped. His meaning became clear. "You want me to give you *my* notes? For *your* masterwork?"

"Seems like a good way to save time." Jaime did not have the grace to look the least bit sheepish. "And since you're not using them . . ."

Reyna laughed and, shaking her head, walked off.

"Is that a yes?" Jaime called out.

"You're the worst," she said. And went to find her notebook, to give Jaime.

THIRTY

ARE YOU READY?" Levi asked.

"I'm ready." Reyna grabbed her pack from the boat and strapped it onto her back. It held everything she would need for their journey. An adventure, through the jungle and up the mountain, to the sailing ship in the sky.

Levi helped Samuel and Benjamin pull the boat onto the bank. There was no dock here. Only thick, overgrown vegetation and trees that listed sharply toward the water. The small boat with its one sail and two oars would serve as a marker for the *Truthsayer* when it made its return journey from Lunes to bring them home.

But that was not for some time yet. For now, it was just the four of them in the early morning light. The aftermath of Miramar was for others to worry over. They had done what they had set out to do. Reunited Ana and Mei. Seen their loved ones safely off.

Samuel slapped his neck and wondered ominously what other biting insects lay in wait for them. Levi strapped on his pack and rolled his shoulders, testing its weight. He smiled at her, held out his hand.

She reached for it. Every inch of her churned with excitement. With curiosity for what lay ahead. With a burning ambition she held close to her heart.

She would be eighteen by the time she returned home to del Mar. And that, she thought, looking up at the mountain with its magnificent, mysterious ship, *that* was going to be her masterwork.

ACKNOWLEDGMENTS

Although *Isle of Blood and Stone* and *Song of the Abyss* are works of fiction, I relied heavily on my public library when it came to details on mapmaking, shipping, and the Middle Ages. For those interested in further reading, I highly recommend:

- *The Golden Age of Maritime Maps: When Europe Discovered the World* by Catherine Hofmann and Helene Richard
- *The Young Oxford Companion to Maps and Mapmaking* by Rebecca Stefoff
- *Cities of the World* by Stephan Füssel and Rem Koolhaas
- *Daily Life in Medieval Times* by Frances Gies and Joseph Gies
- *Ship: The Epic Story of Maritime Adventure* by Brian Lavery
- *Sea Monsters: A Voyage Around the World's Most Beguiling Map* by Joseph Nigg

There are so many people who have worked tirelessly on these books, not only by whipping manuscripts into shape, but by ensuring they make it into the hands of readers. As always, thank you to my agent, Suzie Townsend, as well as Cassandra Baim and the entire team at New Leaf Literary & Media. At HMH Books for Young Readers, I am grateful to my wonderful editor, Nicole Sclama, and to Emma Gordon, Tara Sonin, Sharismar Rodriguez, Karen Sherman, Amanda Acevedo, and Kiffin Steurer.

I can't imagine what my author photos would look like without Jenny Bowles, who is an excellent photographer and an even better friend.

Sometimes choosing a name for a main character is a tricky business. This wasn't the case for *Song of the Abyss*. I wanted a name that was beautiful and unique and strong, much like the character herself. So I named her Reyna, after a cousin who shared in countless childhood adventures. I hope this makes up for that big fight we had in elementary school, Rey. I love you.

Last but not least, much love and appreciation to my two favorite people: my husband, Chris, and my daughter, Mia, who manages my Instagram account during her school lunch breaks. Thanks, baby.

TURN THE PAGE TO START READING!

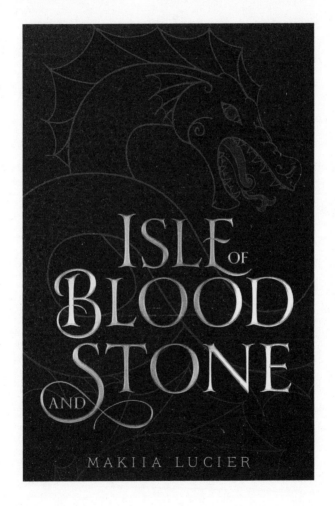

N THE SQUARE, just off the harbor, Mercedes heard the cockfight long before she saw it. A crowd of men gathered in a circle. Thirty deep, they occupied nearly the whole of the small plaza, their shouts reverberating off gray stone buildings. All around them was seawater: salty, pungent, and a little bit rotten, mixed with the smell of fish frying and bodies gone too long without a wash. And rising above the din was the distinct, high-pitched crowing of a rooster.

Dubious, she turned to the man standing beside her with his arms crossed, his expression darkening as he surveyed the scene before him.

"You're certain we're in the right place, Commander?" she asked. "He cannot be here." But even she heard the lack of conviction in her voice. This square, so near to the harbor, was a favorite haunt for pickpockets, charlatans, and travelers lured by cheap lodging and strong drink. They were in an ill-favored part of her cousin's kingdom, surrounded now by the lowest form of men. Mercedes had known Elias all her life. It was likely they were in exactly the right place.

Apparently, Commander Aimon agreed. "Oh?" was his reply. He pulled her aside as a man stumbled out of the throng, cheeks flushed, reeking of spirits. After the inebriate tripped past them, he released her arm. "You are all diplomacy, my lady Mercedes. But let's not fool ourselves." With his face the picture of resignation, he added, "Stay close. Follow me."

Commander Aimon forced his way through the crowd. He was a big man wearing the king's colors and a ferocious scowl; the mass yielded easily. Mercedes kept her head down and her elbows out, absently noting that the oaths and insults thrown their way were in many different languages. These men were Hellespontians and Lunesians and Coronads. A smattering of Caffeesh so far from home. Very few Mondragans, however. They had long since learned the dangers of lingering where they were not welcome.

Someone grabbed her arm. A man with very few teeth grinned and sniffed her hair. His breath stank of garlic and rot. She heard "What a pretty piece! Let me —" before her fist came up, sharp with rings, and connected with the underside of his chin. A pained grunt emerged. Her admirer fell back into the throng and was lost. Onlookers laughed and hooted, but no one else tried to touch her. She continued after the commander and, after much shoving, found herself before a small, dusty clearing.

Her suspicions were confirmed. It was a cockfight. To the right, a bald man with a stained leather apron held up a rooster, turning it this way and that while a second rough-looking character pointed out scratches and gaps in the feathers. She paid them only a cursory glance, her attention captured entirely by the young man to the left.

Elias.

Or, formally, Lord Elias. Only child of Lady Antoni and Lord Antoni, the long-departed Royal Navigator for the island kingdom of St. John del Mar. The last surviving son of a powerful noble family knelt in the dirt, a rooster cradled in his arms like a newborn babe. He wore a loose-fitting shirt and dark trousers, both now encrusted with muck and what she suspected was bird blood. His hair, a rich brown lightened by the summer sun, had grown overlong, so that it settled about his shoulders in thick waves, like a woman's. A battered leather map carrier lay against his back, cylindrical in shape, three feet long. Of his sword, there was no sign. As was usual.

Her breath caught. He'd been hurt. A bruise spread across one cheekbone, mottled and yellow. *What else?* Her inspection was swift: He had all his fingers, his limbs. He moved easily; no obvious injury, then, hidden beneath his clothing. One never knew with Elias, who collected wounds the way she collected secrets and enemies. It was his least endearing quality, this skill he had in making her worry.

Who was that man with him? He hovered over Elias with an anxious expression and deep smudges beneath his eyes. Similar in age and vaguely familiar; his identity poked at the very edge of her memory. Whoever he was, he was out of place: well-groomed and dressed in the dark tailored clothing of an upper tradesman.

The bird was motionless. A lock of hair fell forward as Elias placed his open mouth over its beak and blew gently. Miraculously, the rooster's chest expanded. Wings fluttered, then flapped. Cheers and curses erupted from the crowd. As she watched with appalled fascination, Elias lifted his head and spat out several feathers before sharing a grin with his neatly dressed companion.

She slid a glance toward Commander Aimon. The poor man rubbed his temple with his fingertips as he always did when trying to ease head pains. She could not help but smile, though it felt wrong, knowing what lay ahead. This morning was not going to end pleasantly.

Elias's bald opponent did not look pleased by the bird's quick recovery. "Chart maker!" he shouted, his guttural tones and dull features marking him for a Coronad. "You bird swiver! That rooster is dead. I have won!"

Elias laughed. "It's not dead yet, my friend!" he yelled back. He set the bird on the ground, his hands preventing it from taking flight. "Do you forfeit?"

The Coronad sneered. "We come here; we see del Marian men, even prettier than their women. With soft hands and flower oil in their hair. What do you know of cockfights, pretty del Marian?"

Elias's grin widened. His answer was to blow the man a kiss. Amid the laughter, the other man scowled even more. "Bah!" he said before snatching his own bird from his companion and setting it down in the dust.

A girl ran to the center of the clearing, barefoot, the tattered red kerchief covering her hair a perfect match to her skirts. The child raised an arm high, counted to three, then brought her hand down with dramatic flourish. Elias and his opponent released their holds on their roosters. The girl jumped aside as the birds flew at each other, feathers thrashing.

Commander Aimon's voice was an irritated rumble. "That boy sounds like a lord and looks like a vagabond."

Mercedes leaned close so that she could be heard above the shouting. "He's at ease in any setting. Have you noticed? He blends in without effort. I wonder why Ulises doesn't make use of it."

The commander made a skeptical noise. "Lord Elias isn't like you, Lady. He isn't made for intrigue."

"No?"

"Look at him." They watched Elias cheer on his bird. One arm was hooked around his friend's neck, and they were both jumping up and down and hollering like small boys at the bullfights.

"Hmm," she said.

"You see? Everything he thinks and feels is written on his face for the world to see. A dangerous trait for a king's . . . emissary."

She supposed that was true. Elias in a temper was a rare thing, but it was always memorable, and when he learned of the maps, outrage and insult would be within his rights. Not for the first time, she wished Reyna had not gone to the harbor that day and stumbled upon the map. She wished she herself had not traveled to Lunes and found the other. But what use, wishes? They would do her no good today.

Commander Aimon made to signal Elias. She placed a hand on his arm, stopping him. "We might as well wait until he's finished."

"Must we?"

Another quick smile emerged at his aggrieved tone. "He'll learn why we're here soon enough," she said. "And I've never seen an actual cockfight, have you?"

The commander answered her question with one of his own. "Do you think he can solve it?"

She knew Elias was capable. She wondered only if he would be willing. "It concerns him as much as the king."

The commander studied her with dark, kohl-rimmed eyes, a common trait among the men and women of del Mar's native population in the east. His hair was long and straight, black shot through with gray, and pulled back into a queue. He looked more like a pirate than the commander of the king's armies. "True," he acknowledged. "But that was not my question, Lady."

She didn't answer straightaway, but watched as Elias smoothed the rooster's feathers and whispered what looked like soothing, encouraging words to it. His hands were beautifully shaped. His fingertips, as always, bore the faintest trace of blue paint. Elias cared little for gloves or for the cleansing potions used by most mapmakers. And why was she standing here admiring his hands? She found herself frowning.

"You underestimate him," she said finally. "He's smarter than he looks."

The commander turned away and went back to his mutterings, this time something about being damned by faint praise. She let his words wash over her. Someone prodded her in the back so hard she fell forward a step. Slowly, she turned her head and gave the man behind her a gimlet-eyed stare. Fair hair, blue eyes, skin peeling from the sun: almost certainly a Mondragan.

"Apologies, miss . . ." His smile turned to puzzlement as he took in her own unusual appearance: black hair, golden skin, but with the green eyes and dreadful freckles that no full-blooded del Marian would ever proudly bear. The man glanced at Commander Aimon and then back at her, and she knew from the stranger's reaction that she had been recognized. His eyes widened. Prudently, he inched away until he was gone from view.

She watched him go. Stupid to feel this way, this terrible, skin-crawling shame, when there was not a thing to be done about it. She could not change the blood flowing through her veins. Half Mondragan, half del Marian.

A curse.

Turning back to watch the fight, she held herself apart from the crowd, as she always did, and waited.

The opposing bird lay dead on the ground, his master mourning above it. There was laughter and groaning as wagers were paid. As the crowd loosened, the stink of men dispersed into something that was, while not exactly pleasant, at least far more breathable.

Elias brushed the feathers from a shirt that had once been white. A futile effort; they merely fluttered about in the air before settling onto a different part of his person. Beside him, Olivier danced a small victorious jig, his rooster clutched under one arm.

It was a ridiculous sight, and Elias laughed. He heard "Chart maker!" and looked up in time to see a pouch sailing through the air toward him. He caught it with one hand and held it out to Olivier. "Your winnings."

Olivier took the pouch, unable to hide his relief as he felt the reassuring weight of copper sand dollars and silver double-shells. "You'll take half? It's only fair."

Elias refused. "It's your bird. Give it to your wife, with my compliments."

Elias had just disembarked from the *Amaris* when he'd caught a glimpse of Olivier, a parchment seller by trade, standing at the back of the crowd with a birdcage in his hand. Elias knew desperation when he saw it. He suspected its reason. Olivier's daughter suffered from a prolonged illness. Keeping his work-shop profitable and paying off the leeches could not be a simple thing. Everyone knew these fights were a quick way to make money. Or lose it.

"You're certain?" Olivier asked.

"Yes, take it. I can't afford to lose your services. I don't care for the way Master Hernan prepares his sheepskin."

Olivier tucked the pouch away, then knelt to place the bird in its cage. "I'm grateful that you happened by, Lord Elias, and that you know so much about gamecocks." He eyed Elias curiously. "*How* do you know so much? It's an odd talent for a geographer."

"Most of my talents are considered odd. Or worse."

Olivier laughed. He shut the cage with a snap and, with final thanks, hurried off, the rooster swinging in the cage by his side.

Elias hitched his map carrier higher on his shoulder and glanced up, still smiling. Cortes was the capital city of St. John del Mar. An ancient settlement built on a hill with a round, walled castle at the very top and the parishes, or neighborhoods, spilling downward on slanted streets. The castle was his home. He had not seen it in months.

In his mind, he ticked off all he would do as soon as he reached the tower. First he would bathe, then eat. He would find out if Mercedes was on island, report to Lord Silva, deliver his maps to Madame Vega. Ulises would be in some council meeting or another at this hour of day, but he could visit his mother and the rest of —

He felt her before he saw her, absently touching the back of his neck, then turning fully when he glimpsed pale green silk at the edge of his vision.

Mercedes.